Falling
Kashmir
Roses

Gwen B

For Lalla, the darling of Kashmir,
who danced into my life.

'I didn't trust it for a moment,
but I drank it anyway,
the wine of my own poetry.
It gave me the daring to take hold
of the darkness and tear it down
and cut it into little pieces.'

Lalleshwari

one

Hong Kong 2009

UNTIL A TEMPESTUOUS NIGHT in a hotel room with a view of the Pearl of the Orient, Lily and Oliver had been meeting periodically after work at a Parisian-owned bar called Mingle. It was on a steep and noisy back street in the heart of Hong Kong's bustling Soho nightlife district. The bar was luxurious, with plush velvet chairs nestled in intimate booths, lit with candle flames twirling in the shadows.

Mingle was a place where clandestine affairs began, where a palette of voices with accents from all over the world would mesh into the hookah pipe air while whispering intimately veiled stories of passion. Mingle's one unique bathroom was unisex – inside there was an inviting chaise longue neatly pushed up against a burgundy wall-papered wall. Charcoaled sketches of erotic black-and-white nudes decorated the walls, and the obligatory crystal chandelier hung effortlessly from the ceiling as if it had just sauntered over from the Palace of Versailles. One could only imagine what had taken place on Mingle's infamous chaise in the twilight hours. The bar was filled with the chatter and laughter of lovers, and sometimes even the sounds of lovemaking.

Lily's evening walks up to Mingle were always an adventure. The busy streets with badly paved walkways and wonky stairs had thousands of feet to fall over. So many people, all rushing about in a buzzing metropolis. Red taxis hooted in chaotic traffic, and the pungent smells of car fumes, incense from shrines, delicious Asian food, and sticky summer frangipani sky filled up the nose in a waft of thick, humid air. Lily would be damp and exhilarated by the time she arrived. She was usually dressed in a black tailored skirt suit and a meticulously pressed crisp white blouse – unless she was having a day out of court. Then she would add a menagerie of colour.

It was customary for Lily to turn up early, order a glass of Sauvignon Blanc for herself and a Pinot Noir for Oliver, and then she would sit in a secluded booth with her heart hammering, hoping that no one would recognise her. She stood out in most places in this city, her long blonde migrant hair a contrast amid the sea of dark-haired Asian beauty. *I shouldn't be here. This is wrong.* But somehow her heart just wouldn't let her leave and she refused to argue with its wisdom. If Lily had one core trait, it would be stubbornness.

She hadn't planned this, the whole crazy event – it just fell out of the sky the way a random lightning strike had killed her sister's boyfriend during a hike on the Highveld in southern Africa.

Lily hadn't paid much attention to Oliver when they first met. Work consumed her thoughts, drowning out the rest of the world. She was in the middle of a gruelling high-profile murder trial, and her days and nights had disappeared into one. A close friend, Saima, had rung up and begged a favour. Saima's friend Oliver was embroiled in a protracted divorce and custody dispute, and needed a helping hand. Lily had agreed to meet him over coffee to evaluate and direct him to a 'suitable' family lawyer, and as compensation, Saima had agreed to organise a talk therapy session for Lily with someone top-notch. Lily's anxiety had reared its despicable head again, and she was so damn over it.

Initially, Lily had found Oliver irritating – even the graceful lift of his coffee cup. She liked sturdier men. Oliver's flawless English pear-shaped vowels reminded her of the social stratification she had to suffer through in England as part of her education. She had encountered a plethora of men with similar accents in the corridors of the Middle Temple – one of the exclusive clubs which she had to join to practise as a barrister. All the unavoidable dinners she had to tolerate with tipsy Sirs, QCs, and Lords who 'unconsciously' slinked their sloppy hands up her skirt or grasped her knee beneath the long oak table as they discussed the peasants' issues.

'You just have to grin and bear it,' she was told by her Pupil-Mistress. *Even if it brings bile into your mouth.*

Oliver's unpretentious poshness was contradictory, and it crawled up Lily's skin. He was something to look at, yes. Tall, yes – but that was simply irrelevant to her. Lily was devoted to her tumultuous marriage, her heart wrapped up in its chaos. She had eyes for no one but Luka – her husband, for seventeen beautiful and fucked-up years.

That is until, in a luxurious hotel coffeehouse in Central, over their second shared skinny latte, something about the melancholy of Oliver's eyes made her soften to him. There was a turning, and he rushed right in. It happened so quickly that Lily hardly had time to catch her breath or wrap her heart in layers of cotton wool. It all boiled down to one very confusing, unremarkable, remarkable moment when Lily caught a glint in his eye and Oliver caught a glint in hers. The universe screeched to a grinding halt. Heaven had reached down to earth and offered them both a gift. Hollywood in Hong Kong. Oliver had a piece of her heart and she would never be the same.

On that same day, as the meeting drew to a close, in a glitzy elevator adorned with elaborate marble tiles, Oliver leaned in and, with his left hand on the close-door button and his right hand gently stroking Lily's face, he kissed her. It was noon on a weekday and an unfamiliar man had stolen a place in Lily's heart and kissed her with such gentleness that she felt the delectable taste of his smoky sweetness would never depart from her mouth.

Stuff like this didn't happen to women like Lily.

It takes less than a millisecond for lightning to strike. One minute and it seems a whole life can implode. Seventeen years of Lily's faithful devotedness had just slid down the proverbial drain.

After their initial meeting and a torrent of text messages, they agreed to meet at Mingle – Soho's most controversial bar. Oliver would arrive on those evenings with a flair that belonged only to him. His strong and languid limbs made his stride unmistakable. His clothing was flawless, befitting an Englishman who had spent years in theatrical production.

Fuck, he is everything! The sight of him made Lily's insides squirm.

He had eyes that twinkled. They were framed by laughter lines that told a story of a life well-lived. A slither of grey wisdom or grief touched his short dark wavy hair – Lily wasn't yet sure which – and he had a dimpled chin that Lily couldn't resist resting her thumb on. It was the most perfect crease she had ever seen, the perfect fit for her finger – as if some talented sculptor had placed it there just for her to find.

Oliver and Lily would sit bathed by Mingle's flickering candlelight for hours, lulled by the decadence of wine and world music. They spoke as two people falling into those unpredictable cracks of love speak. Right there, in those moments, they solved the world's problems. They were alive together. Connected by a vast miraculous web that they could not see. They discussed politics, philosophy, relationships, poetry, art, and every other topic under the moon. With every conversation they shared, their love grew a little more. They became inexplicably bound. Occasionally, they would get lost in drunken kisses, a gaze, or a touch, nothing more.

For a while, it was simple.

two

ON ONE SWELTERING AND bustling Mingle evening, Oliver unburdened himself of all he had been carrying. Lily could see the anguish on his face – he had talked about his divorce from his Italian wife, Kat, and the fear of losing custody of his daughter Daisy, but she was unaware of the intensity of the sorrow he was carrying, or the cause of this deep-rooted pain, until that evening. On that night, she understood the expression she had seen in his eyes on the day they had first met in the hotel coffee shop in Central. The expression that had drawn her to him.

They sat bathed in candlelight shadows – huddled on Mingle's velvet corner couch, just out of earshot from the nearest patron. Oliver fumbled with his hands. Lily sensed something big was coming.

'Sadie was everything,' said Oliver.

'Sadie?' replied Lily.

'My first love. She could fill my empty spaces. She knew when to leave me alone and when to comfort me. We were crazy together, and crazy in love. We met on the theatre scene, both plying our trade. I had just graduated from Guildford, a disappointment to my parents who wanted me to go to Cambridge and read law like my brother.'

Lily took a large sip of her sauvé. She couldn't imagine Oliver disappointing anyone.

'I knew it was her,' he said, his eyes smiling, 'when she walked onto a set wearing her grandmother's slippers. Christ, she was funny. She just didn't give a toss.' His shoulders dropped with a heavy sigh. 'She was vulnerable and wild and witty and brilliant on stage – gifted at everything. I could – watch her for hours. She was so much better at acting than me.'

'Really?' Lily flashed a flirtatious, mischievous grin.

'Yes, I'm crap on stage, but Sadie was going places.' Oliver's voice was tender. 'Everyone knew it. We had such a good life together. To make ends meet, we travelled all around the UK and took all the small-town theatre jobs we could. That's when I started working more on the production side.' His hands were jittering, and his feet were tapping out a nervous staccato. Oliver was not someone who sat still. 'We weren't always working in the same town, but when we came back together it was intense – the sex, the intimacy, and everything else.' The emotion in Oliver's eyes was crystal clear. 'We fought too – it never lasted long, we just couldn't maintain conflict, we always had to find a way back to each other.'

He stopped to reflect.

'Sadie was my happy-ever-after.'

Lily's eyes widened. 'You believe in happily-ever-after?' She noticed a flirtatious couple darting into the unisex bathroom for a quickie out of the corner of her eye.

'Of course. I'm not a cynic.' He smiled, his fingertips grazing Lily's warm, rosy cheek.

Lily wasn't sure if that was a subtle dig. But she gave him the benefit of the doubt.

Oliver inhaled deeply, taking in the wine's aroma before swirling it in his glass. He was steadying himself.

'When she came home after a stint of working apart and told me she was pregnant, it was such a shock.' He paused for a sip. 'We were both young and making our way – I was worried that our amazing lifestyle was going to end, and my reaction hurt her. God, I wish I could change that.

'I remember her eyes, the sadness. But she forgave me. That's just how she was.'

The hurt inside Oliver was palpable. It seeped into the air between them and touched Lily.

'I always knew it was her I wanted to have a family with. It was just the timing. Everyone was excited, our friends – even my stuck-up accountant father. He thought Sadie was incredible. We all did.'

Lily smiled, her lips curving into a gentle, peaceful expression. She thought Oliver's love was beautiful and she could tell it was tough for him to be so vulnerable.

'I was working on a production in Bath when I got the call.' His face went blank. His knee was drumming the table, making the wine glasses wobble. 'They rushed her to Chelsea Hospital; the pregnancy was ectopic. I got there just in time to see her on the bed, before they took her away. She was cold. There was nothing I could do to keep her warm. I held her so close. I can still smell her hair – coconut oil.' He audibly gulped, his throat dry as he swallowed hard. 'I begged her, but she just wouldn't come back. She couldn't hear me anymore and she just wouldn't come back.'

Oliver closed his eyes for a moment.

'She will never hear me again. My fucking sperm killed her!'

The tears leaked out of his eyes, just tiny ones in the corner. You could hardly see them in Mingle's opalescent light. Lily felt tears, too, they were pricking hard behind her eyes.

'Oh, Oliver.' She huddled closer but offered no more words. She could not imagine the grief of losing both the love of your life and your child on the same day.

'I fled for two years,' he continued in a soft, choked-up voice, 'all the way around Europe – didn't even say goodbye to anyone, didn't even go to the funeral. I just travelled from place to place, getting as pissed or fucked up on drugs as I could.

'I think Sadie's family hates me. I don't blame them.'

Lily reached up and felt the wetness of his tears against her thumb as she wiped them away.

'I'm sure they don't hate you. Hating you is impossible,' she said.

She wrapped him in her arms and they sat there all curled up in each other until he was ready to continue. He took a big glug of his Pinot and finished what he wanted to say.

'All that running. An old mate got me a job in London after I ran out of money. I was making progress – throwing myself into my career. The West End was where I made it. I paired up with James on the big productions. It was fun. I was getting somewhere; I was something, Lily.'

'Of course you were something.'

Lily placed her thumb on the dimple of his chin. She couldn't help it. Everything about him was asking for a loving touch.

'Then I met Kat,' he continued, 'a fiery cockney-Italian blonde.' There was a spring in his voice now. 'She was a make-up artist on set. She distracted me from everything that was going on inside. Kat is a wild, temperamental thing who can cook better than any chef I know. I don't know if I loved her, but there was something between us. We got married, and we had Daisy.' Relief flooded Oliver's face. Saying his daughter's name brought him comfort. 'Daisy is the best thing in my life.' He smiled. 'Life was good as a family, but now Kat's leaving because I'm an asshole.' His smile faded. 'And I am a fucking asshole. I slept with someone else. I've been sleeping around since I left Chelsea that day, since I started running, always looking for Sadie in some random woman's eyes.

'I stopped for a while when I met Kat, but then we started fighting all the time and the emptiness came back, and I just carried on being a self-destructive bastard.'

There was so much anguish in his expression.

Lily wouldn't judge him – he was human, just like her. Fallible. And she realised he understood the gravity of what he had done. His brutal self-judgement was punishment enough. She wished she could make it stop – that he could see himself, how she saw him.

'You are not a bastard, Oliver. You were acting out of a hurt that hasn't healed. Grief makes us behave in unimaginable ways.'

She saw the horny couple she had spotted earlier slink out of the bathroom.

'M-Maybe, I guess I need a therapist. It doesn't matter – I'm going to lose Daisy, the only thing I've done right in my life. I brushed her hair every morning. I don't know what to do when I wake up anymore … My beautiful girl. I miss her so much.'

'You are going to get through this. You are going to get up every day, and you are going to fight to stay in her life, so that she knows how much you love her. You aren't broken, Oliver. Far from it.' Lily's voice was firm.

He almost believed her.

Oliver stared at her through the hazy, humid air. They were both quiet. Lily could sense that there was a lot going on in his head. She was lost in thought, too. The silence between them was comforting, like an old leather glove that had worn perfectly to fit the shape of the owner's hand.

'Marry me, Lily.' The words shot out of his mouth before he could rein them in.

Lily nearly spat the wine out of her mouth.

'Oliver. W-What?'

She dabbed a napkin against her clothes, trying to soak up the red wine.

'We are both still married,' she said. 'And we have only known each other for five minutes. I-I'm fifty shades of fucked up, too, and I know you feel me, but you really don't know me at all.'

'I know you,' he replied with a solemnity that was hard to refute. 'When this is all over, and we've come out the other side of all this shit, marry me?'

'Why me, Oliver?' She watched his expression intently.

'Because when I look into your eyes, I'm not searching for Sadie.'

Lily felt her heart sink in her chest. She leaned in and pressed a gentle kiss on his forehead. She couldn't reply, and this was hurting. Oliver had crawled right into her bones and he was warming all her frozen places. She watched as he savoured the taste of the

Pinot, gulping it down with one slug. *Please don't let me be in love with an alcoholic.*

Vulnerability is a powerful aphrodisiac. And the night that Oliver opened up to her was the night that Lily decided she would love him to the end, even if he wasn't the only man she loved.

They left Mingle together; they walked to the ferry pier where Lily caught the boat home every evening to Lantau Island. It felt like another life on that island with its jungled hills and temples and … Luka. Hand in hand, they meandered down the steep cobbled roads, the smell of the salty sea air filling their nostrils. Finally, they found a spot on the cracked pavement to sit on, their backs against the gritty cement of a wall. It was the most natural thing in the world, to be dressed up and sitting on the pavement watching the world walk past them, their feet intertwined. His handcrafted Italian leather shoes, her patent leather courtroom stilettos. They looked up at the city's spectacular clashing nightlights, then spotted an elderly homeless woman with an umbrella hat. She smiled a toothless smile as she pushed a trolley of meagre belongings.

Hong Kong was full of wild juxtaposition. Unaware of the danger, Lily and Oliver, two oblivious starlings, thought they had found the perfect nest, but they were perched on a precarious ledge. There was a fall coming, but they carried on regardless, spiralling into each other's hearts.

three

OLIVER WOULD BURST THROUGH the door any minute now, and Lily was having doubts about this rendezvous. Real doubt. Courage is feeling the trepidation but taking the plunge. Foolishness is the same.

Lily sat on the edge of the perfectly made hotel bed, its white striped linen so pristine she wondered whose loving hands had made it. Gazing out of the giant glass-panelled windows in the room, she smiled at all she saw. From the thirtieth floor, the panorama was spectacular. She peered out at the darkening sky as ominous clouds rolled over the horizon across her beloved fragrant Victoria harbour. Fragrant because this harbour was infamous for the seafarers who had travelled these waters for centuries, trading the most precious incense from a tree called Aquilaria Sinensis.

In Hong Kong, they believed that the wood of the Aquilaria trees, agarwood, possessed a potent life force or qi that could heal a life, change fortunes, and awaken the deepest soul mysteries.

Today Lily's heart was taking time to find equilibrium. Its thump filled her throat, and her jade eyes scanned the room for her bag. Perhaps she should take out her little brown bottle of Oud, an essential oil extracted from agarwood, and dab a few drops of the precious watered-down essence on her wrist – its delicate amber-toned smell calmed her. She strolled over to a marble table in the foyer, her long strawberry-butterscotch locks swaying with her ample hips as she went. She took the bottle out of her bag and dotted a few drops on her wrist. The soft aromatic woody scent climbing up her nostrils was the balm that brought the calmness she sought.

Lily found it intriguing. It wasn't the clean wood from the tree that contained these calming medicinal properties; it was the rot. And not just any rot, it was the heart rot. The tree's soul had to be inhabited by a burying beetle that would infest and wound it, causing a perilous mould to grow in its heartwood. The tree would then protect itself by releasing a miraculous healing resin – a tree antibiotic. It was this infected healed heartwood that was the basis for its potency. This diseased agarwood, denoted as Aguru wood in Sanskrit, was viewed as the wood of enlightenment. *This is the power of Mother Earth's extraordinary alchemy – a painful and poetic symbiosis synthesising into medicine.* Lily's heart returned to a soft and steady beat. She wondered if Oliver felt as nervous as she did.

Once upon a time, this entire island had been engulfed in a fragrant cloud of qi, as the Chinese junk boats with their distinctive red sails carried the holy teacher's wood across the waters to countries as far off as Arabia. The mystical was something Lily often pondered, even though there was less time for it these days. As a criminal defence lawyer, her leisure periods were few and far between. At times, she longed for childhood when she was free to run kaalvoet in the wild veld. A place where her vivid imagination thrived. Little Lily had been obsessed with the stars and all things animal and magical. Especially the Tokoloshe, a nefarious dwarf man who had come alive in Lily's imagination through the stories of her Xhosa Nanny, Lulama. Lulama had told Lily that if she didn't behave, the dwarf would visit her in the night with his bag of unimaginable terrors. Instead of being evil, as Lulama would have her believe, he'd manifested in her mind as a sweet, mischievous gnome. The idea of crossing his path excited her. Anything magic excited her – like Oliver.

Unbeknown to anyone else in her Hong Kong circle, this penchant for the mystical remained alive and well in Lily as an adult. Besides the bottle of Oud in her gifted Louis Vuitton bag, Lily carried a sliver of agarwood tucked away in her worn brown leather money purse. A wrinkled and bald saffron-robed monk had given it to her on one of her early morning visits to a Buddhist monastery on the top of a jungled hill on Lantau Island where she lived. As Lily had yet to master Cantonese, the language of this southern Asian region, the exchange had been wordless – but the monk's eyes knew her. His stare had burrowed right into her, like the burying beetle that eats the wood of the Aquilaria tree. Lily had gratefully accepted his gift. She would take the agarwood out sometimes – usually on sad days – and run her fingers over its earthy grittiness, letting its delicate scent come alive in her nostrils. Lily wondered if she, too, like Aquilaria Sinensis, had the power to alchemise her heart's sorrow into medicine.

Sitting on this soft plush hotel bed in her Jimmy Choo stilettos, looking out at the vast gateway to China, glancing at her watch while waiting for Oliver to arrive – Lily couldn't help the giant whiff of nostalgia that descended. She'd arrived in this world on an insignificant day, in a small box house on a quiet unpaved southern African road. The road was hot and dusty and belonged to a one-horse, gold mining town named Welkom. Welkom wasn't welcoming at all – Lily had survived its stinging storms and its warm and cold apartheid stories. Some memories still hurt, but there were beautiful things in that place, too. There were plush pink flamingos and Sunday ice creams and a head full of childhood dreams that had brought her here to this beautiful view of Hong Kong.

Lily, a small-town girl, was now a big city woman barging into courtrooms.

On court days, she dressed in black barrister's robes and white-collar bands. She had bought them, along with her Argentinean horsehair wig, in Ede & Ravenscroft – which had been open since 1689 on Chancery Lane in London. She'd never imagined a life in Asia. But here she was, in a hotel room, about to do something she may regret – sniffing agarwood to calm her building nerves and staring out at the South China Sea.

Today those crossing waters in Victoria Harbour were choppy, and the boats were heading into the storm shelters. The iconic green and white Star Ferry bobbed across wakes caused by crossing large vessel traffic. Lily imagined with a smile the ferry passengers sliding on their slippery varnished wooden bench seats from side to side. The ferry made a safe crossing as it had each day for decades through many types of weather. Tourists and commuters packed the vessel's seats as it crossed from the Kowloon peninsula to central Hong Kong Island. It was an iconic and unforgettable ride that most visitors who travelled to these parts had taken.

As Lily readjusted her seat on the hotel bed, she gazed at the Bank of China Building – an elegant, imposing skyscraper composed of diamond-shaped mirrored glass tiles. Like a theatre stage, it was hosting a troupe of dark foreboding clouds, each pirouetting in an impromptu dance across the slick surface of its smooth, reflective mirrors.

'Black Storm Warning, Black Storm Warning, take immediate action!'

Weather news flashed in lights across its neon skyscraper board.

Even the weather signs in this part of the world were Mao Tse Dung dictatorial, and for good reason: black storms are ferocious. They turn the brightest day into an ominous blackness. In Hong Kong, storms were classified according to severity, with 'black' being the worst. Lily had only ever experienced one black storm, and it was black enough that she didn't want to experience another. She wondered if this caution was an omen – a sign that this rendezvous wasn't meant to take place.

Her palms felt slippery and the smell of the soft flowery perfume she had dabbed between her ample breasts, which were now peering out from her balcony bra, became overpowering. Lily could feel a sickly sensation rising in her belly. And a sticky excitement between her legs. And then she heard it, the simultaneous crack of black storm thunder and the soft gentle tap on the door. Oliver had arrived. He was sliding his keycard in the door and bringing with him a bounty of contradictions as wild as the weather outside.

four

OLIVER WAS BESIDE HER in one nervous heartbeat, looking at her with eyes full of longing. She wondered if he would notice her internal war. And then, with his pear-shaped vowel accent, he said, in the most beautiful way,

'Hello.'

Oliver took Lily's hand as she stood beside the bed and met his gaze. He lifted her chin with his finger. They both smiled in anticipation. She could smell him, and he was delicious. His aromatic aftershave lingered as she nuzzled her head against his chest. She was invincible with her head pressed against his crisp cotton shirt. Oliver gently traced his index finger over the smooth skin of her face and landed on the top button of her blouse. She released a nervous giggle as he unbuttoned it.

Oliver was as illuminating as the moon in the night sky. He understood the pain of her grief even if she hadn't shared it. She knew she would. She was safe with Oliver. He heard her. He lit up her dark places, and somehow when she was with him in those quiet hours in Mingle, the brutal world stopped, and a softness sank in. There was no before, no after, no pushing and propping against the tide – just a sweet surrender to that providential moment when two worlds connect.

That is why she had agreed, on a Friday evening in Mingle, to meet him here on the thirtieth floor of a five-star hotel in Causeway Bay. This wasn't a decision she had taken lightly.

Her hands were shaking, and her heart felt tender because Luka's mahogany obsidian eyes were haunting her.

How does a human not feel guilty?

Christ, why am I behaving like a schoolgirl? She didn't want Oliver to notice her coyness. She was a powerful, confident woman, and the feel of his fingers against her skin was making her lose control.

Oliver slid off her blouse. He was so adept she didn't even notice that it had dropped to the floor. He unhooked her bra at the front, revealing her ample breasts. The La Perla ivory-white lace bra landed on top of her blouse on the floor. She only wore it on special occasions. Lily looked away in embarrassment, and Oliver promptly turned her head back towards him.

'Lily, look at me.' He was tender.

She didn't have an answer, but she met his eyes. He devoured her semi-nakedness with them. There was nowhere to hide, and a tingling warmth rose in her belly. Oliver's breath quickened – the animal in him was awakening. Lily felt his wanting, and her heart raced as her nipples hardened in excitement against the coolness of the air-conditioned room air. She felt ripe and gorgeous standing in front of him like this. Being watched made the wetness rise between her legs. The anticipation was unbearable.

'Stay there, don't move.'

Oliver grumbled under the quickness of his breath as he walked towards the mini bar and picked up a bottle of wine and two glasses. He poured them each a glass. They both sipped the rich oak-vanilla red – watching each other.

'Fuck, you are beautiful, Lily. I'll watch you before I fuck you, okay? Take off your skirt.'

Lily loved the authority of his tone, but she challenged him with a mischievous look while she stood still in defiance. She was getting her confidence back.

'Take it off,' he insisted with a playful smile.

She hadn't heard him speak this way. It made her want him. Lily unzipped her skirt and let it fall to the ground in a heap.

She felt her cheeks flush. *God damn it*, she thought, *why am I still so self-conscious about my body?* She wanted to hide her wobbly thighs and her rounded belly. But when she looked up, she saw Oliver's face. His eyes were blazing. Lily had never felt so wanted.

Oliver removed his clothes as fast as he had removed hers. Lily found him irresistible, and before she knew it, they were lying on the floor between the bed and window. Their chemistry was as ferocious as the black storm raging outside. They made love in every way, with their eyes and bodies entirely in sync. Oliver took her in all the ways he wanted. Bent over and kneeling in front of him, on her back, watching her swollen red lips release delicious moans as he thrust himself inside her. Lily's face was expressive – anyone watching would know her bliss. They ebbed and flowed together like the waves of the sea. Gentle and rough, rough and gentle. She rode him. He fucked her. Their lovemaking was exhilarating, wild, happy, and free.

Between the passion and awkward condom wrapper moments, there was a feeling of comfort. As though they had been doing this for an eternity. Lily loved his playfulness.

'You've had no one suck your toes?' he asked with a mischievous smile, putting her left big toe in his mouth.

'Never!' Lily squirmed as she pulled her foot away from his slippery tongue.

Oliver swiftly turned her over, playfully spanked her bottom, and fucked her some more – in a way that meant business. Lily came over and over, writhing on the small patch of carpet floor beside the bed while looking out at the magical night sky through the tall glass-panelled windows.

After several hours, the passion abated, and the tenderness began. Oliver poured them another glass of wine. They sat on the floor with the duvet wrapped around their naked bodies, watching the lightning show over Victoria Harbour and listening to the night sounds, and they talked.

Sex is only part of real intimacy, which comes from something far deeper and more challenging to the human psyche – truth. Making love to Oliver had been as effortless as a floating leaf following the trajectory of the river in which it fell. But opening her heart and offering the truths that were as integral to Lily's life as the stitches that hold together a garment – took courage. An act of courage that she couldn't find until this moment. And when she found it and her voice with him, she could talk about it all, even the darkest places.

She told him about the life of a girl who had been abused by the man she loved most – her father. She told him about the grief of losing him two years ago, a father that she had never really had, but, for some incomprehensible reason, she loved more than any human alive. She told him about burying an old man under an African sky, and she knew she could tell him because Oliver understood what it means to lose the things you love the most. She told him about Lulama, the one person who knew her, the one who could see inside of her, even the not-so-nice parts, and loved her all the same. She told him about Luka and their marital problems. The only thing she could not talk about was her baby, Jessie.

To do so would betray some part of her soul.

On that night, on the place between the bed and the wall, on the floor staring out at the multicoloured lights of the city until they diminished with the penetrating light of a golden sun rising over the South China Sea – Lily remembered what intimacy was. They remained covered in each other's limbs until the morning light painted the horizon. Until the traffic on the highways beneath hummed with a steady flow.

five

South Africa, August 2007

LILY KICKED THE DUST with the tip of her takkies. *Crap!* Papa hated dirty shoes. But today, it had to be done. This red earth was the smell of home. And it had been a long time since Lily's feet had touched South African soil. The flight from Hong Kong had been an easy one with a smooth landing at dawn, which offered a wondrous view of a candy floss-coloured southern African sky.

She stood beside her luggage on the manicured curb of her parent's new home. They lived in the Western Cape, in a small seaside town called George. The lawn was perfectly mowed, the smell of freshly cut grass lingering. The driveway was lined with hydrangeas in a vibrant mix of blues and pinks, and the sweet-salty sea air was filled with the delicate scent of rose petals and fynbos. This new suburb was pristine. Beautiful spacious homes with tended gardens – a complete contrast to the density of Hong Kong housing that Lily had become accustomed to for the last ten years.

She noticed the weeping mop head tree positioned on the side of the face-brick house. As she stood in Papa's new garden, she looked down at her dirty trainers and remembered Sundays after church – Papa would pull out newspapers and brushes for shining and polishing shoes. Lily would sit beside him as he explained the polishing routine. She could hear him and smell his rum and maple tobacco breath as if it were yesterday.

'We use this flat brush with the long bristles for polishing. Dip it in sparingly, my girl,' he cautioned, 'then apply it in an anti-clockwise direction.'

Papa always had an authoritative tone.

'Okay, let's set the shoes to dry for a minute before we use the brush with the shorter bristles to shine them.'

He peered at Lily over the top of his spectacles, expecting acknowledgement, his hair slicked back with Brylcreem.

'Yes, Papa,' she said, beaming. Grateful for any time she could have alone with him.

'When we shine, we use even strokes from left to right.'

He called out the directions, 'Left, right, left, right,' with a firm voice.

'You try,' he ordered, handing the brush to Lily.

When Papa attempted the task, it seemed incredibly easy, but she soon realised it was a lot more difficult than it appeared. For weeks, Papa observed Lily's every move as she polished until he was content with her technique. It took time – her little hands were not dexterous.

'Keep going, my girl. One day you will perfect it!'

Lily recalled the last step being the arduous task of buffing the surface until it gleamed. She used a velvet buffing cushion – it was silky soft and smelt like petrol bubble-gum.

On one lucky Sunday, Papa deemed her capable enough to shine her shoes. She would never be good enough to shine his.

'Remember, Lily, if you do a job, do it properly or don't do it at all,' he said.

Lily wasn't sure that this graduation was good, and she was right. From that day, if Lily's shoes weren't perfectly polished for school, she would get a thorough talking down or a stinging slap on her bottom. The Flannery family was blemish-free, so the presentation to the outside world had to be shiny shoes. Shiny shoes, pearly whites (Papa sometimes used ash from the braai to make sure they were spotless), and manicured nails.

As a child, Lily deplored shiny shoes. She found the etchings of dirt so much more gratifying, like the intricate placement of paint on a blank canvas. On most of her childhood walks home from school, Lily would jump into puddles and kick the hard red dust until her shoes were filthy. When she reached the driveway of her house, she would slip them off and hide them in her old brown school satchel, only retrieving them later to clean them out of the sight of Mama's cornflower-blue eyes. Mama thought Lily was protecting her shoes when she turned up with bare feet at the door. Lily loved this minor rebellion. It made her feel alive.

Her nanny, Lulama, was wise to her antics. She would watch Lily from the shadows and mumble to herself. 'Sjoe! This little Pikinini is a rebel.'

Now, as Lily examined the door of her parents' new home, she knew Lulama wouldn't be on the other side, and she felt a flood of sorrowful missing. Lulama – the only one in the family who accepted Lily for who she was and showed her unconditional love, despite enduring the agony of being apart from her son. Lily remembered the droop of Lulama's shoulders as she washed the dishes, cleaned the laundry, cooked, and ironed the Flannery family's linen for all those years. Lulama would see her son Nelson on the last weekend of every month. She named him after her hero: Nelson Rolihlahla (troublemaker in Xhosa) Mandela. Lily would watch her leave, her head held high and her energy renewed. Despite understanding that she would soon be reunited with her, Lily could not cope with their distance.

Lulama was her comfort blanket. She would cry when she was gone. She had whiled away many nights cuddling with Lulama, calming her bad dreams. It was also in those late evening hours that Lily had heard the stories of the freedom struggle.

Lily asked Lulama countless questions, and she understood from listening to the answers why Mama kept a separate tin cup and plate for Lulama under the sink. She also understood why Lulama lived in a separate room outside the main house, and why Lulama could never use the house toilet or eat dinner with them – even though she had prepared it. She understood why the police would sometimes come and check that Lulama was home, and why there were parks and beaches with signs that read NET BLANKES (Whites Only) that they couldn't visit together. She understood why black and white people weren't permitted to love one another.

Yes, she knew why. And it would remain a solemn secret. She knew if she spoke it, there would be severe consequences. Papa would yell and show his stinging hands. So she never would. At least, not until she was a grown-up, and she was as strong as him.

Lily felt a burning love for Lulama. It was the ember of strength that kept Lily fighting, and it was this spark that ignited her curiosity in the law.

The wave of missing Lulama hit Lily hard as she stood on this new southern African soil and looked down at her dirt-speckled shoes that were quite impossible to clean. Bugger. Here she was, an adult woman, still seeking Papa's approval in the most arbitrary ways – clean shoes, sparkly teeth, and manicured nails. She had tried to fix her appearance in the airport toilet, but now she had ruined it.

An abundance of scented roses framed Papa's lawn. She wondered as she gazed at their beauty and the beauty of the Outeniqua mountains beyond if the aching need to please Papa would ever leave her. Lily ran her tongue over her smooth, sparkly white teeth and walked towards the neat front door.

Shoulders back – 'Papa, Mama, I'm home!'

The door burst open. Mama was the one who opened it.

'My kind!' she cried, tears welling up in her eyes.

Lily ran to her mother, and when she felt the warmth of her embrace, she exhaled a sigh of relief. They stood in this embrace for some time, both women sobbing the tears of reunion, which in this case were bittersweet. It was good to be home, enveloped in her mother's fresh scent – a mixture of eucalyptus and flowers. But when she pulled away, she noticed how Mama had aged. She looked frail. Lily's heart sank to her belly. Mama was disappearing.

'Mama, where is Papa?' Lily asked as she stroked her mother's soft silver hair.

'He is not here. He was sick last night, and the doctor insisted on admitting him to the hospital.'

'But I spoke to him yesterday. Why didn't he say it was that bad?'

'You know your papa; he didn't want to worry you! I'm so glad you are here, Lily!' Mama was shaking. 'I can't get through to the hospital. No one seems to know what's going on, and I can't drive anymore, so I can't get there to find out. I haven't heard a word since Papa said goodbye last night.' Her eyes were distraught.

'Don't worry, Mama, I will find out what's happening. You sit down, and I'll make you a fresh cup of tea. And then we'll sort this out.'

Lily dumped her bags in the entrance hall and walked to the kitchen. There was such a familiarity to it, even though she had never lived in this house. The kitchen was in perfect order, just like she remembered from her childhood home. The tea tin clearly marked – she opened the lid, and the smell of fresh rooibos hit her. Another waft of childhood. Lily turned the kettle on and placed a tea bag in a regal white porcelain Royal Doulton teacup with gold rims. These were Mama's special occasion teacups, and this was a special occasion. It had been two years since she had been in her mother's arms.

Mama settled onto the sage-green sofa, and the sound of the cushions rustling filled the room. The lounge room was cosy and inviting, with its plush furniture and the mosaic of colours from the carefully chosen decorations. Lily noticed the family photos arranged on side tables – the silver frames glinting in the light. The faces of childhood peered out at her from behind the spotless glass. Her two little brothers beamed with glee, her big sister's hair styled in a '70sinspired look, with a passive expression. Lily's heart warmed. Despite its imperfections, her childhood was filled with heart-warming memories.

There were Christmas Eves, where she would sit with Papa and wrap all the presents he had chosen when she was old enough to know that Father Christmas wasn't real. Hearty family meals made by Lulama and days spent tending the garden beside Papa. Mama read the bedtime stories at night and worked at the local post office during the day. There were caravan holiday adventures; best of all, there was sleeping under the stars.

As Lily stirred the tea she was preparing for Mama, she thought about how much she loved those nights, in the old garden, the adventures of setting up camp. All the siblings wrapped up in sleeping bags, with Papa narrating the path of the constellations. He welcomed their questions and answered each one of them. It was hardly a surprise that her baby brother, Thomas, had become an astrophysicist. Papa had awakened a curiosity about the universe and its conundrums in all of them. The siblings possessed quiet confidence; Papa believed them capable of great things, and they could all feel that. Those nights under the stars awakened Lily's insatiable appetite for pursuing answers to the *big* questions. And her thirst for adventure.

Papa was a complex character with many sides, sometimes Jekyll and sometimes Hyde. As loving and encouraging as he could be, there were also dark days cloaked by his outbursts. Lily loved him more than anyone else, but she knew she couldn't rely on him. And that's why she'd decided early on that she would become self-sufficient.

Lily felt her jaw tense as she admired the intricate patterns he had carved into the garden from the window. It was like the one Papa had made in Welkom, the town where the Flannery family had grown up. A town filled with a hot yellow desert sun, bulbous white clouds, and flocks of pink flamingos. It had a grid of unkempt dirt roads and simple box-like houses containing a community of ordinary folk with toothy smiles and working hands. There was nothing posh about it. Women were observed with curlers in their hair, chatting with their neighbours. Many of the men left home with miners' boots. Papa was their boss. Children played with one another in the streets, their bare feet treading the heat of the dusty, unpaved roads. The sky would roll with thunder, leaving the veld smelling like fresh rain. A smell that would linger for days after a big downpour. Welkom was also a place of choking red dust storms.

When Lily was little, she sometimes waited at the crisscross wire gate of her family's box house for Papa to come home. Her long golden locks framed her pixie face as she stood, counting daisy petals, singing songs, or kicking the dirt. Lily was perplexed because she never quite knew which Papa would come home. This was because he was as charming as he was treacherous. Her fear never stopped her from waiting; he would be happy to see her. And that was worth the gamble.

Papa's good moods were better than sunshine. He was handsome, gentle, and generous in spirit, that is – until his dark moods came. They made him ugly. His outbursts would arrive like Welkom's insatiable dust clouds, blowing with a ferocity that would leave everything in their path stinging and covered with thick red dust. Blood. Yes, Papa could be violent. He loved with a consuming fierceness, but his darkness was equally torrid. In his rage, he hurt his children and even his beloved wife.

Papa was a broken man. And he needed to be fixed. As all four-year-old girls know, it was Lily's job to put him together. Like Humpty-Dumpty.

Not a single memory was erased in this new house. New carpets and curtains didn't change a thing. Lily walked over to Mama and set the fragrant rooibos tea down beside her. She knew she wasn't responsible for the pain in Mama's eyes. Despite that, she would have done anything to erase it.

six

THE DAYS THAT FOLLOWED were a blur of activity. There were challenging phone calls to all the siblings and all-day visits to the hospital where Papa lay in a cold room. He was unconscious. Emergency surgery to repair his intestines had failed. There was sepsis. He lay in silence, limbs cold and limp, connected to tubes and drip lines, heart and respiration monitors. He lay immobile, unresponsive, eyes closed to the pain of all those who loved him.

Lily brought Mama to the hospital as much as she could. Mama's eyes were becoming vacant – a hollow ghost. She was disappearing into another world, a place that would keep her safe from the reality of a dying partner. Lily felt a weight lift when her brothers and sister arrived. They were a close and loving bunch. Thomas from New York, Edward from Johannesburg, and Sarah from London. At any other time, they would have been happy to see one another. But in the sterile hospital halls, their embraces were tentative. They all appeared broken in their unique ways. Papa might have been a storm, but he held them all together like the glue of a gum tree. He had become a wise council in his later years when the violence inside him had abated. Papa did the miraculous thing that some humans do – he changed. And he did his best to make amends. Contrary to popular belief, those who grow up in Africa know leopards can change their spots.

Lily did her best to cope with the momentous days surrounding Papa's end. There were drops of Oud dabbed on her temples and wrists; late-night incense burned in her room; and there were many attempts at meditation. She had been reading about it in a book titled *Cultivating Calmness*. Lily no longer prayed.

And then there was one memorable night with her older sister, Sarah. They had driven to the Dutch Reformed Mother Church on the corner of Courtney and Kerk streets – slap-bang in the middle of the town of George. The Cape Dutch architecture unique to this part of the world held a simple but striking beauty. The windows were composed of stained glass; the ceilings were decorated with intricate wood-etchings; and the gardens were dotted with roses – Papa's treasured blossoms. He kept all his gardens full of them. When Lily was a child, he would bring her his lovingly tended yellow Germiston Gold, the red-and-yellow Durban July, or the autumnal peach Just Joey. The elegant

Kashmir Rose, his red crowning glory, would be reserved for apology days – for his red outbursts. He said nothing on those days; he just put a single red rose on Lily's pillow. A place he visited too much. Over the years, there were dozens of red roses.

Lily and Sarah walked hand in hand into the church – its floor covered with red carpet. It seemed strange to Lily – *the Christian God is an invisible celebrity.* The sisters always walked this way when they were together, holding onto each other for dear life. There wasn't a competitive bone between them. As children, they had barricaded each other from the harshness of their world – from Papa's black clouds. As adults, they encouraged each other in all their pursuits. No matter how crazy. Sarah, the arty one, had once wanted to be a stripper, Lily, the academic, a war correspondent. The sisters were confidantes, and even though they lived in different countries, when they were together, it was as though not a day had passed. Sarah was three years older than Lily, but no one noticed because they looked like identical twins.

'I can't believe this is happening.' Sarah's voice was a whimper.

'I thought of him as invincible; I thought he would outlive us all. I've never imagined a single day without him in our world.'

'I know, Sarah, I know.' Lily clutched her sister's hand.

They made their way to the front pews and sat down. The church was empty, and they were both grateful for that. Lily sat in silence, staring at the flickering candles on the altar and the image of Jesus nailed to a cross. It sent a shiver down her spine. *How cruel.* Sarah bowed her head and prayed. Her intermittent sobbing outbursts broke the quietude.

'I don't want him to die. I don't care about the past. I forgave him a long time ago. He lived through hell. I don't want him to die, Lily!'

Lily wrapped her arms around Sarah, staring at the bloodied Jesus behind them. This hurt so much. Nothing she could say or do would lift the heaviness of it all for any of them. Not for Sarah, not for Thomas or Edward. Not for Mama.

God, she wished Lulama was here. She would know what to do. She would break Mama from her daydreaming and keep Lily from feeling as though she were carrying the entire load. She would make light of what was so heavy – she was an expert at that. *Please, Lulama, if you can hear me, please find your way here. I can't do this without you.*

Lulama lived in the village where she was born, beyond the river Kei, known as the Transkei in the Eastern Cape of southern Africa. Squeezed between the Drakensberg, the Mountains of the Dragon, and the Indian Ocean, is the Transkei. Here, the Mountain Pipit sings its songs to the morning sun, and the Indian Ocean's warm and turbulent waves crash on the white sandy beaches. Lily had offered Lulama a mobile phone, but Lulama refused to use it. Neither did she have a landline. She was isolated from the modern world. Lily understood why. Lulama wanted to be rooted where she lived. The place she'd been deprived of for so many years as a forced migrant worker. She didn't have any of the modern amenities that lived in her son's home next door. No television, no computer – nothing to divert her attention from her rightful place on the hillside, in her traditional African home with the most breath-taking sights of the untamed and rugged ocean – the waves so powerful they could erase entire worlds.

Lily had made only one trip to Lulama's rondavel. It was a contemporary adaptation of the ancient Transkei circular houses that were shaped like beehives and made of mud. The old rondavels had conical thatched straw roofs and floors made of polished cow dung. Lulama's walls, made of straw bale, were thick, insulated, and coated with a bright sea-green plaster. Her floors sparkled with shiny stone embedded in polished concrete. Inside was an artist's dream. Lily was enamoured by it all. The floor was warmed by traditional Xhosa hand-woven rugs, and the wooden kitchen shelves were adorned with vibrant, hand-painted pots. Every day, Lulama carefully strung together colourful beads to form beautiful designs, which were then sold as souvenirs at the local tourist spots. Her life now was simple, creative, and full. Full of the voices of her extended family and childhood friends, and full of the joyous grandchildren that her son's wife, Nomsa, had birthed. Lily was overjoyed to witness it all. Lulama stepped out of her rondavel to a garden of ripe, succulent edibles, accompanied by the sweet smell of sweet flowers. Fresh, juicy pineapple, carrots, spinach, eggfruit, broad beans, and runner beans filled the garden. The free-roaming chickens roamed around the yard, providing a delicious breakfast as the resident rooster proudly announced the sunrise with his loud, crowing call and his halo of ruby feathers. On warm summer days, Lulama would open the bright red front door and the sound of the sea breeze would fill her room, lulling her to sleep. Once in a while, a scorpion or snake would escape the heat of the summer sun by slithering into the cool refuge. Lily noticed that Lulama didn't even flinch at the presence of scorpions or snakes.

'Poor things!' she would say. *'Why would I deprive them of shade?'*

Lulama would leave the rondavel for an entire day rather than chase the snakes away.

Lily had no means of contacting Lulama. So, on the first day she arrived in South Africa, she sent a postcard and an urgent email to Lulama's son, Nelson.

She should have been here by now.

Lily felt exasperation as she pulled away from Sarah's embrace. The church was filled with a chill that seemed to seep into her bones. Sarah was intent on prayer, her voice a quiet whisper in the room's stillness. Lily waited, trying not to get too lost in hopeless thoughts.

Lily was unaware that Sarah and Nelson had been talking and had made a plan to keep Lulama's arrival time a secret. It was their plan to surprise her. And the reason for this church visit was more than just to pray. The intercity bus stop was situated directly across the road.

Half an hour later, as Lily and Sarah stood to leave the old church, they noticed an ethereal silhouette in the doorway. Lily thought she was hallucinating. She let out an involuntary squeal.

'Lulama!'

She stood regal as a queen, wearing a colourful headscarf and matching dress. Illuminated by the candlelight near the doorway, she looked like a ghostly apparition. Lily rubbed her eyes hard to make sure she wasn't dreaming. The sisters ran into her wide-open arms. She had space for both of them. Lulama's arms could hold the world.

Three days later, in the Sunday morning hours, Lily heard the gentle chime on her phone and woke from a dreamless sleep. She noticed Lulama was already awake, kneeling in prayer in front of the window in the room they were sharing. She was staring out towards a tiny sliver of moonlight and mumbling words that Lily didn't understand. Still, by the way she said them, Lily knew they were significant.

The Night Duty Sister was firm. 'You should all come now. He hasn't got long.'

Lulama had already packed a small bag to take to the hospital. Lily set about waking her brothers, sister, and Mama, and they all tumbled into the dark and distressing night.

The following day, Lily woke up crying – small sobs, followed by the shuddering cries of grief. She got up to wash her hands. Over and over. Sobbing and washing hands – she could still see blood, smell blood, taste blood. A bleed out is a shocking thing.

The tide of grief receded, and Lily got dressed and walked out to the park across the road. She had left the others inside; they were still asleep. At last, the air smelt clean – recent rain on the earth, a distinct smell in Africa. She sat on a wooden bench, staring out at the empty sky. It had lost its colour. And then a curious thing happened. A dark-haired woman walked towards her. She had something in her hands. She placed it in Lily's lap without saying a word.

Could this be? Is this real? Am I still dreaming?

And then the stranger walked away before Lily had time to thank her.

A single red rose – its red velvet petals as soft as cashmere.

Oh, Papa! You can't apologise for dying.

seven

AFTER PAPA'S ROSE, LILY felt a comfort as sure as the daily sunrise. She didn't know how he did it. But she knew it was him. Papa had placed the rose in the stranger's hands. And the stranger had placed the rose in hers. The rose, now coloured with death, would be kept alive in her heart, in Lily's diary – where it lay pressed flat between the pages, telling a story of forgiveness.

Carrying its comfort, she set about doing the thing she did best. Organising. She arranged the funeral, Mama's finances and Mama's blood pressure medicine. She met with the probate lawyers to settle Papa's will. Flowers and eulogies, coffins and cremations. A photo wall of memories – Lily did it all. Doing was all she thought about – it worked for her because it allowed her little time for being still.

There were occasional silent moments when she noticed a cold emptiness creep in – especially moments like now when she was watering Papa's crafted garden. Looking at Papa's landscape, she thought about how lovingly his hands had tended the bridal proteas, the roses, African lilies, daisies, hydrangeas, and Mama's favourite – Yesterday, Today and Tomorrow. This garden was full of life, and Papa's hands had abandoned it in death. Right now, it was an African-English garden. *What would it become – Bushveld?* Maybe that was right, but it felt wrong. She imagined Papa turning the compost pit, a satisfied smile spreading across his face when he saw the healthy, wriggling earthworms. He took pride in regenerating the earth. She remembered his words.

'Without healthy dirt, we die.'

Lily remembered him harvesting the sweet Hanepoot grapes that hung from the pergola and the hard-shelled granadillas that clung to the trellis on the side wall of their old garden. She remembered him tossing her juicy coral peaches, tart nectarines, and sweet blush strawberries. She remembered the sweet, sticky feeling of the mulberry juice as it coated her teeth and hands after hours of gorging on the ripe berries that he grew. Papa's anger evaporated when he was tending his plants. As if the soil drank from his wounds. Everything that was good about Papa was here on the little piece of land. Lily wasn't ready to let Mother Earth reclaim it.

A Buffalo Thorn tree cracked in the wind, its branches heavy with age as a southerly wind swept into Papa's garden. Lulama appeared beside her, and Lily jumped. She was holding a crimson plastic raincoat.

'The rain is coming.' Lulama draped the raincoat gently over Lily's shoulders. 'How are you feeling, my little Pikinini?' she asked.

Lily placed the hosepipe on the ground with a soft thud.

'I forgot how suddenly these storms arrive; I've spent the last half hour watering for nothing.' She sighed, her feet dragging on the ground, as she walked towards the tap.

'Not for nothing; you needed to be still, and plants need company – they get lonely, too.' Lulama looked at Lily with an understanding glint in her eyes. 'How are you feeling, Lily?' she repeated the question.

'I've just got so much to sort.' Lily turned off the tap. 'I can't stay here forever. I have to get back to work.' She wound the hose around a reel. 'Who is going to water the garden when I'm gone?' Lily said. 'Everyone has lives to go back to. Sarah's boss is an arse. I'm surprised she's even allowed her to attend the funeral. And the boys have work and families who need them. We need to hire help. Mama won't cope.'

'There is still time, Lily. I will stay until it's all settled. Stop trying to do it all and accept the help that's being offered. It will make things easier for you. Your brothers and sister are just as capable as you.' Lulama raised her eyebrows and gave her a piercing look.

'Oh, Lula, thank you!' Lily ignored her admonishment. 'I am worried about Ma! I wish I could take her back to Hong Kong with me, but I know she won't cope in such a foreign environment. She's never travelled abroad.'

'We will find a solution. Many qualified care nurses are looking for work.' Lulama's tone was reassuring.

'Do you think she will wake up out of her dream? She feels gone, Lula – like the wind has taken her.' Lily's teeth scraped her bottom lip.

'She is gone, Pikinini. She is visiting a quiet place, a necessary place. The truth here is too painful for Mama.' Lulama pointed to her heart. 'But there will come a moment when she is brave enough to see, and that is when she will need us the most.' Lulama placed a comforting hand on Lily's shoulder. 'I won't leave until then. I understand if you must go back to work, but try to stay as long as possible.'

Lily nodded in agreement.

'Pikinini, you still haven't answered my question. How are you feeling? Are you okay?'

Lily felt a lump in her throat, unable to make a sound. She grabbed the crimson raincoat, the fabric crinkling as she put it on.

'I have to rush off to buy groceries,' she stammered. 'The shops will close soon. We are running out of rooibos and buttermilk rusks, and that is unacceptable.'

Lily scampered off in a flurry of leaves before Lulama had a chance to respond.

Lily didn't know why she was avoiding Lulama's question. She suspected it had something to do with hard truths. She was avoiding her feelings. She avoided everyone, too – Sarah, Tom, Edward, and Mama. Their eyes all said too much. And Luka. Her husband. She looked at her phone – fifteen missed calls and twenty-one texts.

The morning of the funeral arrived. Lily woke up before dawn and was relieved to get out of bed. No more staring at the ceiling. She felt the gnaw of anger in her stomach.

Luka should have been here today.

She made a cup of coffee, grabbed a rusk, and went to sit outside on the porch. The view was something – just as the sun slipped above the horizon, the shadow of the peaks arrived. It was breath-taking. She understood why Papa was so adamant about moving here.

George and Cradock Peak were mountain guardians that stood proudly in the early light. These Outeniqua ranges had stories to tell. The name Outeniqua means 'those who bear honey'. A Khoikhoi tribe who once walked in the mountains had named it. This sweet land was abundant with fertile bounties, providing nectar for the bees. In the foothills, leopard would chase klipspringer. In the crags, meerkats and rock hyrax would play deadly 'hide and seek' games as the black eagles circled overhead, searching for prey. On the southern slopes lay the sub-tropical Knysna forests with their treasure trove of native trees: Ironwood, Stinkwood, Outeniqua Yellow-wood, Cape Holy, White Pear, Cape Beach, Assegai tree, and even the Cape Bastard Saffron with its rugged, round leathery leaves, purple berries, and its orange-copper saffron-coloured trunk. Cape Bastard was a furniture maker's dream – producing chairs and tables with golden-amber hues.

These forests were home to a menagerie of birds and animals, including Lily's favourite – the noble African elephant. In a high school set work, Lily first discovered that elephants have funerals. Sometimes they bury their dead under foliage. Sometimes they just circle back to the remaining carcasses of their loved ones and stand in circles and mourn. She wished human funerals were as simple as burying bodies under leaves or leaving them to hungry animals to feed. It seemed so gracious – giving the dead back to the earth this way. There was no fuss. Everyone could just get on with the business of grieving and remembering. And Mother Earth could get on with her decomposition work.

Lily hated funerals. The last funeral she attended was made even more sombre by the small box coffin. She shuddered at the memory – as if it were made for a doll.

She spotted a single leaf lying sunken in the earth between the grass and the porch paving. It was crackled by the sun, spot-eaten by chewy insects. It lay gnarly and imperfect. The leaf took up its space without pretence or shame. It settled where it was meant to be on the earth. Even though it was dead, its organisms would continue to live for decades in the perfect rhythm of time's unfolding. Becoming earth, becoming nutrients, becoming a myriad of life forms that would circle this way for an eternity. *Sooner or later we all fly from the tree.*

By the time Lily returned to the house, everyone was up. Lily noticed Sarah sitting in the lounge's corner nook, her face illuminated by the morning light. Sarah with her ballerina's toes, so regal and so beautiful. Dressed in a cream linen dress decorated with colourful African beads around her neck, wrists, and ankles, she was a picture. She sat next to Mama, her elegant fingers intertwining with hers as she stroked her hand. Sarah would never know how lovely she was because she was the type of woman who only saw beauty outside herself.

Lulama was in the kitchen, preparing breakfast for them all. And there were many of them since Edward's and Tom's families had arrived for the funeral.

'Sit, Lily,' she said as she shoved a plate in front of her. 'Eat. You need your strength. You'll be busy for the rest of the day.'

Just as Lily was taking her first mouthful of scrambled eggs, Edward burst into the kitchen, still wearing his striped pyjamas.

'Has anybody seen my suit?' he bellowed in desperation.

'No,' Lily replied, 'what's happened?'

'I hung it up in Papa's wardrobe. It was the only place where I could find any hangers.' Furrows of worry creased his forehead. 'It's disappeared, and it's the only suit I packed!'

Oh my God, the truth dawned on Lily's face, *what have I done?*

She reached for her phone and dialled the funeral master's number.

'Um, good morning. Is that Mr Van der Merwe?'

Edward's eyes bulged out of his head in disbelief.

'I am s-sorry to disturb you so early,' Lily continued, 'but can you please describe the suit that Papa will be buried in today?'

She listened to his response.

'Oh sh— Mr Van der Merwe, I sent you the wrong suit. It b-belongs to my brother. It's the only one he brought with him. All the way from New York. Is there any way we could change it now?'

The room was silent. Lily could feel everyone's eyes on her.

'Oh, crap! Thank you, Mr Van der Merwe. I'm sorry to disturb you.'

Lily ended the call and Edward glared at her in disbelief.

'Lily, what the hell? Papa's wearing my suit?'

'I'm afraid so. I'm so sorry. It was hanging in his cupboard. I just assumed it was his. Nothing I can do. He's already in the hearse.'

Edward looked at her with disgust, and then his face softened as his eyes sparkled, a hearty chuckle rumbling from his chest. Lily giggled, too. Lulama, concealed behind the fridge door, snorted and cackled hysterically, while Sarah gave a loud howl that sounded like a wolf baying at the moon. Even serious Thomas was beside himself with hysterics. Papa was being buried today in Edward's pants, which would be way too short for him, and his favourite conspicuous red socks.

'I'm sure I can sort you out with something to wear, old boy,' said Thomas with a smile that could swallow the sun.

'Thanks, boet,' replied Edward, between all the fits and snorts.

And so Papa's funeral day began with rainfalls of laughter.

Lily felt blessed to have a family like hers. They had weathered many storms but endured them together, which was all that mattered. She was sure that Papa would smile from his place in the stars. Lily noticed a tiny twinkle in Mama's eyes, too – life was returning to her in the most unexpected way. They would bury Papa in trousers four inches too short, and the heaviness of grief that had stung the air for days had just dissipated.

eight

Hong Kong, October 2007

LUKA WAS RIDING THE escalator up to Exit A. Chek Lap Kok Airport was a morass of people rushing. Luka stood still on the right side, holding the handrail, and the commuters, who were in a hurry, walked past on the left. Everything was a model of efficiency in this city, and Luka liked that. *Polite efficiency.* His lips curved into a smile, a stark contrast to the wild energy of the woman he was about to meet. His enigmatic wife, Lily, was wise and wilful, her presence a constant source of fascination.

His hands were slick with sweat as he gripped the cold, black handrail. Things had been strained between them. She had said it was okay if he didn't attend her father's funeral. It was a lengthy trip amid his most demanding period at work. The world was about to dip into recession, and he was putting out fires. Lily had stopped taking his calls after that conversation. He had tried to reach her in her midnight hours – time zones were a bitch. But the least she could have done was respond to his texts. Sometimes she behaved like a petulant child.

Luka's heart was heavy with sadness at the thought of Lily's father's passing. He felt a kinship with Charles Flannigan. The thought of him not being here felt strange. *Quite unreal.* He knew Charles had been a source of pain for Lily in her childhood, but Luka had only ever known him as an older man, and Charles had been kind and generous to him. When Lily spoke of Charles's violent outbursts, it was like she was talking about a completely different person. Sometimes he even wondered if Lily had made it up. Lily was great at embellishing; she had a talent for it. She was such a gifted lawyer.

Luka loved watching her in a courtroom – always a big surprise to her adversaries. He was proud of his Kick-Ass Woman. The way she went in for the kill on a cross-examination – who would have believed his delicate-faced girl could be so fierce, her verbal blows ringing out in the air? He had never seen that side of her at home, except in bed. Lily could be a firecracker. She was gentle and devoted to her loved ones and those she took under her wing, yet never hesitated to fight for her cause. Lily's world was an ever-present battleground. Luka didn't mind. He loved it that Lily was so full of life, so full of causes and contradictions. He treasured their life together – at least he had, until that fateful day two years ago. The day their baby girl, Jessie, died. He felt a tightness in his chest as the thought dawned on him.

Lily's pregnancy had been normal. He had loved watching her tummy grow. Nothing had made Luka happier than the thought of their child. He would snuggle close to Lily every night, his hands on her belly, feeling the baby's first infinitesimal movements and feeling Lily. Pregnancy sex was sensational. Luka felt an enormous sense of pride – his wife would be a wonderful mother, and he would do everything to raise a happy child. Unlike his demanding parents, he would have no expectations of this baby. He was already in love.

Lily's twenty-week scan occurred on a cold, blustery November day in a private hospital close to the top of Hong Kong's Peak. There was a heavy blizzard in Beijing, and rumours circulated that Hong Kong might expect its first-ever dusting of snow. As the obstetric gynaecologist conducted the scan, her gaze shifted from efficient to deeply worried.

'I'm sorry, I'm not picking up a heartbeat.'

Luka shivered at the memory of those words, never to be forgotten. No one would ever know why their baby had stopped living. They induced Lily into labour that same day. They inserted pessaries every three hours – it took her all day; she just didn't want to let Jessie go. His gorgeous, stubborn Lily. It was almost unbearable to watch her suffer like this, knowing their baby would be born blue. All this was happening amid a conversation no parent should have. Did they want to hold her? Did they want a post-mortem? Would they like to arrange a burial or cremation?

As the moon was high in the cold sky, Lily's water broke, and Jessie was born in silence. Luka remembered cradling her tiny limp body in his arms; she was perfect. All ten fingers and toes and Lily's pixie nose. He felt like his insides had been hollowed out, leaving him an empty shell. She hadn't even seen a day. Stillbirths were eerily quiet. Luka didn't understand why you loved something that hadn't even lived in the world with such a consuming passion. But you did. And this is how he knew souls are immortal. Every time the memory threatened to overwhelm him, he would line up a dose of coke to numb the pain. Good thing he had a reliable cocaine dealer and his beloved companion, his hand-carved and hand-oil-polished cello. It wasn't a Stradivarius. There were only sixty-three in the world, but it was close enough.

Music had always taken Luka away from darkness. His fingers were reverberating butterfly wings on the cello's strings. His notes arrived, landing in between heartbeats, in the places where humans were open. He made people feel things. He was gifted, and after graduating from school, he'd been offered a place at the prestigious Royal College of Music. Unexpectedly, he'd refused it – the music industry couldn't give him the life he wanted. Instead, he accepted an offer to read

PPE (Politics, Philosophy, Economics) at Kings College London. That was a significant decision because he was now a Portfolio Manager at a Hong Kong branch of a large American hedge fund with offices in all the major financial centres of the world. And Kings was also where he met Lily.

Luka made more money than he'd ever dreamed and played in a small but prestigious Arts Centre Orchestra. They had a six-concert season, which required only three to six rehearsals for one concert, and which meant he could balance his work and his passion. He spent his sparse spare time running in the jungle-covered Hong Kong mountains or making love to his wife – but since they'd lost baby Jessie, that had all changed.

Luka stepped off the escalator onto the concourse and walked to the flight information board. Damn. CX9203 was delayed. This meant waiting for forty minutes. Time he didn't have. Luka walked to the nearest coffee shop, ordered a tall black, pulled out his Blackberry, and began responding to emails. He was so engrossed in work he hardly noticed that a woman had arrived at his table and was sitting opposite him. When he looked up, he saw Emily Chu, with a massive grin on her face, staring at him as if he were the last man on earth.

'Emily!' *Shit, shit, shit.* He felt a sudden jolt of fear grip his stomach.

'Luka, it's been a while. I thought I'd say hello.' Her eyes were full of playful flirtation.

'Hi.' He smiled. He couldn't help himself. Emily was sexy in her red-and-white cabin crew uniform.

'Where are you flying off to today?' he asked.

'Bali for the weekend, you wanna come?' Her voice had a lilt, and she flashed the most inviting smile she could muster.

'Ha, if only ... I'm so bogged down with work, can't remember what it was like to have a weekend free.' Luka ran his fingers through his sun-streaked hair.

'Pity, you know how much fun we have when we haven't seen each other for a while,' she said.

'Mm ... I do, but, Ems, I can't. Lily is about to land. She's flying in from SA. You know she is my priority.' *Damn it. Does she have to be so gorgeous?*

'Ah, finally, she's taking a break from work?' Emily's jaw clenched as her expression fell.

'Yeah,' he said, offering nothing more.

'Well, you have twenty minutes to change your mind. Drop me a text if you do.'

She stood up, turned around, and walked away with an audacious swagger.

Luka was relieved to see her go. He didn't like close calls. He had kept his succession of mistresses hidden from Lily. Luka knew he should feel guilty. He just didn't. All his male colleagues had mistresses – it was what they did in Asia.

On Luka's first welcome bash to the Hong Kong office, the managing partner had introduced him to the Girlie Bars in Wanchai. They were beguiling places. A burly bouncer stood at each entrance, along with a couple of short-skirted and platform-heeled beauties waving potential customers inside.

'Hello, handsome, welcome!' the women called out in successive unison each time a patron walked through the door.

Each bar entrance had a makeshift shrine beside the door. Aromatic joss sticks released smoke that would ward away evil spirits and evil humans. Arranged flower petals, hibiscus or frangipani, and sweet tropical fruit would feed and please the gods of fortune. There was always a statue of a happy arm-waving cat – the ultimate good luck trinket. Once inside, the Mamasan (a retired escort) would greet first. She would negotiate a price for her ladies dancing on the bar next to cold steel poles with a number affixed to their bikini bottoms. You chose a number and paid. A simple transaction. Effortless.

On Luka's initiation night, the managing partner had negotiated a deal with a delighted Mamasan. The entire Girlie Bar would be closed to the public and reserved for Luka and his colleagues. The night was a baptism of women. Softly oiled, naked skin of all proportions was available for him to touch as he pleased. Gorgeous plump boobs and tight, pert asses were all Luka's for the taking. He felt uncomfortable in the beginning. He wasn't into it. It was overwhelming, all this naked flesh. He'd never acted out on desires until Lily started rejecting him. But after their heartbreak, and a couple of Tsing-Tao beers and encouragement from workmates, Luka soon lost his inhibition. Life was good in Asia – it pushed your limits.

Luka seldom went to Girlie Bars anymore. He preferred more sophisticated and educated women; it made the game more fun. His conscience plagued him – most of the women working in the bars were from impoverished parts of rural China. They would receive an immediate two-year custodial sentence if they were caught prostituting. The Hong Kong government had introduced this law to deter illegal foreign workers, prostitutes, and traffickers. Despite the Mamasans appearing to be understanding and caring, Lily had informed him that these young women were being mistreated. Lily had represented many prostitutes, and she often took on pro bono work. Knowing that the young women didn't have free choice and could be locked up kept Luka away.

It wasn't as if he had to look hard to find anyone. There was the receptionist, Maggie, at work and half of the cello section – Jemma, Ange, Lulu, and Mei. There were the flight crew on business trips, the groupies at concerts, and the front staff at hotels. For a man who looked like Luka, with music in his fingers, the women just appeared. He was transparent with those he played with – his wife was his priority. And nothing in the world would ever change that. Luka was attentive to the needs of his women. They were treated to extravagant bouquets, precious jewellery, days of pampering at the spa, exotic overseas adventures, and ample money to support their families. He was a generous guy with a ferocious sexual appetite. Besides, Lily was always too busy and, in the last two years, too hurt. She was fragile, and it made him sad. If she were available, she would be his first choice every time. Their lovemaking was connected. It was never just about fucking. There was a time when they had all-day sessions and all-night sessions. Sessions on boats, beaches, taxis, nightclubs, and rooftops of buildings. But it seemed those days were over, and he had found a very satisfying solution. What Lily didn't know would never hurt her, and he was brutally honest with everyone else.

Despite all that had gone awry between them, Lily was still Luka's world. And he hoped that time would heal what had broken for both of them. He was looking forward to holding her in his arms today. He missed her when she was gone. Luka checked his watch – ten more minutes until her plane landed. He felt a familiar excitement. He still loved her just as much as when they had first met on a campus in England as foreign students. The first time he heard her voice, he knew he would marry her. And Luka always got what he wanted. On that auspicious encounter, Lily was reading poetry to her friends. She was practising for a recitation under a shimmering maple's dappled light. Lily's voice was powerful and reaching. Her dark-rimmed glasses and simple white summer dress with a V-line silhouette gave her an air of eloquence. It surprised him to learn that she was a law major. The surprises never stopped with Lily. She was layer upon layer of revelation. Lily filled the empty parts of him, and she would achieve all the altruistic things in the world that he didn't have time for but also cared about. She gave his drive and his money a purpose. Yin and yang. Music and poetry. They were a perfect balance.

Lily was a good wife, and he was looking forward to taking her home.

nine

SOME PLACES LEAVE A pit in your stomach when you leave them behind because they are part of you. Lily struggled to get her feet off southern African soil and onto the plane. Today she was flying back to Hong Kong – a place she would never tire of. East and West intertwined in a slow love-hate waltz. The world waiting for them to break up. From refined French bakeries to hot pepper Szechuan eateries, Hong Kong was a culture soup.

The journey was a fight against time. Lily checked the clock on her phone.

Why was it passing so slowly?

She tried to fall asleep, only to be dragged into a nightmarish slumber, until she finally stayed awake. Unable to concentrate on books or movies, she pulled out her diary and wrote. This was the only way she could get rid of the heavy thoughts in her head. By the time they were over South East Asia, Lily had completed dozens of pages. She pressed her face against the cubbyhole window, the glass cool against her skin, as she looked out at the rolling mountains beneath, dressed in a thick canopy of lush vegetation. You were close to the ground when you could make out the silhouettes. Sunset Peak came into view just as the plane dipped towards the sea – then all the colourful boats, cargo vessels, ferries, naval ships and maybe a sampan with an old angler standing upright in his bamboo hat, cutting a solitary figure rowing treacherous wakes, so determined to hook that fish.

As you descended towards Lantau Island, you could see the turquoise waters stretching to the horizon. It felt like you were landing in the sea. Chek Lap Kok Airport on Lantau was completely unlike the older Kai Tak Airport on Kowloon – the runway where only the most skilled pilots in existence could land. When Lily first got to Hong Kong, it was an eye-opening experience – descending among the skyscrapers, pondering if the plane wing would get snagged. Flying right among the neon sign-lights of the city. Amahs could be seen bustling around kitchens, cooking dinner. You became a voyeur, looking into the intimate parts of people's lives. A man asleep in bed, a child in pursuit of a cat, a woman slouched at a desk, hard at work. The runway was dangerously close to the sea's edge. A few planes had nose-dived right in. Lily was thankful for Chek Lap Kok as she looked out the window and saw the safety it provided, unlike the old Kai Tak landing, which had been so thrilling and risky.

She flew in and out of the city many times. On work trips, holidays, and family visits. She was a platinum card frequent flyer. As the plane descended, she felt like she was watching her life from outside her body, as if another person was inhabiting her. Some stranger who viewed the world with less optimism. Lily had lost something. Now and then, she would see Papa's blood on her hands. She supposed this was another kind of grief.

The plane shook and rumbled as it navigated through the nimbostratus clouds, which stretched to the sky like mountains. The clickity-clack of the food trays ringing in her ears, Lily closed her eyes and took a deep breath of stale airline-food air – the turbulence on descent always got her. As the air hostess instructed, she packed everything away and got ready for the final descent. She had no choice; she would have to face where she was going. Luka would be waiting at Exit A – armed with his generous smile and 'come to bed' eyes to greet her. In the past, she would feel a rush of joy at the thought of being in his comforting embrace, but now all she felt was a dull, aching hollowness.

'Lily!'

She heard Luka's voice echoing through the hall as she pushed her luggage-laden trolley with its tell-tale squeak through the exit. He ran towards her, and she felt his powerful arms wrap around her in his customary bear hug. The woody scent of his fresh aftershave hit first. Lily's arms hung motionless at her sides. Her body was as limp as a rag doll and her face was expressionless, like a woman whose heart had grown cold.

Lukas sighed in disappointment, his shoulders sagging.

'I know you have been through a lot,' Luka said, 'but I'm here now; please don't push me away – you always do that when you need me most.'

He reached for the trolley, but Lily wouldn't let go of it; her knuckles were white.

'I needed you most three weeks ago. Let's not make a scene.'

She pushed the trolley past him towards the car park with a force that belied the hurt in her eyes. Luka scurried behind. As they settled into the matte black luxury sedan, Luka pressed the door lock.

'I'm not driving until we sort this.' He was wearing a determined scowl.

'Luka. I'm exhausted, can you not—'

'You know what's happening at work? You know how impossible the timing was with this recession looming. I am under pressure, you know that. You don't think I wanted to be with you?'

'Some things take precedence over work.' Lily's voice was deadpan.

'But you said it was okay if I didn't come. Don't you mean what you fucking say? I'm not a mind reader.'

Lily's eyes became vacant. Her voice was calm.

'Do you love me, Luka?'

'Of course! More than anything.'

'Then please take me home; I need to go to bed.'

Reluctantly, Luka started the engine. He navigated them home on the winding roads of the valley, going past concrete village dwellings, deserted shrines, unordered household landfills, metal cargo carriers, and hills with the pointed tops of flame trees appearing above the jungle cover. With each turn around a bend, Lily felt the chasm between them growing. She had nothing to say to him, nothing at all.

Reaching their architect-designed three-storey home in the back of an old Chinese village, a profusion of tropical forest trees encompassed them, including the valuable Aquilaria Sinensis. The locals cherished these trees, worshiping them as sanctuaries to their ancestors and the tree poachers, held them in similar regard, searching the incense trees for their aromatic resin. In the darkness of night, smugglers came from Mainland China to cut down trees and smuggle them back across the border. The fragrant trees on the island were quickly diminishing. Lily shuddered at the thought – no more Oud, or Chen Xiang as they knew it in this region. A century had gone by for the trees to generate a first-rate resin. The hapless smugglers were extinguishing the last sparks of a thriving metropolis.

What would Fragrant Harbour be without fragrance?

Lily fled the confines of the car and walked along the path that led to the guardian Aquilaria Sinensis tree at the back of their property. She stepped along handmade concrete pavers with a leaf design, listening to the loud chirping of cicadas, passing by spider lilies and trees with epiphytes, to a place she had been many times since living here. The sweet smell of frangipani and hibiscus hung heavy in the air. She noticed that incense in the clay pot beneath the tree had recently burnt out, the pungent aroma arriving like home in her nostrils. Her deep sigh came easily – a release from the tormenting conflict between her and Luka. She lit a joss stick with old matches that some kind villager had left in a notch of the tree. She missed her family. It was so hard to say goodbye. Someway behind, Luka watched from a distance. She was meditating. She would be calm by morning.

Her breath steady, Lily went inside – straight to the guest bedroom. She carelessly tossed her travel-worn clothes into the wicker wash basket and headed towards the glossy black Italian marble shower. The warm rain shower cascaded over her body until her skin was wrinkled from the water. She would stay here for as long as it took. She needed to wash it all away. The blood, the journey, the grief, and Luka's insensitivity.

Eventually, Lily's exhaustion caught up to her and she collapsed into the freshly washed sheets, smelling the comforting scent of home. She wanted to sleep forever. That wouldn't happen because, in twelve hours, she had to be back in Chambers. She set her phone alarm, changed the ringtone to a gentle harp, and drifted off into a restless sleep.

ten

IF THERE WAS ONE thing that Lily was certain of, it was that love could be a fading light; as quickly as it lit you up, it could darken you. She felt that this morning as she made her way to Chambers. Lily was looking forward to the distraction that being at work brought. Her job required a hundred per cent focus, and any uncomfortable feelings would disappear as she examined her caseload. Lists would be made, files would be requested and prepared for trial, research would be done, phone calls would be made, and client meetings would be arranged.

Lily sneaked out of the house before Luka woke, careful not to make a sound. With no ferry leaving this early, she took their only car. She needed space. Love's rollercoaster is why she kept a measure of herself for herself. Lily was capable of love and care and commitment, but she wasn't a fool in love. She had learned from watching Mama that seeking a home for yourself in another soul was unwise. Papa fabricated stories in order to manipulate and control Mama. Stories about her worth, place, and duty as a woman. Without realising it, Mama was so affected by her circumstances that she kept herself enslaved. Lily would live free from the misogynistic madness prescribed by the society she had grown up in. There were no men at the head of her table and there never would be. She refused to be dependent on or taken advantage of by any man, no matter the strength of her feelings for him. Despite that, she understood the worth and significance of relationships, and she didn't wish for her marriage to fail. Luka wasn't Papa. He had always supported her dreams, and that was the reason she had agreed to marry him. When they lost baby Jessie, Luka's heart was shattered, his sorrow matching hers. She saw the loss in his earnest copper-flecked eyes. She saw it every time she looked at him. And she loved him fiercely for it.

Lily felt the tension in her shoulders ease as she drove over the sweeping Tsing-Ma suspension bridge towards Hong Kong Island. Two hundred and six metres up, she was stunned by the vastness of the Ma Wan Channel, the view bringing an amazing sense of perspective. The cold-blue sea was smooth and glassy, gently lapping against the shore in the distance. When Lily arrived at the underground car park of her over-the-top glamorous gold-glass work building, she felt the stress of the previous day evaporate. As she was about to get out of the car, a soft slip of red fabric caught her eye on the floor of the front passenger seat. She leaned in to investigate and heard the distinct sound of knuckles tapping against the car window. It was Mr Wu, the car park attendant.

'Welcome, Missee, Jo san!'

'Jo san, Mr Wu.'

It was indeed a good morning. Mr Wu's toothy-smile radiated warmth and positivity, lighting up the day. The sight of him brought a comforting smile to Lily's lips.

As she entered through the glass doors of Chambers, Lily was drawn to the new statue in the lobby, its intricate carvings reflecting the light. It was a garish marbled figurine of a female warrior holding a sword. She smiled to herself – the head of Chambers was a quirky SC with a penchant for comedy. No doubt he had placed this here as a tongue-in-cheek encouragement. They were the only set of chambers in Hong Kong that were female-heavy. Alexander Chau SC was proud of it. Lily let out an audible chuckle. It was good to be back in a place she belonged.

An enormous pile of papers lay waiting on her desk; she tackled them with her usual methodical efficiency. She was almost done when she received a call in the late afternoon asking her to take an urgent statement on a pro-bono case – another welcome distraction. The deposition was for an Afghani refugee family's asylum application to the United Nations

Refugee Agency. Refugees could not remain in Hong Kong. Despite this, if the agency approved their application, they could be sent to a country providing them with long-term sanctuary – perhaps Canada, New Zealand, or Norway. Lily agreed.

Jacket on, she went downstairs to the lobby and hailed a green cab to Kowloon side.

She made her way to Chun King Mansions, a derelict high-rise that housed Hong Kong's refugees. The building's lack of maintenance made it an extreme fire hazard. Electric wires hung loose from the ceilings, and paint peeled off dirty walls soaked in cooking oil from kitchens with no extractor fans. The floor tiles were weathered and cracked, and cockroaches skittered along the passageways, the air filled with a dizzying array of scents from the global cuisines cooking in the kitchens. The smells hung heavy in the humid air of the populated building. No one who lived here could afford to air-condition, which in a city as hot as Hong Kong in the summer could be a death sentence. Each apartment had iron security gates across the doorways and windows reminiscent of the ones that Lily had grown up seeing in South African houses. Chun King Mansions was one of the few places in Hong Kong considered unsafe.

Lily concluded her interview with the destitute family on the ninth floor. She hoped that the data she recorded would provide the ammunition they needed to win their application. She could hear the despair in their voices as she informed them that their chance of success was small. Lily made a point of being as honest as possible in these situations. Even if it was difficult. There was always hope, and she would do her very best for them. She made sure they understood this well. Hope was something that couldn't be taken away from anyone.

With her spirits low, while waiting for the clanging cage lifts, she spotted a poster on one of the iron security doors. It read: '*The only prison is your mind. Find freedom within. Join us at 7pm for yoga practice.*'

Lily's curious nature compelled her to look at her watch – it was six forty-five pm, only fifteen more minutes, and she could be free. She waited outside the door in the oppressive heat, beads of perspiration beginning to break out on her forehead.

Seven pm arrived, and Lily was drenched in sticky sweat. Her clothing was inappropriate for yoga; at least she was wearing trousers and not a skirt. She knocked on the door, and it swung open. A young South Indian woman with luminescent eyes appeared, welcoming Lily with a gracious smile and ushering her inside a tiny room with several grass mats on the floor. Underneath a window, a sculpture of a naked woman with several outstretched arms was displayed on an altar. She was dancing. There were bright orange flowers laid in a pattern beside her, a delicate crystal bowl of water, some delicious-looking ripe star and dragon fruit, and a floral-smelling incense throwing loops of smoke rings into the muggy air. This picture enamoured Lily, and she hardly noticed the room filling with other people.

Each person was led to a place on a mat and given a pillow to sit on. It was silent, no one was talking, and Lily felt the long-held tension in her muscles beginning to dissipate.

I don't have to talk to anyone. What a relief.

Emulating a man in front of her, Lily sat down on her pillow with her legs crossed beneath her. The woman who had greeted her at the door took a seat beside the altar. She looked far too young to be the teacher, but she was. Two young women with long plaited ebony hair and toes adorned with gold gem rings flanked the teacher's left and right side, each holding an instrument that resembled a tambourine.

The teacher sang in a language Lily couldn't identify. Her voice was soothing, the melody was rhythmic and penetrating. With each note, Lily felt her body hum as if alive with electricity, every fibre of her being resonating with the melody. Lily's eyelids closed, and the noise of her busy mind fell into blissful silence. At some point, she tasted the saltiness of tears streaming down her face. Relief washed over her the way a typhoon clears away a polluted sky or the mighty Yangtse river empties its banks of vegetation in flood.

The teacher's haunting voice had unlocked something inside of her. Lily had become summer sunshine. She was filled with a warmth that was so comforting, it was indescribable. Hypnotised by the repetitive mantra, she could discern that the young women with instruments were dancing around her. She could sense their movements even with her eyes closed. *How peculiar.*

Lily's torso swayed from side to side in a soothing rocking motion and then in spiral circles. As the music reached a crescendo, Lily felt a bursting rush of orgasmic energy rise the length of her spine – and an indescribable feeling. An ecstatic bliss. A sensation so overwhelming that Lily couldn't contain it. She passed out.

The young teacher smiled at her as she awoke. She was holding a cup of sweet-smelling liquid to Lily's lips. Honey, chai, milk. She stroked Lily's forehead with a mother's tenderness. The wisdom in her eyes betrayed her youth. She was otherworldly. *Perhaps a goddess.*

The vestiges of Lily's atheist worldview crumbled that day in that hot, sticky, cockroach-laden building on Kowloon Side. It took her some time to regain her composure and discern what had happened. A deep peace remained with her all the way back to Chambers.

With her windows down, she drove over the Tsing-Ma bridge back home to Lantau Island that evening and marvelled at the vibrant colours of the sky. The sunset over the ocean sparkled like jewels, the bird's songs seemed angelic, and the mountains shimmered with a viridescent hue. The world was a dreamscape.

Lily pulled into the driveway, and the frangipani tree's white and yellow waxy flowers created a honey-like aroma around her car. Her sense of smell was heightened. She realised she was excited to see Luka. She wanted to embrace the man she loved. Right now, their squabbles seemed inconsequential. She opened the passenger car door to retrieve her bag, and a piece of fabric slipped out onto the frangipani-petalled drive. She leaned down to pick it up. Her eyes widened. A pair of delicate red lace G-string knickers lay stark against the white gravel in the soft evening light.

eleven

LILY DROPPED THE CARDINAL red knickers on the kitchen island. Their red was emphasised by the sleek white granite countertop. She was calm. Despite the realisation that this delicate slip of lace may be the final nail in the coffin of her marriage, she still felt an underlying sense of peace. The yoga class had brought her equilibrium, and she was grateful for that. If this had happened a day earlier, she might have fallen apart.

She poured a glass of sparkling wine and watched the tiny bubbles dancing up the side of her glass as she sat legs crossed on the grey upholstered kitchen bar stool and waited. Luka would be down in a minute. He would have heard the familiar screech of the car tyres on the driveway.

On cue, Luka swooped down the stairs with his usual sure-footedness. He carried his prized cello in its ebony case and set it down on an aged brown leather sofa in the lounge.

'Hello, gorgeous.'

His face brightened as he laid eyes on Lily in the kitchen, the smell of his musky-toned aftershave wafting in the room. Her mass of blonde shimmered in the window's light.

'Are you feeling better?' he asked.

'Yes, thanks, Luka. Are you on the way to rehearsal?' Lily's fingers gently tugged on a strand of wild hair.

'Yep.'

There was a softness in Lily's eyes. Luka was about to walk over and wrap his arms around her until he saw the bright pop of red on the counter. Lily noticed his eyes widen, the vein in his neck bulge, and his shoulders give an involuntary twitch. She watched him like a falcon homing in on its prey. Or a trial lawyer assessing her witness.

How very telling. He knows.

Her stomach flipped. She swallowed, a sudden wave of nausea rising in her throat.

'Wh— What's that?' The look on Luka's face said it all.

'I was hoping you could tell me.' Lily took a slow, deliberate sip of her bubbly wine, the bubbles popping on her tongue.

'Are you in the mood for love?' Luka's eyebrows shot up, the corners of his lips curling into a playful smile.

'Definitely not.' *God, he is smooth.* Lily's stomach churned. 'I found this on the car floor. Who is the owner, Luka?'

Luka's face darkened. 'They're not yours?'

'Have you ever seen me in red lace?'

'N— No, but I'd like to. Lily, I don't inspect your underwear drawer, okay?'

His eyes still held a whisper of mischievousness. 'If they're not yours, I dunno whose they are. And I don't appreciate your insinuation.' Voice clipped, he continued, 'Maybe you should ask Pete. He borrows the car. I don't have time for this shit. I've got to get going.' He walked towards his cello, ready to flee the room, sanctimonious anger colouring his face.

'Good idea, I'll call him right now. In fact, I'll call Angie. I'm sure she'll want them returned.' Lily grabbed her phone.

'Don't do that, Lily. Do you want to drop Pete in it? What if they don't belong to Angie?' His shoulders twitched in beats.

'If they don't belong to her, she should know. No one deserves to be in a dishonest marriage.' With shaking fingers, Lily searched for Angie's number and pressed the green dial button. Luka reached across and snatched her phone.

'Stop it! You are not being rational, and you're tired and emotional. You don't destroy a relationship on a whim.' Luka rarely raised his voice, but it was rising now – his desperation showing.

'Luka, if you don't give me my phone, I'm going to walk over to their house and ask in person. I'm sure there will be an innocent explanation.' *Two can play this game.* She marched towards the front door, ready to dash to the neighbour's house.

Luka's shoulders sank in defeat. 'Stop!' he yelled. 'Please don't do this.'

Lily reached for the cold door handle.

'Okay, okay, enough,' he half shouted. 'I know who they belong to.'

Lily turned around. *Here it is.* She felt calm, like a bystander witnessing someone else's fifteen-year marriage fall apart.

'Lily, i— it's nothing. It means nothing.' His eyes were brimming. 'I … I am so sorry.'

'Means nothing to you, maybe, but I'm sure it means something to whoever she is, and it fucking means something to me.' Tears were pricking behind her eyes. Swallowing the lump in her throat, she refused to let them spill out onto her cheeks.

'Lily …' His voice went soft as he combed his fingers through his hair. 'I love you, please believe me when I say this was a stupid mistake. I was lonely, ever since Jess—'

'Don't say her name, just don—' Lily's tone was steel.

'For fuck's sake, you can't hide from this forever. You are not the only one who lost a child that day. You haven't let me touch you since then. I've tried everything. I've done everything I can to help you –

you refuse to let me in. I need, I have … have urges, Lily. Jesus Christ, I'm a virile man in the peak of his lif—'

'Oh, so this is my fault. Your cheating assholery is my fault.' She felt her fists clench into tight balls.

'C'mon, please look at this from my perspective. Damn it, Lily! Why is everything about you? There are two of us in this marriage.'

'Evidently, there are three or four or five or six – you think I don't notice, Luka? The perfume smells, the lipstick stains, the fucking excessive trips and hotel bills on our Visa?' Her eyes were ice.

'Lily, I … I—' He was lost for words.

'You married an intelligent woman, Luka, don't for one minute think I don't know what's been happening. I just haven't had the heart or the energy to confront it. Are you delusional? Or just a naïve idiot? Whatever it is, there is something inside of you that doesn't give a fuck. And frankly, I don't give a fuck anymore either.'

Luka went quiet. Her words had cut through him.

Lily swirled the last sip of effervescent wine in the crystal glass and gulped it down.

'I'm leaving, Luka. I'll book a serviced apartment in town. I need space. Please, if you care about us, don't contact me.'

'N— No, please don't run. Please, Lily. I know I can fix this.' He shook his head in disbelief.

'It's not about fixing, Luka. It's about healing. And I don't know if that's possible.'

Lily picked up the car keys and walked away. She wasn't sure where she was going. Right now, she wanted to walk into another life.

Luka stood in the kitchen, tears streaming down his face in rivers. As he heard the tyres of the car crunch against gravel, he sank to the floor, and for the first time in his adult life, instead of reaching for his cello, he knelt his head and prayed.

Some things make a city what it is. In Hong Kong in the year 2007, it was high tea at the Mandarin Oriental. It was the dirt cheap and delicious food in the street Dai pai dongs. It was Sam's Shoe Polishing and Repair located up the noisy back lane behind the Peddar Street building. Uncle Sam repaired thousands of well-loved shoes and broken heels, and his cheery smile could repair even the saddest of days with a glimmer of his customary kindness. Another iconic Hong Kong thing was the soothing waft of ginger-lily home fragrance floating out the doors of Shanghai Tang on the same street. It was Lily's favourite shop – a contemporary Chinese fashion and home store filled with embroidered silk blouses, shawls, wraps, and modern Cheongsams in the boldest colours of the rainbow. It had exquisitely hand-painted chinoiserie wallpaper depicting tiny birds, perfectly painted flowers, and Lily's favourite silk-covered writing journals in chartreuse green, tangerine orange, and amaranth red.

When Lily had chosen a serviced apartment, it was no surprise that it was near her favourite store and the pulse of the city. There was still beauty in the world, and she needed to see it. She needed to see the raptors gracefully diving between the high rises, their calls echoing off the walls. She needed to watch the smoke from the street shrines, its acrid smell stinging her nose as it spiralled up into mysterious ghost shapes. She needed to be outside of herself.

As the sun set each evening, she trudged along the winding road home from Chambers, week after week. Every night was the same. She would light candles in the bathroom and soak in warm bath-salt water, eat a takeaway from a local street vendor, put on oversized soft cotton pyjamas, pull out a silk-covered Shanghai Tang Journal, and write until her eyelids drooped and the joints in her fingers ached. She woke every morning with a pen in her hands. A black and gold Montblanc – an anniversary present from Luka.

She wrote it all out. The memories that coloured her mind with uncertainty. She wrote about the things that hurt and the things that healed. She remembered, on the rough textured paper pages, Jessie's perfectly formed toes before they took her away. She remembered Luka's cries behind the bathroom door and the overheard phone calls made by Luka to the therapist begging her to help his wife. She remembered, in ink, how he had kissed her brow in the middle of the night, changed the sheets, washed the dishes, and mopped the floors when she had forgotten how to do all those things. She remembered, in cursive writing, how he had tried to touch her and how she had pushed his hands away. She remembered his eyes before it happened – how they pierced her when they made love and how he would call her name in the dark when he had nightmares. She remembered when the ink ran dry, how much Luka loved her and how much she loved him. And so, one evening, she put down the fountain pen and called him.

'Hi, it's me.'

'Lily, oh my god, Lily, you don't know how good it is to hear your voice.' Luka choked up.

'Do you want to meet for a drink?' she asked as she gazed out the window at the dancing city lights.

'Can I come over now?' he asked.

'No, but I can meet you in Soho for a drink.' She wasn't ready to be alone with him.

'Okay, I can be there in fifteen.'

And so it began, a tender and tentative reunion. They dated at first – hand-holding and candlelight dinners and slow forgiveness. After a few months, Lily moved home to Luka's welcoming arms and the sweet scent of frangipani that lingered around the house they had built together on Lantau Island. She moved home to nights of anxiety, asking herself if he was truly late from rehearsals or if he was really alone on his business trips. Work was a distraction from unwelcome thoughts, but somehow that wasn't enough to quell the uneasiness inside of her. Forgiveness was easy, but trust was elusive. How could she forget the brightness of those red lace knickers, and the way they had appeared on her kitchen counter when she was still reeling from the loss of Papa?

There was no comfort here, no Lulama or Mama or Sarah. She had good friends in Hong Kong, especially Saima, but Lily was private – she kept the struggle inside. She attempted to go back to the yoga class in Chun King mansions. She wanted to find that indescribable peace she had found on that defining and perilous day. She was disappointed when she found that the Goddess was gone – the authorities had deported her back to Pakistan. And so Lily had searched for a substitute, but the yoga she found had more to do with perfect poses, tight buns, and designer wear than heart and soul and peace.

Despite regular therapy sessions, the lingering uncertainty carried on as months turned into almost two years, or rather, the moment Oliver turned up in an elegant hotel coffee shop in Central with his sparkling eyes, dimpled chin, and perfect English vowels. The uncertainty continued until Lily did what she had vowed she would never do. In a hotel room with views of a tumultuous black storm, she shared her heart and her body and her soul with another man.

twelve

2009

OLIVER AND LILY'S AFFAIR continued at pace. Their romance was velvet chocolate – oozing sticky sex, sweet promises, and a dizzying yearning for more of each other. More lingering gazes, more intimate whispers, and more desperate hands touching each other and reaching into those spaces that make you feel alive. Lily spent hours tracing the shadows on Oliver's back – index finger on the curves and the lines that the sun leaves behind. She was reading the story on his skin; it made her forget her own.

They met in a myriad of places. Under the pastel pinks of sunset over the islands in the Andaman Sea, in art galleries in the old quarter of Hanoi, walking hand in hand in Singapore's orchid gardens, and they fell asleep near the banks of the wild Yellow River. They danced at nightclubs, on beaches and bus stops, and between the crisp cotton sheets of hotel rooms. They ate in roadside cafes, seaside eateries, Dai pai dongs, curry houses and Michelin-star restaurants. They ate off each other, and some days, they didn't eat at all. Instead, they drank delicious lime-infused Mai Tais and cherry liqueur pineapple Singapore Slings for breakfast. Tsingtao and Singha beers for lunch. And in the evenings, they sipped mandarin gin and tonics, ripe Merlots and crisp Sauvignon Blancs.

Lying became easy. There were so many site visits for cases and so much research to be done. Lily's clients now lived in the most romantic parts of South East Asia. Luka never questioned his good wife, and he had no reason to. The rebound from the Global Financial Crisis of 2008 meant that he was spending more and more time in his firm's New York office. At least two weeks a month.

The timing couldn't have been better. It enabled Lily to spend time at Oliver's apartment on Hong Kong's Peak with a balcony overlooking the tall vined banyans on forested hillsides and the silhouettes of the city's skyscrapers. On a clear night, the land sparkled with colourful city lights – the sky twinkled with stars, and in the distance, the ship's night lights skipped the waves of the South China sea.

Lily loved those evenings. She would catch a red taxi up Magazine Gap Road, along the twisting bends of the narrow mountainside roads, to Oliver's place after an exhausting day at work. Oliver insisted on cooking dinner; it was the way he relaxed. She'd watch him. He was usually in torn jeans and a white cotton shirt with a linen apron, and wearing his sexy smile. Oliver would dance around his kitchen between sips of wine, looking like someone in love with the world. He was the only man who had ever cooked for her, such a simple gesture, and it made her feel so loved.

Despite her happiness, the physical and emotional strain of maintaining this lifestyle was taking its toll. The fog of hangovers, the burden of lies, and all the late-morning sex hindered Lily's job performance. She could sense things slipping – a forgotten fact – which could determine a lighter prison sentence, a crucial technical error which could mean her client's freedom. On a sweltering Tuesday morning, she was beckoned into the head of Chambers' office. Alexander Chau SC was not a man who minced words.

'Good morning, Lily. Please take a seat.' His voice was direct.

'Morning, Sandy.' She used his nickname to soften his mood.

With her finger, Lily twirled a strand of her hair as she walked towards the shiny chrome and leather office chair. Alexander's office was enormous, with windows stretching from the floor to the ceiling, letting in the salty scent of the nearby harbour and giving him a picturesque view of Kowloon side.

'Look, I'm just going to say it.' He adjusted his gold cufflinks. 'You've been making a lot of unfortunate mistakes. Mistakes that barristers in these Chambers don't make. This isn't like you, Lily. I want to know what's going on?'

She kept her gaze averted, unable to meet his eye. She felt a wave of shame, and her cheeks flushed with embarrassment.

'I'm sorry, Sandy. I know I've made a few minor judgment errors—'

'Minor! Lily, you almost cost a client his freedom last week.' Alexander slammed his manicured hands on the table. 'What the fuck is going on? Is it that prick, Luka? Is he fucking you around again?'

'Luka,' her head jerked in shock, 'nno, he, um – how did you kno—' Her eyes searched Sandy's.

'I know everything that happens in these Chambers. Last week Caitlin was finger-fucking her girlfriend on the conference table. The week before that, Mei Ling stole the copy room's hole punch. I make it my business to know everything that happens between these walls. I told you two years ago that you shouldn't be married to that cello-playing cunt, but you refused to listen to me.'

He shook his head, sighed, and shrugged.

Lily scanned his office for cameras. 'He's not a c-cunt, Sandy. Please don't use that god awful wor—'

'Look, Ange told me you smelled of booze all of last week. I've taken your case list and passed it on to Benson. He'll manage your clients while you are away. It's good that you are not listed for trial in the next fortnight. You'll take a week off – and you'll decide what you want during that time.' Reaching behind him, he pulled a file off the shelf.

'W-What! Benson. No—' Lily wound a tendril of hair into a tight twist.

'Are you going to let that prick ruin your career? Think about it and get back to me. You're one of the best here, Lily. You give a shit about clients. It's time to give a shit about yourself.' He flipped through the file on his desk.

'Sandy, I don't need time off.'

'This isn't negotiable. I've booked you into the Four Seasons for a week. You're having a break. You'll have lots of massages, and I've booked you in with a therapist.'

Alexander pulled out a key card from his drawer and presented it to Lily; it was the key to one of the most luxurious hotels in Hong Kong. 'And you're going alone. Don't take that prick with you. And not a drop of alcohol crosses your lips before you walk through these doors again.' He shut the drawer with a loud thud, the force of it rattling the furniture. His lips were set in a line of resignation. 'There's a reason we are the best criminal set in Hong Kong. And I won't let you fuck up the reputation I've built and you've built. I won't let you fuck up your life because of a philandering asshole. Okay?'

Lily sighed, her hands falling to her lap. 'Okay.'

She was cornered and had no way out. She didn't have a choice – and deep down Lily knew he was right.

As gruff as Alexander Chau SC was, she knew he had her back.

'Good.' He smiled.

Something about how Alexander's brown-flecked eyes looked at her reminded her of Papa, and she felt her throat tighten and her eyes brim with tears. She dashed out of his office and into the ladies' room, where she felt a sharp pain when she stubbed her toe on the metal corner of the designer cubicle door.

'Fuck,' she yelled and stumbled towards the white porcelain loo, the door slamming shut as she curled up into a ball and wept. The weight of the grief and the guilt that she was carrying were equally heavy.

As the taxi wound its way home to Oliver's that night, she applied a few drops of Oud to her wrists and at the base of her neck.

Breathe; just breathe.

While the car climbed up the Peak, she stared out the window, contemplating the tough choices she had to make. The soupy air felt thick and oppressive, and she knew this night would not be tranquil.

Oliver opened the door, smelling like woody spice. *He is so damn delicious.*

'Hello, my love. Have you had a good day?' He gathered her in his arms, and she felt the warmth of his body against hers.

'Not really.' She nuzzled into the comfort of his embrace.

'Well, I've poured us some margaritas. Go shower and meet me on the balcony. I have a surprise that will cheer you up.' He planted a kiss on her forehead, his touch lingering on her skin before he swaggered away to the kitchen.

Lily stood in the shower, feeling the coolness of the water and the tension of the conversation with Alexander slowly draining away, and she thought of the discussion she would soon have with Oliver. The walls of their bubble were breaking down, no longer able to sustain them. Something had to change. She threw on a pair of jeans and her soft jade silk summer blouse, and ran her fingers through her still-wet hair. Stepping out onto the balcony, she was met with a gentle breeze carrying the scent of delicious food.

Oliver had put a plate of canapes on the teak outdoor table. Prosciutto, olives, juicy plum tomatoes, and bouncy mozzarella topped with fragrant basil and drizzled with aged balsamic and olive oil – all beautifully arranged beside freshly baked sourdough and icy summer margaritas. Life beside Oliver was picture-perfect. His long limbs carried him onto the balcony with minimal effort.

'Hey, beautiful. Tell me what's up.' He looked at her with concern, picked up a margarita, and handed it to her.

With a gentle touch, Lily set down the salt-rimmed drink. 'I don't want to drink tonight, Oliver. Can we slow down on the booze?'

His eyes narrowed as he squinted against the glare of the setting sun. 'But it took me ages to make these. C'mon, hon, you need a pickup.' A charming smile spread across his face.

'I don't want a drink,' said Lily.

Oliver's face was crestfallen, the disappointment radiating from him.

'Okay, can I get you a water, some iced tea?'

'No, thanks. Can we talk?' She touched his arm and took a whiff of the Oud on her other wrist.

'Sure.' Oliver leaned against the railing of the balcony. His instinct was to steady himself.

'Alexander called me into his office today. I've messed up at work. I'm not focused. All the booze and late nights, Oliver – it can't go on. It's not just about me; it's about the people I represent. I've dropped the ball, and it's making me feel like shit.'

'I didn't realise—' His shoulders sagged.

'Oliver, how do you maintain focus at work with all the drinking?'

Lily had read up on high-functioning alcoholics and wondered if he was one of them.

'I dunno. It doesn't affect me, I guess.' He gave her a lazy smile. 'Steel liver.'

'Well, it affects me; I can't do it anymore.'

'Lily, I've never forced you to drink.' Oliver's eyes were sombre.

'Of course you haven't. It's been so much fun, so wild and crazy. But it's not sustainable – my job requires intense focus. And I'm not giving it up. It's too important to me.'

Lily brushed a lock of hair away from his forehead.

'No one is asking you to,' Oliver said, looking at her as if she was crazy.

'Okay.' She relaxed her shoulders and smiled.

'What was the surprise you had for me?'

'Wait here.' Oliver ducked inside to grab something. He returned, an A4-size brown envelope rustling in his hands, and placed it on the table. 'Look,' he said with smiling eyes.

Lily pulled a white document out of the envelope and looked at the header. DECREE ABSOLUTE. Her lips curled into a wide smile.

'Congratulations! Your divorce is final.' She flung her arms around him. 'Now you can move on.' She squeezed him.

'Yes, Lily, Now *we* can move on.' His sea-coloured eyes twinkled.

They made love to celebrate. Oliver had polished off his margarita, her margarita, and a couple more. Lily sipped on some icy cold water. It felt strange – new. She instinctively turned her head away from his strong alcoholic breath; the scent was repulsive. He tasted sour and acrid. Lily couldn't look at him, couldn't kiss him. Their movements fell out of time – a disjointed, broken tango. He was staccato; she was pianissimo. Beads of alcohol-laced sweat dripped on to her dry body. From the corner of her eye, she noticed a white box with a blue label on the bedside table. Viagra.

Ah, so this is how he does it.

She felt pain rip into her chest as Oliver jerked in orgasm. As his semen leaked onto her thighs, she merged into a black hole of loneliness. Her eyes scanned the white ceiling, her body icy and limp – like his flaccid penis now pressing against her stomach. Oliver collapsed into sleep on top of her and then rolled off to the side. Their heartbeats were no longer in sync. Snoring echoed loudly through the room, an unfamiliar, jarring noise.

As Lily noticed the last ray of daylight fade behind the curtains, the truth dawned, unfurling as effortlessly as the petals of a rose teased out by the light.

thirteen

LUKA WAS ON THE Airport Express, a slick silver high-speed train that took commuters from the airport into all the major Hong Kong city stops. He went straight to the office. He'd slept well on the flight back from New York, a perk of business class travel. The train stopped underneath the International Finance Centre. Stepping off, he took a lift straight up to his office on the forty-eighth floor. The awe-inspiring view of the city, a vista of towering buildings and bustling streets, amazed him. It made him feel like he was at the top of his game. The office was full of cold steel and black leather. One gold-framed picture of him hugging Lily stood on a mirrored shelf, beside an onyx statue of a carved cello. He walked straight over to the coffee machine and poured himself a double-shot espresso. His nose was hit with the sharp, pungent smell before he tasted the bitter beans. He let the hot liquid slide down his throat before he allowed himself to remember, in fleeting cinematic pictures, the fun that he had over the last two weeks.

He hadn't intended for it to happen. It had started with an innocent jog in Central Park – part of his morning routine when he worked in his firm's New York Office on Park Avenue in Manhattan. She appeared on the park bench, the warm sun shining down, as she played Vivaldi's "Spring". Her dark, smooth skin shone in the light as her muscular forearms moved gracefully, like a maestro in harmony with their instrument. With perfect precision, she moved the bow of her violin; the sound creating a seamless harmony with her hand. She played from that mysterious part of herself that connected to a music oversoul, allowing the rich, melodic sounds to wash over her listeners like a wave. She was mesmerising. Her fingernails were clear and short with no varnish and her face was clean of make-up. And she was striking with a strong nose, deep soulful brown eyes and an Afro that caught sunrays and sparkled in the fresh light. A small crowd gathered around her as she busked her magical notes into the cool morning air. Luka noticed an amethyst trilby full of notes and coins next to her elegant bare, toe-ringed feet. It wasn't unexpected to spot a nearby artist drawing her sharp, chiselled cheekbones as his eyes looked at the enigmatic musical muse with the same enthusiasm that was bubbling in Luka.

In his desperate attempt to make an impression, he remembered running past a flower cart. Luka spun around and raced to the flower stand. He chose a lilac rose to match her amethyst trilby. It was as fragrant, delicate, and striking as she. Out of breath and in between music pieces, he arrived in perfect time. He nestled the flower in the middle of her hat, accompanied by a short note that said '*I'm curious*' and his phone number. He signed it with a cursive L, wanting to appear a little mysterious. She noticed. He saw the way her eyes darted across his face, revealing her spontaneous smile. Luka stood for a second longer. He needed to drink her in, and then he jogged off into obscurity – her interested gaze piercing his back.

The call came that evening.

'Hi, I'm Imani, the musician,' she said.

'Hi, I'm Luka, the musician,' he replied.

The next two weeks flowed with an unexpected, turbulent excitement. She was magnificent to fuck, her dark skin luminous against the crisp white hotel sheets. Her boobs melons, with dark ripe nipples bouncing on top of him. Her ass was round and firm as apples. And best of all, her throaty, soulful laugh as she came screaming into the night. She was the most vocal fuck he'd ever had. At another point in his life, he might have fallen in love with this wild and mesmerising creature. Imani was a soul who lived and breathed music. Untethered. Someone who understood how to make love in legato. She was a pragmatist, independent and intelligent, and he was sure that he wasn't her only lover, and that was okay with him. She was a darting swallow — not the type of woman you would want to cage. Luka didn't feel that way about Lily. The thought of her with another man made him want to vomit.

There was something about Imani that spoke to his soul, the way she moved her hips, the way her heart connected to music. The way she snorted more cocaine than him, it seemed in a way that they were lost together — the music and sensational sex an outlet for their pain. At night when she was sleeping, he would watch the rise and fall of her chest, sometimes gently placing his hands on her heart. He wished he could heal her; he wished he could heal himself, too. He didn't know why, but he couldn't shake the feeling that something about their connection was predestined.

God, those weeks had flown by. He almost missed Imani's wild and wonderful eyes as he gazed out over the bustling harbour, spotting the red sails of a junk boat. The coffee had given him the energy boost he needed. After tying up all the loose ends in the office, he would head home to surprise his gorgeous wife. It was Saturday. Hopefully, she wasn't working. She wasn't aware that Luka would be back today. He thoroughly enjoyed surprises. The hours spent choosing Lily's gift were worth it — an emerald pendant, to match her brilliant eyes. He felt a stab of guilt opening the box and staring at its inanimate beauty. It had been almost two years since he'd last fucked a woman other than his wife. Imani was irresistible. He'd thought it would be easy to go back to being the loyal husband, but Lily seemed vacant. They still weren't connecting the way they once had. She wouldn't look in his eyes when they made love, and Luka felt helpless. Imani made him feel alive the way Lily once had. She made him feel wanted. He would never abandon Lily, but he wouldn't abandon himself either.

Luka closed the black velvet box and tucked it into his tailored blue blazer pocket, rolled up his white cotton shirt sleeves, and got to work.

It wasn't long before an over-enthusiastic intern spotted him through the glass wall of his office. She tapped on his door.

'Do you fancy some lunch?' she asked. 'I'm just popping to Starbucks downstairs. Can I bring you anything?'

He looked at her and felt a strange stab of duty – he'd once been an intern.

'Let me finish here and I will take you to lunch. Working on a Saturday – you deserve a break.'

The flush of pleasure on Ling's face was clear to see. Twenty minutes and Luka was done. He was hungry – lunch was not that big of an inconvenience. He grabbed his blazer and called out to Ling, 'C'mon – we are going to the best Italian in town.'

She was beside him in a millisecond, wearing a proud smile of accomplishment. They got the lift to the upmarket shopping mall beneath the office. Luka's confident strides led them across marbled floors to a hidden white door on the third floor. The entryway opened to a glamorous interior with sweeping views of the ocean. Everything was pristine white – the bar's Agaria marble surface, the laundered tablecloths, and the bulbous contemporary light fittings. The contrast of the white interior with the lapis lazuli blue of the sea was startling, and the waft of garlicky basil air made Luka salivate.

The enthusiasm on Ling's face was touching. She was a sweet girl, and he would do his best to offer her some guidance and support. Being an intern at a hedge fund was shitty. Long days, little sleep, and a shitload of stress. He remembered those days well, and he would do whatever he could to make it easier for Ling. He was fond of her. She was as bright as a button with a Masters from Oxford. He didn't want to lose her. She would be an asset to the firm. A deleterious wave of sadness washed over him – Jessie would have grown up to be as bright as Ling, he was sure of it.

Luka ordered a bottle of crisp Italian Pinot Grigio, hoping that the vibrant floral aroma would snuff out the ember of sadness that Ling had ignited. If it didn't, he had some magical white dust in his pocket.

'Anything in particular you need pointers on, Ling?' he asked with a weary smile as he dabbed freshly baked bread into blotches of dark balsamic vinegar and olive oil.

He knew this would be an interrogation. And he wasn't wrong. Ling fired questions like bullets. Halfway through, Luka excused himself to go to the washroom. The Pinot Grigio wasn't working. Inside a toilet cubicle, his hands worked their magic, manipulating the fine powder into a perfect line, a work of art with a credit card on a small mirror. He inhaled as far into himself as possible, its astringent sting bringing a familiar rush of invincibility over him. He would finish the day strong. And soon the night, too – with Lily, hopefully naked, in his arms. He could still feel sex with Imani in his groin. There was something irresistible about the thought of fucking Lily with the linger of Imani's wild sex still on him.

While walking back to the table where Ling sat, he noticed the back of a familiar dress. It was white with soft lavender florals off the shoulder. He recognised the back of the woman who wore it, and the soft strawberry-blond hair on her neck.

Lily's dress. Lily's neck. Lily's hair.

He was about to march over and scoop his wife in his arms and surprise her; he remembered this was her favourite restaurant in Central, when he noticed that the tall dark-haired man sitting opposite her had his fingers intertwined with hers.

What the fuck.

fourteen

IT WAS NOVEMBER IN Hong Kong, and the wind was biting. Covered in goose bumps, Lily stood on Oliver's balcony and watched the waves of the distant ocean meet the shore. They seemed to sing a sad song. A song of goodbyes. An invisible chill crept into her bones, leaving her feeling hollow and alone. She felt the pressure of the decision she had made, but she trusted her gut that it was the right one, even if it wasn't easy.

Lily made an effort to get dressed today, donning the long white and lavender floral dress she had bought in Florence with Luka, the fabric feeling soft and luxurious against her skin. She paired her lavender dress with a pashmina, the colour matching perfectly, and draped it over her shoulders to shield her from the cooling air. Lily wasn't one to fuss about her appearance, but today she wanted to look good. Maybe it was selfish, but she wanted Oliver to remember her vividly. She wanted to make sure that she would be etched in his memory, an everlasting part of him, because she knew with no doubt that he was an everlasting part of her.

Lily was taking Oliver to lunch at her favourite Italian restaurant with sweeping views of the fragrant harbour and a chef whose flavour would stay on your tongue long after the last bite. They took a red taxi down the mountain, both quietly sitting on the faux leather seats, heads turned outwards towards the skyline views. Both contemplative. Oliver's large hand with clipped nails wrapped around Lily's. It was the perfect home for her small, delicate fingers. She looked down at their intertwined hands – how could something so connected, so perfect in places, be wrong?

Lily didn't have all the answers, but she knew what she knew. It was time to trust her intuition. Oliver was a great love, but they weren't a forever story. She noticed a sadness in his eyes today. He knew it, too. And today he was saying it with his silence.

Hands clutching onto each other for the last time, they walked into Il Piacere with the look of new lovers. The Maître d' led them to a private seat in the corner with a sweeping vista of the bustling harbour.

Oliver delicately unfolded the crisp white napkin and placed it over his lap. He toyed with the polished silver utensils. 'I know you brought me here to tell me something significant, Lily. Please, just spit it out. I can tell when you're holding something.' His eyes were gentle, the redness a reminder of the previous night's drinking.

'Oliver, I love you,' she began, 'so very much. I just don't think that we belong together.' She swallowed hard, tears welling in the corners of her eyes.

'Can you tell me why?'

He reached across the table, almost knocking a glass of water off as he grasped for her hand. Lily looked down at their intertwined fingers again. *Perfect.* And then into his forlorn eyes.

'You have a drinking problem.' Her words were stark. She felt the warmth of Oliver's hand as he squeezed hers, before his gaze settled on the harbour. 'I have drunk more alcohol with you than I have in my entire life. I'm spiralling, Oliver. You are taking me down a path I won't come back from, and I just can't do it anymore. There is too much at stake – my career, everything I've worked so hard for. I can't lose it because I'm in love with a man with an addiction.'

Her sigh stung the air with its heaviness. Oliver was silent, Lily's word 'addiction' piercing him like an arrow. The sky was pewter grey.

'Look,' Lily continued, 'I know you carry grief with you and that's why you need to escape, but you can't escape forever. And I can't erase your wounds. No matter how much I want to and how hard I try. That's up to you.' She studied his face, her eyes lingering on his. They were vacant. 'I can't make that choice for you

Oliver, but I can choose to heal myself. And that's what I'm going to do,' she said.

He took a sip of the cool water in his glass and let out a sigh as he cleared his throat.

'I function perfectly well, Lily. I think you're overstating it. I just like to party hard—'

'Have we ever had sober sex?' she interrupted. 'A night together when we were both sober?'

'We can do that right now – let's go.' He gestured to the waiter with his free hand. She noticed he hadn't let hers go.

'I'm not leaving with you, Oliver,' she said. 'I can't do this anymore. We are not good for each other – we feed off each other, and then we spiral out. We're too intoxicating.'

'Damn it, Lily, isn't that what being in love is? Intoxication?'

'Oliver, not in this way.' A single tear slipped down her cheek.

'Jesus, Lily, have you ever felt a connection this deep?' She could tell his anger was beginning to rise. Oliver pulled his hand away, leaving hers feeling naked.

'I don't know what it is with us.' Lily wiped her cheek. 'I don't know why we feel each other the way we do. I don't know why you finish my sentences or why you know what's in my head before I do. But I know – don't ask me how – that this is not our time.'

He reached for her hand again. 'Is this about Luka?' he asked. 'Do you want to stay with him? He doesn't deserve you. He won't see you the way I see you.

Christ, he doesn't even see what's right in front of him. The man is blind.'

'This has nothing to do with him. This is about us. This is about you.' She absentmindedly scraped her bottom lip with her teeth as she gathered her thoughts. Her words were slow and deliberate. 'Sometimes we need to look at our demons. I'm looking at mine, and you can choose whether to look at yours,' she said.

'I think you are making a mistake, Lily. I may need a little help, but that doesn't mean I'm a write-off. Connections like this, like we have – they don't come round often. Trust me, I know. I've been with many women.'

'Of course you're not a write-off – you are quite the opposite.' Her tears were streaming now. 'This is one of the hardest things I have done. I know you need time to sort yourself out – and frankly, Oliver, I need time, too. I need to process everything that's happened over the last few years, and I need to do it sober and alone.'

Despite the rivers of tears streaming down her face, she was calm and wearing a determined expression – it told him all he had to know. There was no leeway here. This really was the end. Lily used the bleached, starched napkin to blot the tears from her eyes. The hard fabric was unpleasant on her salty skin.

'Oliver, I will always love you.' A sudden desperation touched her voice.

'I will always love you, too,' he said.

Oliver's eyes reached into her heart and pulled out a part of her. She wondered if she would ever reclaim it. This beautiful man, with his dimpled chin and perfect vowels, and his kind heart and velvet morning kisses. This man who fiercely loved her would never hold her hand again. She stroked his finger with her thumb, not wanting to let go but knowing she had to, or she would drown in his sorrow.

Before she had time to gather herself, Lily saw him out of the corner of her eye. Luka. He was stalking towards their table with a mad glint in his eye, and she felt her heart quickening with alarm.

'Lily, so nice to see you, dearest. I see you've missed me.'

Luka was furious. *Dearest.* She'd never heard him use that word.

'Would you like to introduce me to your friend, and while you are at it, can you explain why he was holding your fucking hand?' His voice was thunder.

'Luka, please calm down.'

She glanced over and saw the anger in Oliver's eyes – she needed to defuse the situation. The last thing they needed was a brawl.

'Calm down.' Luka's hands were shaking.

Lily stood up and met his crazed stare. His pupils were dilated. *Shit, he's as high as a kite.*

'Let's go outside onto the balcony, Luka, we don't need a scene.' She noticed a young woman at a table nearby. She was watching them. Lily recognised Ling. 'Isn't your intern waiting for you, Luka? Surely you don't want her to see the managing partner lose it?'

Lily walked in strides towards the sliding balcony doors before hearing his reply. She would not give him any options. He followed. Lily wanted him as far away from Oliver as possible. She didn't know what he was capable of in this state. She walked along the balcony corridor until she was out of sight of the restaurant's patrons. Luka was right behind her – his foreboding presence looming larger than life.

She turned to face him – and then she felt it. The hard sting of his hand sweep across her face. The force of the blow made her stumble backwards. She took a deep breath and steadied herself. As warm blood trickled from the corner of her mouth, she remembered Papa. She remembered the violence of her childhood – it all came at once, flooding her senses with horror, with fear, with grief and despair. And then with raging anger.

Luka toppled forwards, the weight of what he'd just done washing over him like ice. The startled confusion in Lily's eyes was searing. He looked down at his shaking hands.

'I'm so so sorry, Lily. I'm so fucking high. Please help me – I'm out of my mind and he was holding your hand! My wife's fucking hand.'

Lily remembered these turbulent feelings so well. Papa had brought them often with his violent storms. It seemed Papa had turned up in Luka today – just another man whose uncontrolled emotions manifested in violence, whose internalised pain shattered into shards of glass, cutting all those who dared to tread around them. Men with minds like razor blades.

Lily had made a promise to herself decades ago, and it was one she would never break. She would set aside any feelings she had for Luka. It was time to protect herself. She pushed past him without saying a word and walked back to find Oliver. She noticed the empty chair, and the tell-tale sign of his departure – a neatly folded napkin, lying on the table.

Lily kept walking out the door of the restaurant, out of the building, out onto the busy street beneath. She walked through the noisy, polluted city roads until she reached the fresh salty air of the ocean promenade, and then she took off her shoes and ran. She ran for miles. She stopped when she had nothing left, no breath, no energy – not an ounce of strength left in her muscles. Collapsing against a stone wall, she could see the rise and fall of the steady ocean. The constant ebb and flow. Wave after wave washing the marked sand clean.

The metallic taste of blood lingered in her mouth. She nervously lifted a trembling finger to her lips, the blood smearing on her chin.

There is only one thing you can be sure of in life – nothing stays.

I Will Weep and Weep For You, O Mind

'I will weep and weep for you, O Mind;
(My Soul) The world hath caught you in its spell.
Though you cling to them with the anchor of steel,
Not even the shadow of the things you love Will go with you
when you are dead. Why then have you forgot your own true
Self?'

Lalleshwari

fifteen

THE THERAPIST'S HANDS WERE firm. She was kneading all the tension out of Lily's taut muscles and the room smelt like rose oil and eucalyptus, each breath in a balm to her aching lungs. The organ that carries grief. Lily felt far away from everything, even though her whole life was only a few kilometres away. The timing of her 'involuntary' holiday couldn't have been better. She'd checked into the Four Seasons, as per Alexander Chau SC's instructions, on the same evening that Luka had left his bloody mark on her face. She hadn't gone home, and she wouldn't be doing so until she could be sure that there was an adequate window of time when Luka would be gone, and she could safely collect her belongings without running into him. He did not know where she was. She deleted the dozens of calls and messages she received from him each day without a millisecond of hesitation. There was nothing to talk about, no resolution possible. Goodbye had been said with a blow from the back of his hand. Chambers staff were under strict orders not to answer his questions, not to forward any calls from him, and security was briefed to turn him away at the door.

Lily released a deep, guttural groan as the masseuse's skilled thumbs worked to ease the tension in her neck.

'You are very tight, missy. It's no good,' she said in a disapproving tone.

Lily lay face down on the massage table, her silent tears slipping down her cheeks as she stared at the fragrant bowl of water, topped with frangipani petals, that was placed on the floor beneath. She was grateful her face was concealed. She didn't want anyone to see her pain. The repetitive ping of her phone broke the serenity. She knew it was Luka; she could feel it. His energy was looming – like a dark shadow.

'Missy, do you want your phone?'

'No, thank you,' Lily replied.

Luka's clinging desperation made her shiver. Her body went cold at the memory of what had happened. The only message Lily wanted to see on her phone was one from Oliver. But it hadn't arrived. Not a single call or text. He had slipped away from her life as effortlessly as a warm sun disappears from the horizon line, or a colourful autumn leaf falls from a tree. The image of the white napkin Oliver had folded and left on the restaurant table was a haunting memory. His absence was like a physical weight in her stomach, a clenching, burning feeling that made it difficult to eat. She knew her decision was right. They'd been dancing in a dark room, and it was time for them both to find their light. But it wasn't easy. Losing a love of your life never is, and she had lost two.

After Lily's massage, the masseuse swaddled her in warm towels and sent her to the sauna, where she could feel the penetrating heat seep into her muscles. Her body ached, every single joint, every fibrous tissue and, most of all, her heart. When she was done, she wrapped herself in the warm, fluffy towelled robe and sank into the inviting softness of the super-king bed in her room.

The first nights were restless. Lily checked out every single pillow option from the pillow menu at the hotel, trying them out one by one. Still, sleep was elusive, and big dreams plagued the little she had – the kind that linger in your psyche and leave you feeling uneasy for days.

The sessions with the talk therapist were disastrous because Lily had nothing to say. All she wanted in this moment was the warm comfort of Lulama's hugs, yet she was so far away and unreachable for Lily, making her ache all the more. Alcohol was off the menu. The only liquid that touched her lips was herbal or sourced from a crystal-clear alpine stream.

Lily tried every treatment offered at the spa. She'd been coated in thick clay, which was then sealed in cling film and weighted with hot stones for the ultimate exfoliation, using Himalayan salt. She'd luxuriated in the sensation of a massage with pink peppercorn, amber and fig as it cleansed her body. Lily had sat in a eucalyptus-filled steam room, lavender saunas, bathed in cold pools of frangipani scented water. Her body had been pummelled, rubbed, stroked, kneaded, and pricked with acupuncture needles.

By day four, she felt more settled, her body calming down. On the fifth day, she slipped into a deep and rejuvenating sleep. She slept for a solid fourteen straight hours.

On the sixth day, she woke up with a raging appetite and an inexplicable urge to visit a temple. Many times, over the last few months, she had thought about the experience she'd had with the South Indian Goddess in the cockroach laden building on Kowloon side. The blissful peace that had washed over her as she had sat cross-legged on a grass mat in a tiny insignificant room with iron bars on the windows. The longing to experience the indescribable peace again was growing. It was a yearning – the way you long for your mother as a child, or the summer sun in the winter, or your bed after an exhausting day.

The existential mysteries intrigued Lily. Since childhood, she had looked up at the night sky and asked questions. Why am I here? What is the purpose of life? Who am I? Who is anyone? Life had made her forget her inquisitiveness, pain had made her forget, but that day in Kowloon, the Goddess had reminded her. She had planted an almost imperceptible seed in her soul. A cotton thread of the Divine, barely tangible, but perceptible enough to entice Lily to begin a new search.

Lily decided she would visit the Po Lin Buddhist Monastery, a place she had been frequently. Today she would arrive with fresh eyes. She got dressed, called the concierge to arrange a car, left her mobile phone in the bedside drawer, and went downstairs to wait for her ride.

The monastery had a temple perched high on a forested mountain on Lantau Island. Lily's previous visits had been in the early hours before sunrise, when the bald saffron-robed monks would sing their chants into the reverberating mountain crags. It was a bright and clear day today, and the view from the top was breathtaking. Verdant hills, covered in majestic banyan trees, the forest dramatically rising above the wild South China Sea.

Lily lit a joss stick, placed her hands together, and bowed before the striking statue of Guanyin, a Bodhisattva (a being who had dedicated her spiritual path to the freedom and happiness of all beings) and one of the few female deities who are given a place of reverence in the Buddhist tradition. She was tall and resplendent in gold, rising out of a lotus flower, her robes like turbulent waves blown about in a storm, her face serene. Lily felt a deep connection to Guanyin, also known as the Goddess of Compassion, the moment she saw her.

Shrouded in enigma, it was almost impossible to work out the exact origin of Guanyin's story. Her Chinese name, Guanshiyin, was derived from a Sanskrit name, Avalokitesvara, which translates to 'he who hears the cries of the world'. Lily had read of a legend where she was a beautiful pregnant shepherdess, summoned by a cruel king to dance for his five hundred victorious warriors. The heartless soldiers had forced her to dance on and on, and it had been too much for her, leading to a miscarriage that broke her. Death had claimed her, and in the afterlife, she became the wife of Hades. To console her for the pain of her life, he'd gifted her with five hundred children. Even then, her pain was unbearable, and she felt no solace, transforming her into a monstrous ghost who haunted children with her shrill cries.

Until one night, after a ghoulish haunting, Buddha appeared before her and said, 'You've been blessed with five hundred children, yet it hurts so much when only one of them is gone. It is a fact that Earth-dwellers typically have a few offspring. Have you thought about how much pain they suffer when they lose one?'

It was said that Guanyin recognised the enormity of what she had done. Guilt flooded her, and she was filled with compassion for human beings. She relinquished her five hundred children to earthlings who had not been blessed with their own and kept praying for the child she had lost. She transformed into a being full of compassion with a thousand eyes to observe those in pain, and to extend her care to all who asked for it. It was believed that she would continuously be reborn as a woman, foretelling that it was the Feminine that was necessary to free this patriarchal society of its sorrow and anguish.

Lily thought about Luka and how his pain had created such monstrous emotions inside of him. She watched the tendrils of incense smoke waft above Guanyin's serene head.

We have a choice; we can turn our pain into something else, just like Guanyin. Perhaps that's why she had come here today to remind herself of this story.

Lily often wondered if the various women she encountered on a bus, a plane, in a soup kitchen, or a courtroom could be the reincarnation of Guanyin, although she wasn't sure if she truly accepted the idea. In other legends, Guanyin was the ultimate source of unconditional love, so that each parent who had a love for their child held a part of her spirit. This made sense to Lily, and it was a comforting thought to think that the noble part of ourselves that loves unconditionally is a drop of the Divine filtering through us. A Goddess-like essence as opposed to a God-like one. A compassionate energy, instead of a vengeful, power-seeking, fear-inducing one.

Her entire life, Lily had been told tales of a male-centric paradigm, a male deity. To be in a holy temple facing the mythos of a female was liberating.

sixteen

'IT'S GREAT TO SEE you back.' Alexander Chau SC was beaming a contagious smile.

'Thank you, Sandy. I am so grateful for everything you have done for me.' Lily was profoundly thankful – words couldn't adequately express her feelings. Alexander had given her a gift bigger than he would ever know.

'Don't mention it,' he said. 'I can see the break has done its job. You look fantastic.' He went towards the mirrored closet in his office to pick up his robes and his black wig tin with his name embossed in gold-lettering.

Lily's eyes sparkled, her skin glistening with a smooth, golden sheen.

'I'm feeling great. It's amazing how much perspective a short break can give. You should try it,' she said with a twinkle in her eye.

'Hah! The next opening in my diary is in summer. Someone's got to run this show.' His grin stretched from ear to ear.

Alexander adored his job. More than his loyal partner Max, his six children (several of which were adopted), and his regal hairless Egyptian cat, Cleopatra. His exuberance washed away any pretence of burden as he prepared himself for court. His dexterous hands expertly tied his bands behind his winged collar, and he flung on his robes with the flair of a magician. He lived for the real-life drama of it all.

'Sandy, may I ask you a serious question?' Lily's shoulders twitched.

'Ooh, I love serious – fire away.'

'How do you remain so enthusiastic? Doesn't it feel meaningless and contrived, especially with conviction rates so disproportionately high in Hong Kong? The latest report says we're close to North Korea.' She tensed her body and waited, her eyes narrowed in concentration for his answer.

Alexander deftly adjusted his cufflinks with his fingers. 'I'm surprised to hear that question from you. Maybe you've had too much time to think?' He was suddenly stoical. He disliked what he saw in her eyes. 'Lily, if we don't defend with all we've got, the whole thing unravels. What little chance they've got becomes non-existent. Even the shitty ones who are guilty as sin.

The law fails by every measure if there isn't equal representation. This system has its flaws, but fighting for justice – for that bigger picture perspective – gives me drive. And it gives you drive. That's why you are here. Some of us are born to fight.'

'Mm …' Lily wasn't convinced. After the time off she'd had for reflection, she was sure that she wasn't born to fight. Fighting was born out of a necessity to survive, not her mother's womb. 'Sandy, the brief on my desk concerns a man with a messiah complex who has been kidnapping young boys and circumcising them in public toilets. I'm not sure that it's possible for me to defend him with all I've got.'

Alexander's booming laughter filled the room. His eyes gleamed with delight as he shook his head.

'Jesus, what a fuckwit. Look. Lily, this job isn't pretty. Life's not pretty. We get to see the dark underbelly and live in the shadows. For every evil motherfucker out there, there are twice as many innocents caught up in dire circumstances. And even the evil motherfuckers have some redemptive qualities. There are very few true sociopaths.' He let out a deep, heavy sigh. 'Try to find the good in him. Work for that,' he said.

Alexander packed his files and wig tin into his trolley briefcase and wheeled it to his office door. Lily trudged behind.

'I'm sorry a shit brief has landed on your desk on your first day back. Approach it as a test of your commitment to justice. I know you will ace it. Lucky bastard.' He gave her a wink and ambled out of Chambers towards the lift lobby. Whoever he was defending today was very lucky, too.

Lily slumped her shoulders. Not every brief felt right – she couldn't shake the ominous feeling that this career was no longer her calling. The break had given her perspective. She was searching for something, and she was sure she would not find it in a hostile courtroom. She thought of everything it took to stand in her black stilettoed shoes today. The hard work at school, which had led to a scholarship at a prestigious UK university. Having to leave her country and her family and everyone she held close to study in a foreign land without support. Papa was furious she had accepted. Lily didn't have a choice; it was the only way to free herself from his reign of abusive love.

She had spent her university days bent over books in libraries, while her peers danced and partied and raved. Luka had been her only reprieve from the mundanity, their lovemaking taking her out of her studies and analytical head. He was so gentle then, so full of love, and hope and promise. She softened at the thought. Lifting her hand to her mouth, she traced the tiny wound that he had left on her lip with her fingers. It was healing, and so was she – and she hoped Luka was healing, too.

Lily walked into her office. She loved this space. The plush cream sofa her work colleagues would jump onto whenever they needed her listening ear. Two Vietnamese paintings depicting women in floral dresses in soft pastels hung on the wall above the rows of shelves carrying law books bound in a rich history. The smell of old pages, and her diffuser blowing essential oils in the air – today it was peppermint. Several state-of-the-art screens were on her desk, and her built-in wardrobe where her dry-cleaned robes, bands, and pressed court blouses hung. Her wig box, which was covered in leather and embossed in gold leaf, sat on its own shelf. She had earned this place with sweat, tears, and exhaustion. With fortitude, perseverance, and tenacity. How could she possibly be thinking of giving it up? She looked at the brief papers lying tied with a pink ribbon on her desk, and she couldn't bring herself to pick them up. She went for a walk instead.

Tropical flora flanked the pathway to Hong Kong Park. It was lined with purple bauhinia, ginger lilies, hibiscus, orchids, frangipani, and Hong Kong irises. The thick air was filled with the sweet, heady scents of flowers – a true delight for the senses. Lily slipped off her patent black stilettoes. She wanted to feel her bare feet on the ground. This drew disapproving stares. Bare feet were not a common sight in the city. Lily didn't care; she needed to feel the earth. She couldn't explain why – it just made her feel alive.

She walked up to the Edward Youde Aviary, the cobbled stone path warm beneath her feet, the late winter afternoon sun highlighting her flamingo-pink manicured toenails. She heard the strange and enchanting calls and whirrs of the wild birds beckoning her nearer. The aviary was an extraordinary place filled with colours, smells, and sounds that filled your senses to overflow. Lily spotted a Golden-crested mynah sitting in the tall branches of a Banyan tree, her orange halo flashing like a warning sign. She was mimicking the visitors below, repeating words in her strange squawking language. Further along, sitting in the branches of a sunshine tree, were a pair of emerald doves, peacefully cooing a repetitive song. She stood there for a moment, listening to the serene sound of their chirping, until a white-crested hornbill with a white mane rushed past and spooked them away. The great Sumatran bird, its wings flapping anxiously, looked out of place, so far away from its natural habitat in the forest. It made Lily sad. These wild creatures were trapped under a roof, unable to reach the clouds, or the sky or the stars. Or home. Perhaps she was a trapped bird, too, in a job and place in time where she didn't belong.

As she made her way back to Chambers, she noticed a man sitting on a bench opposite the old traditional Chinese tea house, with a view of giant lily pads floating on a pond. He was unmistakable: Oliver – with his dimpled chin and eyes from the sea. He was sitting beside a slender, dark-haired woman. She was regal, with almond eyes and a petite button nose. They were pointing and laughing at something – a golden retriever who had run off with a little child's shoe. The sound of his familiar deep voice ignited an unbearable pain in her stomach. Less than two weeks, and he had moved on. While she tossed and turned with aching for him in her friend Saima's spare room bed, he was probably sleeping soundly beside someone else. She saw the woman's hand resting on his leg as if it belonged there. Her stomach lurched, and she turned and hurried in the opposite direction – there wasn't a chance that she would cross his path. The ring of his laughter echoed in her ears until she reached the safety of Chambers.

After closing the door, she turned on the red do-not-disturb light. She stared out the window at the city beyond and allowed the tears to fall. Amazed that she had any tears left, she lifted both legs onto her chair and hugged them for a moment. She soaked the brief papers that lay on her desk with her crying, the clumps of wet sticking the paper to the table. Peeling it off and untying the pink ribbon, she read, hoping to be distracted from the heaviness in her chest. Even the horror written in the words couldn't pull her out of her melancholy. She read it twice, looked out the window, and spotted a raptor diving in between the high rises, then soaring higher and higher in circles towards the clouds above.

A graceful, free, wild flying hawk. Unlike the trapped birds she'd seen in the aviary.

She stared at the brief papers for a few more minutes, letting the typeface dissolve into a blur. And then, as if struck by a bolt of insanity, she tore them to shreds and threw them in the wastepaper basket, grabbed her cerulean pashmina, and walked back out into the early evening air.

It is said that the most suffering happens between the point of knowing something and the point of acting on it. Lily was about to test that hypothesis. She was walking away from a lifetime of conditioned expectations into the unknown.

She was following the hawk and rising towards the sky.

Forgetful One Get Up

Forgetful one, get up!
It's dawn, time to start searching.
Open your wings and lift.
Give like the blacksmith
even breath to the bellows.
Tend the fire that changes
the shape of metal.
Alchemical work begins at dawn,
As you walk out to meet the Friend.'

Lalleshwari

seventeen

Koh Samui, 2010

THE AIRPORT ON KOH Samui was unlike any Lily had ever seen. The outdoor Shala was a sight to behold, with a bamboo and thatch roof and a sparkling pond full of golden-and-white koi fish skimming the surface in gentle waves. Guests could relax and enjoy the serenity of their surroundings in the outdoor seating area. It looked more like a poolside terrace than an airport lounge.

On landing, colourful golf carts painted with purple and yellow flowers greeted passengers. The carts were waiting to drive them to the main building. The travellers came from all over the world dressed in summer attire, hats, flip-flops, and sunglasses, wearing excited smiles in anticipation of an island holiday in an exotic location. Lily wasn't here for a holiday – well, not exactly; she was here to find herself. Whatever that meant.

She spotted two monks in turmeric robes reclining on a sofa beside the pond as she exited arrivals to head for the luggage turnstile. They appeared calm and smiling. The island was full of temples, and she was excited to discover them all.

On the baggage belt, one medium suitcase arrived, filled with all the items she needed for her self-discovery journey – sunscreen, mosquito spray, five light summer dresses, one warm cardigan, one pastel pink summer raincoat, underwear, two bras, a cap, two swimsuits, a sarong, two yoga outfits, running shoes, sandals, a yoga mat, a hot water bottle for her period cramps and her Shanghai Tang Journal. Save for her journal, all these items were new. Lily hadn't been home to collect her belongings. She couldn't face Luka.

Alexander Chau SC hadn't taken the news of her sabbatical well. He said she was being impulsive, that her career was gaining momentum and to have a break now was irresponsible. He told her she would regret it and that he fully expected to see her back within a month. Any other job would bore her senseless and she was too bright to throw it all away. Lily smiled at the memory. He cared; he really did.

She grabbed her tattered black bag from the turnstile with a clatter and dumped it on a trolley before heading out towards the exit. It was chaos. There were throngs of drivers jostling like seals for space and holding placards with passenger names, and others trying to solicit tourists for rides. The name-calling was a cacophony to the ears. Lily scanned the boards for her name and eventually, after ten sweaty and anxious minutes, she found it. In black cursive on a whiteboard: Lily Flannery. She gulped. It had been a while since she had seen her maiden name in writing. Her driver was professional and polite, dressed in a white-collared shirt and long cotton trousers. He greeted her with hands pressed together in a prayer fashion, a bow and a warm,

'Sawadee Khap, welcome to Samui.'

There were prayer beads in his car, along with the delicious smell of white petalled star-jasmine hanging off the front rear-view mirror. Someone carefully placed icy bottles of water in the back seat pockets, as well as fragrant hand towels to mop up the sweat on her forehead. The air hostess on the flight had sternly warned that the only safe water to drink was the bottled water on the island. Lily didn't want dysentery or typhoid; she would heed her advice. The air-conditioned car was a reprieve from the heat that was so oppressive, it felt like a heavy blanket pressing down on you.

She gazed out the window as they wound over bumpy pot-holed roads, with tangles of electricity wires loosely hanging from pole to pole overhead. The views of the west coast were elusive until they reached Chaweng Beach, a bustling tourist spot. The sea was a vivid aquamarine blue with pools of vibrant greens. It was calling her and she couldn't wait to be buoyant in its gentle rhythmic waves. They were heading out to the southern peninsula of the island. Lily had booked herself into a wellness and spiritual retreat that promised a blissful experience, complete with yoga classes and meditation sessions. She did not know what to expect, and looking out the window, it alarmed her to see the chaotic, bustling scene of the island streets. She had hoped to find respite here. The drive through towns with bars, cafes, galleries, massage houses, spas, and clothing and tourist shops was a lot to absorb, especially after a flight. Lily felt overwhelmed looking out the window. She was longing for stillness.

After a chaotic forty-five-minute journey filled with the sound of screeching car horns and the buzz of scooters darting by, sometimes with helmetless riders carrying women and children on the back, they eventually arrived at the Kalalaya Wellness Retreat. It was down a long drive lined with bursts of purple Siamese tulips, sunshine yellow allamanda, coconut palms, and banyan trees with their branches decorated with a variety of orchids. Lily breathed a sigh of relief – it was bliss. The retreat sat perched on the end of the peninsula, comprising a magical little village with bungalows dotted on the steep terraced hillside with sweeping views of the shimmering turquoise Andaman Sea.

A soft-spoken receptionist with white and yellow frangipani in her long plaited hair greeted Lily with a smile. She brought her a fresh coconut, chopped off at the top with sweet icy juice inside and a spoon to scoop out the white flesh of the fruit. *I'm in paradise.* The cool liquid slid down Lily's throat – it was pure relief.

As she was driven in a golf cart to her villa, carefully balancing her welcome coconut, she caught glimpses of intricately carved Hindu and Buddhist statues peppered all over – at reception, and amid the lush, tropical gardens. She also noticed the ponds full of bright indigo lotus flowers, their petals reflecting the sunlight like iridescent gems. They drove past the swimming pools, which had waterfalls and infinity views of the sparkling ocean beneath. Lily's bungalow villa had an outdoor spa-bath scattered with frangipani and hibiscus flowers to welcome her. Richly coloured silk meditation cushions were placed to provide a comfortable seat to admire the picturesque vista, while large mirrored glass doors reflected the oriental decor inside. Soothing music was piped in from speakers hidden in ceilings and heated essential oils in a large intricately crafted pottery burner were mingling with the smell of fresh sea air. It was by far the most sensorial space that Lily had ever stayed in.

She walked straight to the outdoor bath, dropped her clothes on the floor, and sank into the fragrant floral scented water. There was something so wonderfully wild about feeling your naked skin caressed by the water and the ocean winds. The sun was setting – a palette of soothing pastel colours skipping on the waves. As the sky darkened, Lily noticed twinkling lights rising on air currents in the distance. She wondered what they were. *Dancing fireflies?*

There was a palpable magic in the air – a sense that this place belonged to an ancient story. The tightly coiled tension in her shoulder and back muscles was dissipating. As she stepped out of the bath with water-wrinkled skin, out into the evening breeze, she felt her whole body exhale. The torment of the previous months was beginning to find a place to release. Lily stood naked in the quiet, watching the extraordinary landscape beneath her. She felt wild – a voluptuous goddess on top of a landscape of mystery. There was something out there for her, something calling from the sound of the night waves. She could hear it in her heart.

Excitement swashed in Lily's stomach on her first morning at the retreat. She had slept naked, too tired to eat after her bath. She had jumped into the bed, enjoying the luxurious feeling of the four-poster king-size frame and the crispness of the freshly pressed sheets. The morning light had brought the gentle chirping of a gecko on the roof.

'Ge-Kooo, Ge-Kooo.'

The sound brought an instant smile to Lily's lips as she opened her eyes to her first day in Thailand.

Lily pulled on a soft pink maxi-dress and slid her feet into flowery flip-flops. She was so delighted to begin her day, she almost forgot to brush her teeth. She gathered a few essentials and put them in her day pack. It was time to explore. As she was leaving the villa, she noticed a list of instructions left on a hand-carved coffee table beside a plush white sofa. And just like that, paradise turned into a boot camp. Her schedule was packed with back-to-back activities, courses, and consultations.

Shit. She had already missed the opening sunrise meditation. She made a scramble for the dining hall, holding the map of the retreat in her hands she marched up steep pathways lined with birds of paradise, and down curving lanes, left and right and … No, she'd reached one of the many meditation halls. *Ugh.* It seemed she was a lost in the labyrinth of landscaped pathways, and the map was hardly helping.

As she rounded the corner, she was startled by the sight of a turmeric-robed nun – a Western woman, her shaved head as gleaming as her deep cobalt eyes. Lily had never met a Buddhist nun. The woman had many intricate lines weaving a story on her face. Lily guessed she must have been well into her third quarter of life.

'So sorry. I'm lost. First day here,' Lily muttered in between breaths. These hills were killing her. Her calves were on fire. 'I'm looking for the dining hall.' She looked at the nun with pleading eyes.

The nun smiled and pointed to the sticker on her robe which read: '*I'm practising loving silence.*'

Lily sighed. *Damn, what am I supposed to do now?* She wiped the sweat gathering on her brow with her forearm. *And how can silence be loving?*

Unexpectedly, the nun reached out with a small yet firm hand, grasping Lily's, and guiding her down a winding path. She stopped in front of a pond with a floating lotus on the surface. They stood there, holding hands and gazing at the beautiful indigo flower, its petals wide open to the bright morning sun's rays.

Lily knew from her visits to the monastery on Lantau Island that the lotus held significant symbolism in the Buddhist tradition. It represented the womb of the universe, from which all things are born. Usually rooted in mud, it manifested out of the darkness into a thing of miraculous perfection. It was a symbol of struggle through adversity, and a link to the universal soul which Buddhists say underpins all life.

The pond reflected a single bulbous white cloud hanging overhead on the smooth surface of the water, shrouding the indigo flower in a white halo. The longer they looked at it, the more beautiful it appeared to be. It seemed almost holy.

Lily wasn't accustomed to touching a stranger in such an intimate way – hands connected, as though they were childhood friends. But somehow this felt right, as though they had known each other for lifetimes, not just five minutes. The nun felt like Lulama. A lump was rising in Lily's throat as she swallowed, and a physical pain of missing formed in her belly.

She wasn't sure how long they had been entranced by the perfectly symmetrical lotus, but by the time they moved again, she was filled with a comforting stillness, and her breath had returned to a gentle rhythm. A smiling warmth. *Ah, so this is loving silence.* Lily's eyes sparkled with delight as they crinkled at the edges.

When they reached the dining hall, the nun let her hand go. She almost wanted to grab it back but resisted the urge. She felt childlike and needy. Instead, she placed her palms together in the customary prayer position and bowed. The nun did the same. They both smiled acknowledgement into each other's eyes.

Wow, I want whatever she's got. It's magical.

Lily's feet glided into the dining hall as smooth as a swan on a quiet lake, her pink dress billowing behind her in the sea breeze. She had almost forgotten that she was ravenous. What an uplifting way to start her first day. If this was an omen of things to come, she was ready for it.

eighteen

DISTANCE HAS A WAY of distorting memory. Lily lay in bed watching the resident gecko chase a mosquito on the ceiling, his mottled grey-and-black tail flicking from side to side. First light entered the room through the gaps in the curtains, creating an ethereal glow. Lily stretched her limbs with a large yawning exhale. She was looking forward to a silent morning meditation. She'd been here less than two weeks, and the rhythms of the place now came as naturally as sunrise. As each day passed, she grew further away from the hurtful memories of Luka. And Oliver. And Papa. This morning, her life felt like a story in a book written by someone else. As she went through her morning routine – washing her face, brushing her teeth – she noticed that the woman looking back at her in the mirror was less anguished. The scar on her lip was gone, her eyes shone a little brighter, and she was developing a rosy glow on her cheeks. No need for blush anymore. Not that she had worn make-up since she got here, but maybe she would tonight. Today was their first schedule-free day, and she was thinking of dining out this evening in the local town with a lovely friend she had made. Maggie was all red hair and fireballs. She was witty and wise and great company. They'd met in a yoga class both attempting an impossible Astavakrasana (Eight Angle Pose), their mutual clumsiness a unifying characteristic. Both of them had fallen out of the pose and then into fits of laughter.

Kalalaya had a diverse group of guests. Entrepreneurs looking for motivation, people in mid-life facing internal and marital issues, a grieving rock star struggling with substance abuse and worn-out professionals. Lily thought she was a part of that last group, although she wasn't exhausted but wounded by love. The guests all had one thing in common: money. Kalalaya was expensive. As much as she loved this place, that fact gnawed at her. It didn't seem right – buying your liberation.

Kalalaya was set up by a wealthy Stanford grad who had wed a Thai monk. He had left a monastic life to be with her. It made for an exceptionally interesting coupling and business venture. Lily found comfort in the idea that a significant portion of the profits went to helping the local monasteries and other charitable organisations in the region.

It felt strange having a free day. The retreat routine left little time for reminiscing. Lily headed out onto the balcony and settled down on the vibrant orange silk meditation cushion. She had become accustomed to the practice, which was a struggle sometimes. Finding emptiness in the mind was a bit like searching for a needle in a haystack, but Lily found that the less she strived for that, the easier it came. She'd read that stillness was the doorway to the temple of awakening. She liked the sound of that. Awakening.

According to Buddhist philosophy, most of us spend entire lifetimes asleep, in a continuous dream state, until one defining moment when we wake up and reality looks starkly different. And when we see this new place, our hearts open, our minds strengthen, and suffering becomes joy. *A lofty goal, but a worthwhile one.* Lily allowed her eyes to flutter open, feeling the comforting warmth of the morning sun on her skin. The light on the balcony was diffused, making the ocean look opaque. She could hear the rushing waters and native birdsong in her ears. The mornings here were heaven.

As her meditation practice ended, she stretched her almost numb legs out on the creaking wooden balcony floor. She noticed they were getting slimmer and stronger. This was unintentional – a bonus side effect of steep hill climbs and daily yoga. With nothing pre-planned, she would go exploring. She had become accustomed to the maze of pathways on Kalalaya and their mysterious destinations. Today, she would take a path she hadn't traversed. Day after day, she would walk by it and be curious, yet never had the opportunity to discover where it went.

She put on a bright, canary-yellow dress that felt light as she set off. After five minutes of brisk walking, she noticed a bright green snake slide across the pathway. She stopped for a moment, unafraid but wary. Koh Samui had many snake friends – reticulated pythons, cobras, minute snakes – and this bright green one was a harmless rat snake. She had learned from hiking the hills in Hong Kong that snakes don't bother humans; you just need to be loud to let them know you are coming. Lily stomped on. Her stamping walk drawing the smile of a passing guest. He was tall with wavy sand colour hair and a warm smile revealing a small gap in his two front teeth. Lily hadn't met him. *He must be a newbie.*

She arrived at an enclosed opening leading to a vibrant, small walled garden with enormous boulders on one side. It seemed a strange coincidence. The nun whom she hadn't seen since her first day at the retreat appeared to be tending an ailing plant. She was gently pulling off the dead foliage and massaging the healthy leaves with her thumb. Lily stood watching her as the nun spoke to the spider lily with its webbed shaped white blossoms, as if it were her child. Not wanting to disturb her, Lily took a few quiet steps backwards and was about to turn and leave when the nun said,

'Would you like to join me, Lily?'

Lily startled. *How does she know my name? How does she know it's me?*

The nun turned around; she had a soft smile.

'Come sit with me,' she said as she tapped a patch of grass beside her. Her voice was authoritative and motherly.

Lily knelt and sat beside her. The grass was prickly and wet.

'It's good to see you.' The words tumbled out of Lily's mouth. 'I was wondering if I would cross your path again. You seemed to have disappeared.'

The nun's eyes were kind. She tended the plant with the utmost care. Her short fingernails embedded with soil.

'I am happy to see you, too. How is your meditation practice coming on?'

'Oh, you know, it's a struggle. Some days I find the quiet, usually when I'm less resistant; other days it feels like a treadmill.' Lily sighed. 'And then there are moments when I think I'm there and it feels almost scary – like falling into an abyss, like I'm going to fall inside a giant hole and never come back – and that's usually when I stop.'

'You're afraid?'

'Yes, yes, I am.' Lily rubbed her wrist with her finger.

'That you'll lose yourself?' The nun's expression was inquisitorial.

'I know it's silly, but yes.'

'It's not silly at all. Most of us are afraid in the beginning.' The nun stood up and dusted her hands off, her robes scattered with earth. 'Come with me.' She reached out her hand and took Lily's. There was something reassuring about the older woman's wisdom lines, her knowing eyes and the firm skin on her gardener's hands.

Striding towards a boulder, they proceeded into the hill via a passageway behind it. They were in a cave with a small tunnel which led to a wider opening. Lily had to crouch down to avoid bashing her head against the jagged rocks. As she sat down beside the nun, she felt the cold, hard surface of the stone seat that had been carved out of the hillside. In front of it was a ledge with an intriguing shrine decorated with many objects: a statue of a gold, seated Buddha, three flower garlands made of sweet-smelling gardenia, jasmine, and rose. There were several burning candles, lit incense in pots, a tray of fresh summer fruit, a bowl of water, Tibetan singing bowls, mala beads, and several gold framed photos of saffron-robed monks. No nuns.

The nun shut her eyes, her hands positioned in a mudra with her index fingers touching her thumbs – a symbolic ritual gesture shaped by one's fingers used to manipulate prana or life force energy. Lily watched intently as she assumed the lotus meditation position that one of the monks had taught her during the early morning meditation sessions on Kalalaya's secluded white sand beach. The silence in the cave was complete, no birdsong, no whispering breeze, no insect sounds. There was just the soft rhythmic breathing of the woman beside her – it was barely audible.

When all the noise around you stops, silence can be loud. Lily's stomach churned in anticipation, like a million tiny storms swirling inside her. Trying not to focus on the discomfort of her folded legs beneath her, she emulated the pattern of the nun's breathing. After some time, the numbing sensation in her legs seemed to belong to someone else. Lily was floating on a metaphorical cloud. She felt light, almost detached from her body. She was observing herself with a strange sense of curious indifference, like a voyeur looking through a window at an interesting stranger. When she realised what was happening, she panicked. *Am I dying?* She felt the nun's hand reassuringly take hers with a gentle squeeze.

She was very much alive.

She was inside the cave and outside the cave at the same time. A gentle reverberation washed over the room as the singing bowl hummed. Lily fluttered her eyes open and saw a monk shrouded by candlelight shadows. He was seated in the far corner of the cave, playing a Tibetan bowl with a wooden striker. *Why didn't I spot him when I came in?* Lily closed her eyes and was lifted out again, flying like a raptor above the clouds. She felt confused and elated at the same time. *Is this what they mean when they talk about the Mystery? That you can leave your body? That you can be in two places at once? Or is this part of an imaginal world that I've never accessed?*

Something felt uncannily familiar – a golden thread back to her child self, a place so strange yet so familiar.

The monk chanted in a low, deep voice as he swirled the wooden striker on the bowl, the strength of the vibrations in the cave steadily increasing. The sound pierced through Lily's body, and she was lifted out through the clouds into a burst of luminous light. A place of nothingness – completely empty, but totally full. The expansive nature of it all, impossible to articulate in written words. And then, as the monk lowered his powerful baritone voice into singing whispers, the sound waves created by the singing bowl echoed and dissolved into the deep abiding silence. A black hole filled with a warm white glow. They remained there for some time. Minutes, hours – Lily couldn't tell. Shrouded in this full, expansive white silence until the nun calmly rose and walked outside into the sunshine. Lily took some time to rise and walk into the light after her. It was jarring – everything outside felt too intense, too loud, too bright. Her senses needed time to calibrate. She searched for the nun, her eyes struggling to adjust to the bright light, and eventually found her in the same place she had seen her before. She was right back to tending the sickly plant, as if nothing special had just taken place. As if this day were perfectly ordinary.

'How did you know I panicked?' She looked deep into the nun's eyes in search of answers.

'Your heart rate, Lily, sound carries in the cave.' She smiled as she took Lily's hand once more, this time leading her with silent steps to the garden exit. As they reached the exit path, she dropped Lily's hand. 'And if you are wondering how I knew it was you behind me when I was tending the plant – I recognise the sound of your footsteps.'

'But you've only walked with me once, two weeks ago, and how do you know my name?' Lily's voice lifted. Nothing made sense.

'When you spend as many hours in silence as I do, you become hyper observant; your senses are heightened. It gives you a discerning ear for sound and rhythm and pattern. And …' she grinned '… I was curious about you after our first meeting, so I looked your name up on the guest list. Sorry to disappoint you. I'm not a psychic. Or Yoda.' She chortled happily and then, with a wink, she remarked, 'But I know of many who are.' Her face became suddenly serious, her cobalt eyes striking Lily as if hinting at some hidden message.

She turned and walked away.

'Wait.' The desperation in Lily's voice reached the nun's ears. She turned around to face Lily. 'I need to know what happened in there,' said Lily.

'Lily, what happened is uniquely yours. I'm not in your head. But I can say that I think you overcame your fear. There are forces unknown to the western psyche. Forces of wind and forest and fire. Forces of sound and earth and ancestry. Forces that can't be psychologised. Take your time and make of it what you will.'

'But where did the monk come fro—'

Before Lily finished her sentence or blurted out any more questions, the nun turned and abruptly walked away, her flowing robes swaying behind her, making it clear that their conversation had ended.

Lily stood watching her go, her face a picture of astonishment.

The Way Is Difficult and Very Intricate

'The way is difficult and very intricate. Lalla discarded her books that told about it, and through meditation saw the truth that never comes to anyone from reading words.'

Lalleshwari

nineteen

LAMAI BEACH WAS BUSTLING with tourists filling the outdoor Thai eateries dotted on the water's edge. The night sky was illuminated by a dazzling display of lanterns, a festival of moons glimmering in the air, the faint smell of Thai spices drifting through the night breeze. Vibrant world music filled the night air as people danced, their glasses clinking with a variety of cocktails. The night revellers lay strewn about on the soft, silk beach cushions, their skin still warm from a day of hot sunshine and swimming. The sea was calm and rhythmic, the white foam fluorescent, under a crescent moon. Its calm ignored the fire dancers entertaining the crowds on its shores with their twirling flames, half naked skin and sensual dances. The party beach was a contrast from Kalalaya – a vibrant assault on the senses. Maggie O'Hara had insisted they come out and celebrate. In a few days, they would all be leaving. This was their last chance to have a hoorah.

Maggie had booked a table at a trendy bar on the northernmost tip of the white sands. Lily had met all the attendees on retreat, except for the man with the tooth gap and wild sandy hair, who had sat himself down on a cushion beside her.

'Hi, I'm Yohan,' he said through his thick French accent. 'I noticed you are afraid of snakes.' His eyes burned with mischievousness.

'Lily,' she said, offering her hand for a shake. 'Actually, no, I'm not scared of snakes. I just think it's polite to announce myself.' She returned his playful expression. He let out a confident chuckle.

'That's good because snakes are my favourite creatures.' His hand lingered over Lily's longer than it should have.

The server brought drinks – a Mai Tai for Yohan, and a lime soda for Lily.

'How come I haven't seen you in any of the classes?' Lily said.

'Because I'm not a guest. I'm a teacher.'

'Oh.' Lily's eyebrows lifted

'Why do you sound so surprised?' he asked.

'You aren't bald and wearing a robe, and you're drinking a Mai Tai.'

Yohan gave a robust laugh.

'So, what kind of teacher are you?' Lily twirled her ponytail into a knot.

'The best kind,' he said.

The vague kind. Lily was dubious.

'Have you heard of Tantra?' He tipped his head back and took a large gulp of his drink, the soft light of the lantern overhead glinting off his dark eyes.

'The sex thing? They teach that at Kalalaya?' Lily stiffened with alarm, her body responding instinctively.

'It's not about sex; it's about extraordinary sex. It's about liberation in and through the body.' His voice was silky, and something about him made Lily's insides pulse. She wasn't sure if it was good or bad. It was very disconcerting.

'Liberation as in Awakening?' she asked.

'Sort of.' Yohan stirred his Mai Tai with a straw.

'Interesting.' Lily let out a soft sigh.

'You seem sceptical?' He was staring at her.

'I'm a lawyer. Scepticism is my trade.'

'Well,' he said, 'I'm at Kalalaya for a three-day workshop, then I head back to my retreat centre on Koh Phangan. You should keep an open mind – there are many pathways on the spiritual journey.'

'Right.' She nodded. 'You have your own retreat?'

'Yes, I'm well known in these parts.'

He was sure of himself, suave, his confidence approaching arrogance.

'You should come and stay for a few days. You'll love it. Koh Phangan has the best snorkelling – the island is untouched. It's a little more rustic than Kalalaya.' He paused for effect. 'It's a wild place for wild things.' His words were intentional, his gaze was piercing.

'Maybe …' Lily could feel concern washing over her face. 'I'm currently wondering, I … I was thinking what to do next.'

'Well, you know what they say. When you least expect it, the answer arrives.'

Reaching into the breast pocket of his white linen shirt, he removed his business card. Lily noticed several beaded bracelets wrapped around his wrist, rustling against his olive skin.

'Here, all the information you need is on there.' He gave her the card and gulped his drink down. Then, with absolute assurance, he said, 'See you soon.' He got up and walked towards a woman on the beach.

'Did you invite him?' Lily turned and asked Maggie, who was sitting across the table in a sexy emerald maxi-dress, her fiery locks glinting in the moonlight.

'No, my dear, I thought you did,' she said.

'No, I definitely did not.'

The drive back to Kalalaya in the hotel car was relaxing, the scenery blurring past and the scent of flowers in the air. Lily had the window down, her hair blowing in the night breeze. She was watching all the twinkling lights, the tapestry of people, and wondering what to do next. When they stopped at a T-intersection, she noticed a man getting off a scooter in front of a twenty-four-hour convenience store. She could recognise that walk anywhere. Luka.

Does he know I'm here? Is he looking for me?

He couldn't know. She hadn't answered his messages and they had stopped appearing on her phone a week ago. The only person in the world who knew she was here was Saima, and Saima was under strict orders not to tell Luka. Maybe she was mistaken. It was late, and she was tired. He had his back towards her and the surrounding night was dark. This island was doing strange things to her mind. Following her experience in the cave, she had been researching 'waking hallucinations' on the web. Perhaps she was having another one of those.

The sun was setting over the Andaman Sea, creating a kaleidoscope of powder pinks and periwinkle purples. Lily buried her toes in the warm, soft white sand of the beach. She was balancing herself, ready to launch her paper lantern as a sign of respect for the Goddess of the Sky, and honouring the ancestors who had made her path possible. As their stay was nearing its end, Kalalaya guests had been granted the opportunity to join in the sacred ritual.

Her paper lamp was undulating in the evening breeze, willing itself to go. Lily was holding onto it tightly, waiting for the release command to be given. She thought about Papa and hoped that he was at peace, that his soul had found rest from the turbulent emotions that had plagued his life. She thought about Jessie, her little angel flying high, and wondered if she could feel how much she was loved by her earth Mama and Papa; she hoped that somehow their love reached her little soul wherever she was, in some liminal space beyond the stars. She thought about the living too: Mama, Lulama, her brothers and sister, Oliver and Luka. And tonight she felt extremely grateful for them all. She hoped that all the broken parts of them, all their shadows, could escape to a brilliant star and be transformed by fire.

As the cicadas sang, and the water glowed with bioluminescent creatures, guests were ordered to let go of their lit paper lamps. Lily watched them fly – higher and higher, like flitting fireflies against the darkening night. They were letting go of the past, all of them. Releasing hard things so that tomorrow could be a new beginning. The floating sky lanterns disappeared into the night sky and Lily felt a weight lift – she was light and free like her flying paper lantern, and she was ready to begin again.

Following the lantern ceremony, everyone was invited to a farewell dinner with the Buddhist clerics. Lily was excited. She would search for the mysterious nun – Karma Chodron. Lily had used her lawyering skills to research her monastic lineage. Tonight, she would make sure that she sat beside her. She had questions, and after the experience in the cave, she was wondering if the monastic path was the answer.

Something beyond herself had brought her here; it couldn't have only been coincidence running into Karma Chodron. It seemed fated. From the day she had set foot on Koh Samui, she has a sense that she was closer to a destined path – a heart-calling that differed from the one she had been walking on.

The dining pavilion at Kalalaya was a colourful canvas. It was outdoors beneath several curved bamboo pagodas, each seating area unique – some next to ponds, some next to rock gardens, some next to ornate fountains. Wait staff carried the food out on trays wearing traditional Thai silk uniforms adorned with golden embroidery and flower garlands. The chef was French and had a specialty in healthy and raw food dishes. The food was a sensory delight, light and nutritious, and pleasing to the eye. Delicate eastern spices and herbs blended with the freshest fruit and vegetables. The meals were a highlight of the stay, and one of the few times when guests were free to speak their minds.

The monastics were interspersed among the guests, the clinking of their cutlery and chatter ringing. Lily looked around the pavilion and felt a sense of peace when she saw Karma Chodron sitting near a golden statue of Lakshmi. It was a curious thing, a Buddhist nun sitting next to a Hindu deity.

Karma Chodron was welcoming, clearly delighted that Lily had joined her. She gestured with her hands for Lily to take the seat next to her.

'Are you coming to ask me questions?' Her eyes sparked with a knowing delight.

'Yes,' said Lily, maybe a little too enthusiastically. She noticed a man at the same table pick up his plate and leave. Feeling slightly unsettled by his hasty departure, Lily took her seat, and was content to see that Karma Chodron was already halfway through her meal, which meant she wouldn't have to indulge Lily on an empty stomach.

Once Lily got going with questions, it was hard to stop. She began her inquisition with a gulp of fresh watermelon juice and finished with the last morsel of delicious, sticky coconut rice pudding. What she learned that evening surprised her. The path to becoming a female Buddhist cleric was fraught with obstacles. When Lily had let Karma Chodron know of her interest in the monastic life, Karma told her the story of Jetsunma Tenzin Palmo. Tenzin, born Diane Perry, was the humble daughter of a fishmonger and the first western woman to be fully ordained into the Tibetan Buddhist tradition.

She had lived a life of extraordinary hardship and equal determination. As a young woman, Tenzin lived as a sole nun among a hundred monks in a remote monastery in India. Despite her dedication to the practice and her diligent study of its philosophy, for six years her fellow practitioners treated her with disdain. The monks had restricted her access to information and practices that would see her progress on the path to ordainment and full liberation. Despite their kind facade, they informed her that they hoped she would be born a male in her next life so that she could join in all the monastery's activities, and although they slightly blamed her for her inferior birth as a female, they understood it wasn't her fault.

When she heard this part of the tale, Lily shuddered in revulsion. How could a spiritual tradition that was premised on the liberation of suffering of all sentient beings, including animals, be so exclusionary and misogynistic? It seemed the tentacles of prejudice had reached even the most sacred of traditions. No wonder Karma Chodron was content sitting next to a female Hindu Goddess.

At thirty-three, Tenzin, dispirited yet determined, sought seclusion in the upper regions of the Indian Himalayas, where she pursued a profound spiritual practice in the boundaries of a cave with a span of ten feet and a depth of six feet. The cave was high in the remote Lahaul area of the Indian Himalayas, on the border between Himachal Pradesh and Tibet. She remained there for twelve years, three of which she lived in full isolation. During that time, she grew her own food and sat for days at a time in meditation. In strict adherence to the protocols of her tradition, she never reclined, instead slumbering in a customary wooden meditation box in a meditative pose for a mere three hours every night. She survived temperatures of below −35°C, snow for six to eight months of the year, and a blizzard that buried her cave so deeply she had to dig her way out.

Years later, Tenzin received her full ordination in Hong Kong from one of the select few Buddhist monasteries that gave that recognition to women. The Dalai Lama eventually acknowledged her fight for equality, and she set up her own order of nuns with his blessing.

Lily had a romanticised idea of the female monastic's life – this stark reality seemed daunting. She noticed, too, that Karma Chodron cut a solitary figure. While the monks sat together in groups at Kalalaya, Karma was off just a little to the side. Lily felt despondent.

According to Kalalaya's morning meditation teacher, once you have glimpsed Awakening, there is no turning back. You are on the path to liberation, and any other way would lead to a life of immense suffering. Lily could see why – the momentary glimpses she'd had in the cave with Karma Chodron, and with the Yogini Goddess in that cockroach-laden building on Kowloon side, had changed her perception of reality. She'd had a glimpse of the miraculous, and for her there was no turning back. She would have to find another way – sitting in a cave for twelve years wasn't an option. Neither was entering a misogynistic tradition with hierarchical structures whose ultimate purpose seemed to be power and not liberation. Because if it had been the latter, women would not have been excluded from the path.

The premise that being born a woman was a karmic punishment was akin to the notions of Eve the sinner in Christianity, and Lily would have none of that. The way institutionalised religion vilified and subjugated women made her stomach turn.

Sensing Lily's despondency after their talk, Karma Chodron reached out for her hand once more.

'Lily, look for the answers on your meditation mat each day. Find them in silence. Find them in your very own heart and in your very own being. Walk on mountains and in forests with your bare feet connected to the earth. Tend a garden and watch how soil and water create life. Study the ground, the sky, the seasons, and the clouds. At night, sit under a blanket of stars and pray.' She picked up her serviette and dabbed her mouth at the corners before continuing, 'When you've done that for at least a year, come back to me, join me in the order and I'll teach you everything I know. You won't be alone.'

'Who do I pray to?' asked Lily.

Karma Chodron glanced at the statue of Lakshmi, and with a playful wink said, 'Why, you pray to the Goddess, of course.'

An involuntary tear slipped down Lily's cheek as she was leaving the dining pavilion – it seems nothing in this life comes easily. It was so peaceful here in this place. Right now, Karma Chodron seemed the only sane voice on earth. She wasn't sure where in the outside world she belonged anymore, but for now, it was time to move on.

Meditate and
Grow Humble

Meditate, and grow humble.
Watch anger and wanting
turn to ashes.

Study the ground Lalla,
as a sign of attainment.'

Lalleshwari

twenty

LUKA SAT ON AN old, ripped sofa on the deck outside the beach bungalow, his eyes lost in the Andaman Sea beyond. Next to him, a burly Danish man with a clipboard was asking questions. Soren wore a serious expression. This was serious business.

'Do you have any blood pressure problems?' Soren asked, poised to write answers with a plastic pen.

Luka swiped at a mosquito. 'No.'

'Any heart issues?'

'No, unless a broken heart counts.' Luka sighed, and his shoulders slumped. He spotted a couple walking hand in hand across the beach. They looked content, their feet making double footprints in the glistening sand as the cool water licked at their feet.

'I feel you, brother, that's what we are going to fix.' Soren's face said that he knew all about heartache.

Luka was hopeful. He hadn't eaten in weeks and was shrinking rapidly. His cello, the thing that had brought him the most solace, was sitting in its case, its strings untouched. And cocaine – well, his nose was bleeding every day. He needed to sort things out.

'Any history of psychosis?' asked Soren.

Luka thought about his childhood, his mother's sudden violent outbursts. He recalled the sting of his cheeks and his mother's slapping hands. And his father's apathy. He had no will to protect Luka.

'Not that I am aware of, but my behaviour has been erratic and out of character lately.'

'Any hallucinations?'

'No.'

'Extreme anxiety or panic attacks?'

'No.'

Soren was ticking boxes.

'Suicidal ideation?' he asked.

'Sometimes, I wonder what the point of living is, especially after my daughter died. It was a hard day when I realised Lily, my wife, wasn't coming back. I think that's the closest I've ever been.' Luka's eyes were stuck on the lovers. They were sitting on a rock. The waves hitting the edges, spraying them with foam. Each time it happened, they would laugh and pull each other closer. *That's what love is. Two people shielding each other and laughing through hard times.*

'Have you ever attempted to kill yourself?' The question pulled Luka out of his thoughts.

'No.'

'Are you prone to violent outbursts?' Soren was scrutinising him.

'Yes, I hit my wife once, a month ago. It's the first time. That's why I'm here.' Luka's hands were shaking. He covered his face in shame. The memory caused a sudden nausea. Soren had no hint of judgement on his face.

'Were you high, or drinking at the time?' he asked.

'High. And drinking,' replied Luka.

'You told me earlier your drugs are alcohol and cocaine, right? Is there anything else?'

'A little weed.'

Soren smiled. 'Weed doesn't count, brother.' He gave Luka a pat on the shoulder.

'I think you're good. We've covered all the bases.' Soren put his pen in the pocket of his tropical floral print shirt.

'Tomorrow morning I'm going to send the doc down to give you a once over and if she gives you the all clear, you're gonna have the ride of your life, brother.' He let out a deep, hearty laugh.

Luka found Soren's rambunctious laughter a little unnerving – along with all his dragon tattoos and body piercing. He was a fierce-looking guy.

'Just make sure you're clean tomorrow.' Soren's expression grew stern. 'If the Teacher is mixed with any other substance, it will fuck you up, possibly kill you. Do you understand?'

Luka nodded. He understood, he had done his research.

'And no breakfast tomorrow. Make tonight's meal good. It may be your last for a couple of days, but no meat though, brother. The Teacher doesn't like meat.'

'Okay.' Luka sighed. Shit was getting real.

'Right, I'm going to leave you now. Go for a massage tonight, relax; go for a swim in the ocean, or run on the beach. And drink lots of liquids. I left rehydration sachets for you in your room.' Soren stood up, ready to go meet his love for dinner. 'Don't worry, brother, you're in the best hands. Two MMA fighters have got your back. The Teacher and I – we are old, old friends.' Soren flashed him a gold tooth smile, his eyes tender. There was something vaguely familiar about him. As scary looking as Soren was, Luka found his presence comforting.

After a light meal at one of the beach eateries and a painful massage with an overzealous masseuse in a Shala with a view of anchored long boats bobbing with the tide, Luka walked back to his bungalow. The air was fresh, coconut palms were waving in the wind, and the sounds of giggling tourists lingered on the sea breeze. He wanted to laugh again.

The bungalow was modest – a white-tiled floor, a fridge filled with coconuts and bottled water, a bed with a simple steel frame and a large mosquito net, a bathroom with a curtainless shower and a pink water bucket that needed to be filled to flush the toilet. Luka had travelled light. He took out a few possessions from his carry-on bag and put them on the simple wooden bedside table. His wedding ring, a small journal, mosquito repellent, a book of inspiring quotes, and his iPod and headphones. He was afraid of tomorrow, but this was one occasion where you must face your fear to keep on living. He turned on the overhead fan, climbed under the mosquito net and turned out the light.

The day broke with the sounds of the cicada chirping, and a gentle rain tapping on the roof. Luka flung open the door and watched as passers-by scrambled on their way under umbrellas. There were fishermen ready to take their long boats out, jet-ski operators, market vendors with bags of produce, and a few early-bird tourists exploring the beach.

He drank two bottles of water – he needed to be hydrated. The doctor's visit was short and efficient. After she took his blood pressure and checked his vitals, she told him she would return that evening to check on him. She left a card with an emergency number to dial.

Soren arrived with a friend who looked like Jesus, at least the way the West depicted him – with long golden hair, a chiselled chin, and ice-blue eyes. They chatted among themselves, preparing a brew on the deck, while Luka became increasingly nervous.

Today, he would meet Ibogaine, a substance derived from the roots of the African rainforest teacher plant Tabernanthe Iboga. For many centuries, the indigenous peoples of western Africa have ingested iboga as a remedy for fatigue, hunger, and thirst, and in larger doses, as a sacrament in religious ceremonies. In the mid-1800s, they used iboga in Gabon, in the initiation rites of the Bwiti religion. When boys would come of age, around age nine to twelve, they were given large amounts of the root. After they had gone through the two-day process, they were seen as adult men. During this period, older members of the community would stay awake by chewing on iboga roots to care for them. Even at that time, it was known that taking a large dose of the plant could lead to suffocation, heart attacks, and even death. But for them, it was worth the risk. In this holy sacrament, the Bwiti men met with their ancestors who imparted vital wisdom and essential lessons for life.

More recently, the plant had been used to rehabilitate substance addiction. An extreme, but very effective, intervention which was administered by a few underground clinics around the world. One dose, and your addiction could be cured. Most doctors were not willing to take the risks associated with the substance. Luka had found Soren through a musician friend who was successfully rehabilitated from his heroin addiction. Luka knew it was time to clean up his act. It was iboga, or years of therapy. Luka thought the former was a tidy solution. Besides, he liked risk – he had jumped out of many aeroplanes.

Soren brought the dark liquid that had been extracted from the root of the plant in a simple clay mug. He was solemn. He asked Luka to sit and meditate. This was not something Luka ever did, but he complied without hesitation. After five minutes, Soren and the man who looked like Jesus began chanting in low, deep voices – something about the melody was touching. Luka felt a lump in his throat.

He swallowed the liquid. It was bitter. It made him want to retch.

'Hold it down.' Soren's instructions were firm. Luka obliged.

Within thirty minutes, Luka felt his limbs becoming heavy until he could not lift a finger. His body was immobilised. Soren had insisted he go lie down on the bed; now he understood why. Soren gave him a blindfold, his headphones, and turned on his favourite classical playlist on his iPod.

The music was a revelation, more beautiful than he had ever heard it, each note an exquisite bloom unfolding. He began to the see the D majors and C sharps dancing across a movie screen which had opened in his mind. Notes turning into butterflies and birds and dancing vines. The colours were more vivid than he'd ever seen. And then it all went black.

He was wrapped in an oppressive darkness and a continuous humming sound which become louder and louder until the noise was almost deafening. Luka recognised it – the hum of the universe. The sound before life began.

She came to him first as a floating rose out of the darkness, which then turned into her sweet eyes, and then a young girl with dark flowing curls and thickly rimmed spectacles. Jessie – his precious child. She reached out her hand and beckoned him to follow her through fields of wildflowers, cityscapes, and then into a library lined with thousands of books bound in beautiful living covers, which were growing gardens. She sat there, content in a glowing light, paging over stories and sharing them with many other children in the room. Jessie beckoned him to come sit next to her and turn the pages. Together they read the story of a girl whose love was so strong it had brought an astonishing light into the world. The light was magnificent, luminescent, and shimmering. It shone so brightly it became too bright for the world. Its intensity made people blind, so it returned to a place where it could shine without limitation. A place with a living library that carried the stories of all the earth's souls.

Luka was so happy to be there, to see her, to know she was still alive. His tears turned into inconsolable sobs – and then she disappeared, and he was thrown into a horrible, icy darkness, a place of sheer terror. He could feel his soul being ripped from his body and he vomited. Bile at first and then a terrible dark liquid that just kept coming. He was projectile vomiting across the room. He was vaguely aware of Soren mopping his brow, and forcing him to drink, between the bouts of extreme nausea. His body was shaking and gripped by the icy coldness. It felt as though every bad thought, evil act, negative experience that he'd had in his life were being purged from his body. Making him clean again.

When he thought the torturous vomiting would never end, an ecstatic peace descended, and the movie screen in his mind opened for viewing once more. He saw himself as a child, innocent and free, as a bright adolescent, as a loving man. He saw the story of his mother's life and the suffering that had led to her slapping outbursts. Her father's abuse, her grandfather's abuse, her great-grandfather's abuse. He saw too how much she loved him and how ashamed she was of the hurt she had caused him.

And then he left his familial story and was planted in a place where he saw the earth and all the planets in our solar system, and the great endless universe beyond. Luka had become a pinpoint of light – so tiny yet completely expansive. He felt absorbed by a vast, ecstatic love that had been pulsating for an eternity. He understood for the first time that he was part of a symbiotic whole, that he was one with it all. Luka, the man, was the child of the universe and the universe itself. He saw that there was no time, just alternative planes of reality where souls played out experiences – all part of the great turning. Each point of life carried light and darkness.

A funnel of purple undulating light opened on top of the earth's North Pole – inside books were floating up and down funnels. The books contained the stories of all the souls that floated in and out of the world. Lives were just stories, and endings could be changed at any point on their journey.

And then she came back to him. Jessie – she was holding out an oval-shaped green luminescent light. He looked down and noticed an empty black hole in his heart. A hole that was created by his mother's abuse, his father's neglect, and his daughter's death – the empty place he had been trying to fill with dozens of women, booze, and cocaine. Jessie placed the green oval light inside his dark spot, and the light became a living vine, wrapping its tendrils in and around his broken heart and healing it.

His body convulsed; he was having some sort of seizure, foam releasing from his mouth. He saw the face of the most exquisite woman. She turned into a rainbow which then burst into ashes of multicoloured light.

Soren was yelling, Jesus was turning him over, and then he died.

Into the vortex over the rainbow bridge back into the fields of light and then a perpetual loving silence.

He came to with a warm breath on his face. It was Jesus administering CPR. Soren was shouting,

'Bro, you left us. Christ. Fuck, I thought you were gone for good. So, so, happy to see that you are back, man!'

Luka smiled. 'How long was I gone?'

'Long enough. Did you say hello to God for me?' Soren had tears pooling in the corners of his eye.

'If God is an exquisite woman, then yes.' Luka's eyes were shining with a love that was beyond this world.

'Ah, the Teacher has taught you well. She brought you the green light.' Soren hugged him, Jesus hugged him, and the three men cried tears of happiness together that only they would ever understand.

'We did it, bro!' he heard Soren exclaim to Jesus as they left the room to let him rest. 'We brought another soul out of the darkness.'

'No, bru, the Goddess did that. We are just conduits, here to witness the ride.'

twenty-one

THE OLD FERRY ROSE and dipped over wild ocean waves. Up and down, side to side. Lily was thankful that the boat didn't roll. Passengers were holding their vomit bags close – a young girl crying in the row behind, her mother trying to console her. Only fifteen more minutes of the ride from hell, and she would be on Koh Phangan. The ocean had morphed from a brilliant turquoise into a foreboding blackness. Its waves were drumming a war beat on the old ferry's decks, the weathered wood being stripped away into splinters. Lily scanned the boat for lifejackets. There was none to be found. This boat was not seaworthy. *Shit, shit, shit.* She felt the old familiar tentacles of anxiety beginning to strangle – *breathe, Lily, just breathe.*

A man sitting opposite, wearing grey wisdom, gave her a reassuring glance as he spoke to his wife, telling her he had made this journey several times and this was nothing to be afraid of. 'View it as a rollercoaster,' he said.

It had never been more welcoming to view the land. The palms on shore were bent, as if trying to touch the tips of their leaves together, forming a low archway. The wind was blowing a screeching gale. As they were queueing to get off the boat, it took every inch of self-control not to push past the passengers in front of her. She was desperate to have her feet on the ground. Instead, she held onto the railing with a steely grip and focused on her breathing. Four men were assisting passengers to walk over the gangplank and onto the jetty steps – there were a couple of near misses, the churning boat making it hard for them to steady the crossing. But they did it, and Lily was grateful for their helping hands.

'Kap kun kah, Kap kun kah,' she said, and bowed her head in thanks to the young men as her feet found safety on the concrete jetty of the little island of Koh Phangan.

She gave Yohan's card to a waiting taxi driver and negotiated a price for the journey. Koh Phangan was much wilder than Koh Samui. The roads were muddy and sprinkled with potholes. The driver was eyeing her in the rear-view mirror; his objectifying stares made Lily uncomfortable. She kept her hand on the passenger door handle, ready to jump out of the car if necessary. They turned down a windy drive lined with old forest trees, their gnarly branches blocking out the light – he could've been taking her anywhere. They bumped and rumbled over the dusty beach road until they came to a halt. In front of them were several modest bungalows next to a dilapidated main building, its white walls washed brown with sea sand.

The driver unloaded her bag from the trunk, and through yellowing teeth, said in broken English, 'Enjoy your sexing time.' His gaze focused on her breasts.

Lily felt her cheeks flush. The way he looked at her made her feel naked even though she was wearing a very demure long cotton dress with a high scooped neckline. She hurried away, her bags in tow, and made a beeline for the reception office, which was sign-posted in faded letters on an old wooden board.

Sexing time. Oh god, what have I signed up for?

The door to her beach bungalow was squeaky – she had to exert pressure with her shoulder to get it open but was surprised by what she found inside. She had expected it to be a dump, but the door opened to a solid double bed with clean white linen, a soft mosquito net folded to the side, two white cane chairs with delicate floral upholstery, a working rattan ceiling fan, a fridge filled with bottled water, fresh fruit and coconuts, and a clean but modest soft-green tiled bathroom with a rain shower and a bidet. Double doors led to a small deck, which opened right onto a pristine white sand beach. A menagerie of fragrant potted plants framed a white hammock strung across the corner. The bursts of star-shaped frangipani were a familiar comfort, their soft scent being lifted by the breeze. The receptionist said that the bungalow was less than a hundred metres away from the edge of the water in high tide. *Perfect. This is perfect.*

The tumultuous journey slid off her like an oversized silk dress; she had arrived in another paradise, and even in this wild weather, she didn't want to be anywhere else. The densely forested island, with its curves of white sand framed by streaks of crystalline blues and greens, held its own kind of magic.

On her first day, she discovered that a bustling utopia of salvation seekers had filled the dining hall on Samadhi. From the dreadlocked volunteer chefs, muscled and toned man-bun-wearing men to the bikini-clad yogini surfer girls, everyone here was chasing the elusive dream of Awakening, or pretending to have achieved it. Everyone had something else in common too: they were all healthy, fit, and attractive. These guests were by invitation only. Lily wasn't the only one whom Yohan had invited. She felt out of place with her robust bottom, bouncing boobs, and less-than-perfect Bakasana (crow-pose).

The kitchen was vegan, and before each meal, someone would pull out a guitar or a harmonium and lead the diners in a song of gratitude. The place had a rhythm, a mantra of perfectly packaged people, doing perfect things and seeking an even greater salvation. Lily found it unsettling. She was happiest in her bungalow, alone, meditating on a simple grass matt and breathing in the salty ocean. Karma Chodron's voice was still fresh in her memory, reminding her to keep looking up at the sky.

The first class with Yohan took place on a ramshackle circular beach Shala. He sat, resplendent in white cotton from head to toe, matching the pearly white sand beyond. He had brown mala beads wrapped around his neck, wrist, and ankles, his mid-length sandy hair waving in the sea breeze, the faint scent of insect repellent and coconut oil floating around him. He was a perfect shampoo advertisement.

The session began with several breath exercises focused on energising the Swadhisthana, or sacral chakra – an imaginary area between the perineum and the sex organs of the body. As much as Lily tried to bring her breath there, she ended up sending it to other places: her sore leg, her numb bottom, the creak in her neck. She noticed through a crack in her eyelids that everyone else seemed to be in deep concentration. Relief arrived when the Asana practice began. Yohan led a vigorous physical practice, his body lithe and fluid. He shaped himself into the perfect warrior, cobra, dog, crow, and eagle. After demonstrating his prowess, he would walk around poking and prodding people's shapes. His hands were rough and without boundaries. Lily startled as she found him pressing his hands into her upper thighs from behind to adjust her Malasana (squat pose). His breath laced with the smell of weed, he whispered in her ear, 'Great, Lily, nice form.' She couldn't help feeling a sense of pride, though she knew this was wrong. You feel wrong in your bones.

The practice ended in a restful Savasana (corpse pose), Yohan's silky voice leading them into a blissful, near-sleep state. He was an effective teacher. There was no doubt about that.

That afternoon, guests were invited to a philosophy talk – 'The tantric paths that lead to awakening'. The attendees following each word that rolled off Yohan's smooth tongue with awe – *Ah, now I get it, this is what a guru is.* Lily was less than impressed. She had encountered his type in the courtroom – manipulative, intelligent, slick with a compelling pitch. A little like a good car salesperson, but instead of a selling a tangible product, Yohan was selling an intangible awakening through sex. If orgasm was awakening, half the planet would be enlightened by now. I wonder what's in it for him. Lily pinched herself. *Why am I such a cynic?*

Not that the idea was implausible. Orgasm is a transcendent experience that takes you out of your mind and into the realms of an ecstasy. In that moment, the worries of the world cease. There is something holy and beautiful about that. It was this idea that you could live a permanent orgasm – that seemed more like escapism or disassociation than awakening. And she couldn't shake the feeling that there was something orchestrated and manipulative in Yohan's message. Especially when he suggested that trauma and unresolved emotional pain could be healed through sex. Lily's alarm bells were ringing. Perhaps it's time to move on. *Crap, I've only been here a day and I love my bungalow!*

Lily was swaying in her white macramé hammock. She had decided to skip the evening session. Yohan's spin just wasn't for her. Instead, she would write in her journal, and watch the unique colours that washed the evening sky. It didn't disappoint. The sun became a golden globe, floating on orange and amber hues fronted by the silhouettes of feathery palms waving the day goodnight. Here, floating on the evening breeze, Lily felt a contentment.

She had replaced the longing for Oliver with loving memories of him. He would always be in her pocket. There was a little unease about Luka. Lily had an inkling that their story wasn't over. Perhaps that would change when they finalised their divorce, sold their house, and settled all the financial matters. She thought of him more often than she would have liked.

Right now, though, she was at peace, in this place, hanging in the wind with no real clear path ahead. It was good to be alone, to be free to explore and discover, to not be told that there was no time to look up at the stars, or smell the flowers, or to write irrelevant words, or to imagine the stories of the silvery moon that was beaming down at her. She listened to the night breeze – the sounds soothing until later in the evening when she was dozing off and heard the whimper of a woman's voice. Someone was crying. Her sadness being carried on the wind.

The whimpering sound was coming from next door. Lily rolled out of the hammock and up onto her bare feet – she would have to investigate. Not bothering with shoes, she walked over to the neighbouring bungalow; the door was ajar. Lily peeped inside and saw the silhouette of a young woman with a mane of curly black tresses. She was kneeling beside the bed, crying. Lily tapped on the door so as not to cause surprise.

'Hi, I'm your neighbour, Lily, just stopping by to check that you're okay.' She poked her head around the door.

The young woman didn't respond.

'Hi, I'm your neighbour, Lily. Can I come in?' Lily asked again, making her voice a little louder this time.

'Yes, okay.' She looked up at Lily, with eyes that were bewildered, like a startled deer.

Lily walked over and sat beside her on the cool white tiles of the floor.

'You don't have to tell me what's wrong. I'll just sit here with you until you feel better,' she said.

The girl looked at Lily with scepticism.

'Did Yohan send you?' she asked.

'No, I was swinging in my hammock next door, and I heard you crying. If you want me to leave, I will. You just seem like you could do with a little comfort, and you remind me of myself a few weeks ago. I spent a lot of time alone, crying on the floor.'

'Oh, d— did someone hurt you too?' Her face was anguished, her tears collecting in small pools on the cold tiles. Lily resisted the urge to hug her.

'In a manner of speaking, yes, I guess you could say that. But I hurt myself, too.' The gravity of her own words hit her in the chest. Lily sighed.

'What's your name?' she asked.

'I'm Nova.'

'I'm Lily,' she said and held out her hand. 'Pleased to meet you, Nova.'

'Sorry I disturbed your evening,' said Nova while limply shaking Lily's hand. She was trembling.

'I didn't realise that I had left the door open. Can you lock it?' A frozen look appeared on Nova's face that Lily recognised all too well.

Lily stood up, walked to the door, and locked it.

'We can go to my place if that would make you feel better?' She tried to sound reassuring.

'I— It's okay,' Nova said, though clearly it wasn't.

'Nova, who hurt you? Was it someone here on Samadhi?'

'N— No, ah yes, I mean, sort of.' Her shoulders fell, her face turned away. 'It was the owner, Yohan.'

'Do you want to tell me what happened? I'm good at keeping secrets. It's part of my job. I'm a lawyer and I've helped many women who have suffered at the hands of men. Anything you tell me will just be between the two of us.'

Lily's expression was earnest. She needed to win Nova's trust. She wanted to understand what had happened so that she could help. And if it was anything like she suspected it was, she needed to get this young woman to safety.

Nova's eyes glazed over, tendrils of her curly hair sticking to her tear-stained face.

'Okay, I—' Nova burst into tears again.

'It's okay to cry, just let it out. I'm not going anywhere. You take as long as you need.'

Lily sat beside the weeping woman. Nova needed to feel safe. The night had turned from something beautiful into something sinister. Something terrible had happened here. Lily could sense it.

It took some time, but, when her tears dried up, Nova talked.

'During this evening's Satsang, Yohan invited us to be open about any sexual trauma we had experienced. I shared with the group that my father raped me as a child, and I couldn't enjoy sex in my adult relationships. I hoped that coming here would solve that.'

Lily passed her a glass of water she had just poured. Nova took a few small sips before continuing.

'Yohan said the only way to cure sexual dys-function was with sex, that you must use a healthy active energy to dissolve a stagnant energy. He said the trauma had caused a block in my sacral chakra, which needed to be cleared. It seemed to make sense.'

Lily felt a nausea rising.

'When I was leaving the Shala after Satsang had finished, he pulled me aside and said that he had something special for me, something that would fix me. He asked me to meet him in his room. So, I did.' Nova's voice was fading, her breathing erratic.

Lily reached over and places her hand on her shoulder for a moment.

'Take a few deep breaths,' she said.

Nova slowed her breathing and calmed, and then she carried on talking.

'We talked about what had happened to me and my inability to enjoy sex, and he said it was important to approach the solution with an open mind.

Yohan told me he would massage my yoni with his lingam, and that I should breathe as he did. I was scared, but I want to be better at sex and have healthy relationships and a few of the girls had said that intimacy with him was amazing and transformative. So, I agreed.'

'That's understandable,' said Lily.

'It was okay at first. He massaged me gently w— with his thing. The breathing helped, and I relaxed.' Nova bit her bottom lip. 'And then without asking if it was okay, he just thrust it into me. When I t— told him to stop it, that I didn't want this, that we hadn't agreed to this, he said that it was my block talking and not me! He said the only way out was through and that in his room, I had no choice but to surrender. He just kept doing it over and over. He wouldn't stop.'

Nova was shaking. Lily had to get her to safety.

'This is rape. Nova, he raped you. Would you like me to call the police?'

'N— No, I let him do the massage. The police won't believe me. I don't want to go through that. I just need to get away. I don't want him to come near me again. I feel dirty.'

Lily felt a rage rise. So, this was his payoff, the manipulative son of a ... Yohan was a sexual predator disguised as a saviour.

'Nova, I'm so sorry that this terrible thing has happened to you. I need you to listen to me, okay?' Lily paused for effect. 'This is not your fault. This is absolutely and in no way your fault. Yohan has done a terrible thing, a manipulative thing. And if we go to the police right now and do a difficult thing, we can get him locked away. I'll be right by your side.'

'No, no, I'm not doing that. I'm not. I just can't go through any more. I never want to see his face again. I just need a shower to be clean again, and then I need to get away from here.'

'Are you sure, Nova?'

'Yes.'

The look in Nova's eyes told Lily everything she needed to know. There was no point in pushing this right now. The best thing to do was to get her away. She helped Nova pack her belongings into her threadbare candy-striped bags, and while Nova was showering, she went to her bungalow and, with a heaviness in her chest, packed her own belongings too.

She called a driver. It was time to leave; the lesson learned. She would never ignore her instincts again. Lily was learning that the road to self-discovery was full of perilous dead ends, and you don't know that you've reached a dead end until you arrive at one. Your only choice then is to turn around and find another way.

twenty-two

THE STATUE OF GANESH, the Hindu elephant protector god, also known as the slayer of obstacles, stood guarding the door of their beach bungalow. Lily had taken Nova back to Koh Samui, hoping that in time she would change her mind about reporting Yohan to the police. She thought of all those vulnerable women, all seeking help. Most of them looking to make sense of the suffering they had experienced, only to be exploited once more. Seduced by the promise of awakening and freedom from the pain of trauma. They became the vulnerable prey of men with God delusions, men like Yohan. Men who twisted and manipulated an intrinsic beauty into something sinister.

For women, the path of spiritual exploration was fraught with peril. Yet, there was no doubt in Lily's mind that there was a way through the morass. She thought of Karma Chodron, and the indescribable beauty of sitting beside her in the tiny cave on the hillside. The way she had felt in that moment when she realised that her consciousness extended beyond her body, when she realised the difference between consciousness and its contents – that her mind is a portal to the Great Beyond.

And she remembered the Goddess Yogini on Hong Kong's Kowloon side. The surge of orgasmic bliss that had waved across her body causing her to black out. The experience might have had the residues of a sexual energy, but it was so much more than that, and it wasn't dirty. It was more wholesome than anything she had ever experienced. It was liberating and empowering, like being bathed in a vast river of love that's current was too powerful to hold for more than a moment. A river that washed away all the darkness, revealing the underscore of beauty that lives in everything, even the shadows.

These were tangible experiences, and the seed of enquiry they had planted within her were not about to die. She would not allow the Yohans of the world to snuff out her search for truth. But from now on, she would only search for answers amongst women – women who resisted patriarchal notions, religious hierarchies, and ideas that harm, subjugate and denigrate women.

The golden light of the sun through the coconut palms was creating dapples in Nova's ebony hair. She was getting stronger day by day. Tiny sparks of joy returning to her eyes, especially when she played with the young village children on the beach. Nova had a gift with children; she was born to teach. Like Lily, she had fled a father, but unlike Lily, she had ended up in a dead-end job with no fulfilment – Nova worked to survive. She had gone from waitressing and bar tending to a more lucrative job in a retail shop on the high street of Croydon, a large town in South London, England. While working there, a fellow retail clerk had persuaded her to attend yoga classes in their lunch hour, and there she had met a friend who had persuaded her to use all her savings on a spiritual adventure to the exotic islands of Thailand.

As Nova sat stringing flowers and chatting to a vibrant little Thai girl on the deck of their beach bungalow, Lily couldn't help but wonder what would have happened to her if these events hadn't transpired. Would she have discovered the joy she experienced teaching and guiding young children? Lily liked to think she would. That whatever path we are on, the bumpy one or the smooth one – it's always somehow the right one.

'Nova,' called Lily, through the kitchen window. 'I'm heading out for a walk and a swim. Will you be okay here?'

Lily needed the solace. As much as she adored Nova, she longed to be alone. She found living with someone challenging.

'I'm fine, Lily. Anong and I are going to be making garlands all afternoon for her mother's stall.'

She patted the little girl on her head, and they continued counting the blooms, which had to be an exact number dependent on the garland they were making.

'I've got my mobile if you need to reach me. I'll have it with me all the time, unless I'm swimming.'

Lily grabbed a bag hanging over a chair and gathered a few beach essentials.

'I won't need you, Lily,' said Nova.

Lily felt relieved to hear it. She stepped over the baskets of banana leaves, ribbons, cotton, and bright garland blossoms that were on the deck and made her way out to a bright and gorgeous day.

The warm sand felt crunchy between her toes. Lily loved looking back over her shoulder at the footprints her delicate feet created on the beach sand. After walking for a solid hour, past long boats, sunbathing lovers, and children making sandcastles that would wash away with the waves, Lily found a place for her floral beach towel. It was a glorious day, and it was time for a swim. She found the perfect spot beside a giant black boulder, reminding her that this island had once been volcanic. She lay her towel under the shade of an old coconut palm, first looking up to make sure it wasn't full of ripe fruit. Falling coconuts were a hazard, and quite an undignified way to die.

She pulled her phone out of the threadbare beach bag that belonged to Nova and checked to see if she had left a message. She rarely looked at her phone these last few weeks. The people in her life were messaging her less, they were fading out and Lily felt at peace with that. This was the time in her life when she needed quiet, and the universe was bringing it to her the way a wave had just washed up a tiny glimmering mother-of-pearl shell near her feet. Lily picked it up and tipped it in the light. The dancing colours made her smile. And then she heard the *ping*.

She was expecting it to be Nova, but instead, the name she read on the phone screen made her stomach lurch. Luka. He had stopped messaging weeks ago. This was unexpected. She hadn't read a thing from him since the day that she left Hong Kong. Perhaps it was time. The message was succinct.

'Please read your email.'

She went to her email and scrolled until his latest mail appeared. She hesitated for a moment, then double tapped to open it.

My beautiful Lily,

I don't know if you'll read this, but I need to write it. I'm at a rehabilitation clinic in Thailand.

After what happened, after I hurt you, I decided to sort my shit out. There are a thousand ways to say I'm sorry and I know you'll have none of them, my spirited angel. But I'll give you the gift of letting you know, because that's the only way you'll know I mean it – that I'm letting you go. I've spoken to my lawyers this afternoon and I'm signing the house over to you, along with half our investments, and if you want, I'll keep sending half my salary. I'll do anything to know that you are protected from the man that I used to be.

Know that you will always be my greatest love, and you have been my greatest salvation.

Forever yours,

Luka

Who is this man? Is it Luka? He sounds so different, so old Luka. The Luka I used to know. The grief hit Lily like a thunderbolt because in that one moment, she remembered how much she loved him. She had been resisting this feeling for weeks. But here it was again, overwhelming her. This grief that held a mountain of love.

They had amazing years together, amazing memories before it all turned. Everything about them had seemed so right until it all went so wrong. Without thinking, she dropped the phone on her towel and ran towards the ocean. She dived into turquoise and pistachio waves. She swam with stinging jellyfish, and nosey striped tropical fish. She swam so long and so hard and so far, that a concerned fisherman in a sleek longboat followed her. When she had depleted herself with hardly a breath left, she turned over and allowed herself to float. She was bobbing on the waves like a cotton top, looking at the clouds, wondering if she should let the ocean take her wherever it wanted, when she heard the low growl of the longboat's engine.

'Miss! You are too far out, miss, it's dangerous. You need to come back in,' the fisherman shouted, the desperation in his voice apparent.

She snapped out of her grief.

'Oh, I'm sorry, I didn't realise,' she said, as she looked at the fishermen with distraught eyes, and then under her breath she whispered, 'And I'm sorry Luka that I couldn't be the wife that you needed me to be.'

The fisherman hauled her into the boat like a big wet fish. He wasn't angry, just determined that he would take this crazy white woman back to shore. Over time, he had pulled too many dead bodies out of the water, and today was for the living.

As Lily lay recovering on her floral towel and looking up at palm fronds, she thought about angels. They come in many forms. *Today, in a moment of madness, I met one as a fisherman, with powerful hands and a net that cast me in.*

She grabbed her sand covered phone, dusted it off so that the screen was clear, and typed in a text message,

'*Where in Thailand are you?*'

Three dots appeared which told her he was replying.

'*Lily!! I'm in Koh Samui.*'

'*Luka, I'm in Koh Samui, too.*'

twenty-three

LUKA FOUND IT DIFFICULT not to hold her hand. He wanted to touch her. Instead, he kept a respectful distance.

They met on Lamai Beach. He couldn't believe that their beach bungalows were less than a thousand metres apart, something he put down to celestial synchronicity. They had both been on this island watching the same mercurial sunsets, feeling the rain from the same clouds, and neither of them knew it. This was not just coincidence.

A week on from his iboga journey, he was still gaining his strength back, but the insights had continued arriving hard and fast. It was as if he had his own private line to deliverance. For the first time in a long time, maybe even his whole life, he could be accountable for his actions. Knowing that what he had done was wrong, but understanding himself enough to know it couldn't have been any other way. Everyone copes with psychological trauma in their unique manner. The circumstances that shape their lives predicate their actions and choices. Luka had obscured his pain and filled the ensuing emptiness it created with a succession of women, sex, alcohol, and cocaine. None of these things could heal him. They were a distraction from what he was too afraid to feel. Those distractions had caused so much pain, alienating and hurting the woman that he loved most.

Luka understood that continuing the way he had been going would lead him nowhere. And he decided that whatever the future brought him, it would arrive from a place of integrity, and he would never consciously hurt anyone again.

Watching the passers-by, he felt a love for them. He wondered how that was possible – to care about random strangers. Since his journey, he recognised a light in everyone, a magical spark of something, and he had nothing but acceptance for them all, irrespective of who they were or what they had done. There was an ember of Jessie burning in every single one of them.

Luka was at peace. He had found the forgiveness he needed the most – his own. He was okay with whatever life would bring him. He knew that what mattered was how he responded to everything, no longer living with the illusion he could control anything. It hurt, knowing that Lily had been with another man, but he hoped that man, whoever he was, had brought her a measure of happiness. The happiness he couldn't give her when he was wandering in the dark wilderness of confusion.

Above all else, he wanted Lily to be happy and loved.

Luka smelt the familiar scent of her rose oil hair, breathing it in so he could keep the memory. He watched her curved shape, her wild locks of strawberry-blonde, and heard the faint sound of her heartbeat not far from his. He etched the moment like a tattoo on his heart. She had gifted him the best years of his life, and for that, he would be grateful. She had gifted him an angel, too, who was looking down at them right now with a twinkle in her eye from her library up in the stars.

As unexpected as this reunion was, Lily was happy to be sitting beside Luka. It made her feel content. Something had changed about him; she couldn't quite put her finger on it, but there was lightness to him, a peace. His eyes glowed with compassion; his demeanour was almost childlike – like he was viewing the world for the first time.

Lily couldn't ignore the fact that his fingers were close to hers on the sand. Resisting the magnetic pull to him had always been hard. Remembering what he had done with those hands helped her to keep her hands folded on her lap. The sea air between them was cool and charged with chemistry. Both staring out towards the horizon line.

Lily didn't know how to start the conversation, so instead she sat beside him, watching a dog scamper and pounce in the shallow waves, chasing the foam as though it was a friend. Luka was quiet, too, lost in the light maps of his mind. They were both comfortable in their silence. They always had been.

It was a good fifteen minutes before Luka spoke. Fifteen minutes of watching an Asian-palm swift dart and dive above the sand, sticking its beak into holes to find sandflies while nipping at mosquitoes in the air; Fifteen minutes of listening to the bubbling white foam crackle on the shore, and the boisterous dog disappearing out of sight with its owner.

'I love you, Lily,' he said.

She replied, 'I love you, too.'

'I can't make what I did right,' he said, 'and I don't expect you to forgive me, but it would mean the world to me if I could explain what's been going on for me. If you don't want to hear it. I understand. I'll leave.'

'I'm here, Luka,' she said. 'I wouldn't have come if I wasn't open to listening.'

He smiled.

'You look different, somehow more relaxed. You're not bracing, not tensing your shoulders. It's good to see you like this, Lily. Relaxed and sun kissed.'

She smiled. 'Thank you. You look different, too. Content,' she said.

'I've had the wildest experience, Lily. I'm not sure if I recognise myself in the mirror.' His eyes beamed.

'Do you want to tell me about it?'

'Yes and no, I'm still processing what happened, but there are a few things that I've learned about myself that I want to share, if that's okay?'

'Yep, of course.' Without thinking, Lily placed her hand beside his on the sand.

'I didn't have the emotional fortitude to cope when we lost Jessie. It just ripped me up in a way that I didn't understand, and so I went on a destructive rampage. I couldn't talk to you because I could see you were suffering enough, and after what I watched you go through, I didn't feel like I had the right to unload on you. I could see you were lost, and I tried to get help for you, and in that process, I lost myself.'

Lily felt a familiar lump in her throat. She swallowed it down.

'I self-medicated with drugs,' he continued, 'and then sex. It's always been an escape from reality for me, and when you weren't capable of it, after Jessie, I just got it in other places. I'm so sorry, Lily.'

She had never seen him more sincere, but she would not say it was okay. So she remained silent.

'Instead of easing my pain, it just compounded it, and it brought a spiral of shame, which I drowned out with more drugs. When you found out, I stopped, but then I continued. I couldn't help myself. I couldn't face my pain. I didn't know how, or if it was even possible.'

Lily listened, not wanting to miss a word.

'And when I saw you with that guy,' he continued, 'something in me just flipped – like a switch. It was a trigger for everything I'd suppressed – the pain, the rage, the sheer fury that our child was gone. I lost it. I hurt you.

'I know I have no right to say this, but you are the only woman that has ever mattered to me, and the thought that you had abandoned me by being with someone else made me crazy. Out of my mind, crazy. Because I had no control over it. And it's only after I had this experience that I realised how hypocritical that all was. I was treading in sludge, Lily, and I just didn't have the strength to drag myself out.' He sighed.

'But I'm out now …' He sighed again. 'And it feels so damn good.' He ran both hands through his hair.

Not sure how to respond, Lily rubbed her thumb on her wrist and then picked up an empty mussel shell and began cleaning the sand off it. She wiped the tiny grains away while trying to clarify her thoughts at the same time.

'Lily?'

'I can understand that,' she said. 'But it doesn't mean that we can pretend what happened never happened, that it's okay.'

'Shit, Lily, of course it's not okay, I was acting like a madman, and I hurt you. I would do anything to take that day back, but I can't do that so now I must accept what happened and the consequences of that. I'm not asking you to come back to me. I'm just telling you I'm not that man anymore.'

She looked at him for a while, taking in his features, the curve of his mouth, the lines beside his eyes, the way his hair curled around his brow. She looked him in the eye.

'No, you are not that man,' she said. 'You are the man who was beside me for fifteen beautiful years, the man that loved and supported me, the talented cellist with a head full of dreams about making the world a better place.'

She lifted the curl of hair off his brow.

'You are the man who was going to get rich and buy rainforests so no one could destroy them. You are the man who has dreams of fatherhood and family. People cry when they hear the profoundly beautiful music you make. I know who you are, Luka Perez. Please never forget it.' She took his fingers in her hands and squeezed them. 'I was lucky to be your wife.'

And then she stood up, ready to leave.

'Lily, you are the best thing that ever happened to me.' His voice was breaking.

'And you are the best thing that ever happened to me. But understand, Luka – that since Jessie left, I have a hole, too. An emptiness. And I don't know how to heal it yet, but I'm working on it. And right now I can do nothing but that.'

'Lily, do you love him?' The words fell out of Luka's mouth.

'Yes, I love him, but I'm not with him. I'm not with anyone. I can't be in a relationship right now. I can't do that until I find out who I am and what I need. And I'm not sure if I ever want that again.'

Luka was watching her.

'I feel free, Luka, freer than I've ever felt. I'm not answerable to anyone but myself and I'm not sure that I could ever give that up.'

Luka got up, dusted the sand off himself, and stood beside her.

'Can I hug you?' he asked.

'Yes, you can.'

They stood like lovers even though they were departing as friends, holding on to each other for one last moment.

When Lily got back to her bungalow that afternoon, she opened her journal and read an excerpt that she'd kept – a torn-out page of an old, worn book she'd found a few days ago in a second-hand bookshop in Lamai Village.

'*For now, she need not think of anybody. She could be herself, by herself. And that was what now she often felt the need of – to think; well not even to think. To be silent; to be alone. All the being and the doing, expansive, glittering, vocal, evaporated; and one shrunk, with a sense of solemnity, to being oneself, a wedge-shaped core of darkness, something invisible to others … and this self having shed its attachments was free for the strangest adventures.*'

— Virginia Woolf, *To the Lighthouse*

twenty-four

THE RHYTHMS OF ISLAND life ran like a clock. One tick and the golden sun slipped above the horizon line, the next tick and a wave rolled in, another tick and a wave rolled out. A few tocks later, sunset arrived and tricked the stars into shining. Occasionally, a fiery thunderstorm would crack in the sky, breaking the pattern of a quiet day.

After four months, these island cycles were ingrained in Lily's psyche. Her days were simple and satisfying. A morning swim to greet the day, along with the fisherman who were boarding their longboats, followed by an hour of meditation on her worn grass mat, a smoothie breakfast, yoga, journaling and lunch at a nearby raw food café where Yogis, travellers and resident artists would gather to discuss life, philosophy or the latest island gossip. Afternoons were free and

Lily would use this time for exploring, visiting temples, markets, reading, painting, writing in her journal, or gathering seashells – and in the evenings, she would prepare a simple meal for Nova and herself.

Nova had found a job at a local pre-school teaching English, and each day she came home with a big smile and with wonderful stories about her young pupils.

'Anong climbed a coconut tree today and we couldn't get her down, so we had to call the fire and rescue service,' or, 'Aroon brought in a gorgeous baby python for show and tell.'

There was never a dull moment at the Island school. Nova was in love with life. She woke each day with a sparkle in her eyes, and it was a beautiful thing to see. In the last month, Nova had taken particular care with her daily appearance – lathering her skin with coconut oil or dotting her hair with sweet smelling frangipani or a pop of vibrant hibiscus. Sometimes she'd wear a delicate shade of blush smeared on her morning lips. Lily wondered if that extra glint in her eye had something to do with a new love.

The mystery was revealed one Saturday morning when Lily woke to see an extra pair of shoes on their doormat. Strappy white sandals. They belonged to the feet of a woman called Ubon (lotus flower). She was the administrator at the Island school. Nova and Ubon had fallen in love during tea breaks. Their love was generous, spacious, and gentle. The care they took with each other was exceptional. Notes packed in lunch boxes, small thoughtful gifts, hours, and hours of late-night conversation. And laughter – heaps of it. Their little beach bungalow had become a happy home.

Nova was blossoming – in the right environment, even the lotus comes out from under the mud. On the nights when passion flared between the young lovers, Lily escaped the thin walls of the bungalow with late night walks under the coconut palms. She was becoming very well acquainted with the southern stars. The brightest Alpha and Beta Centauri were visible on most nights.

The beaches at night were very much alive with late night romantics walking hand in hand, holiday merry makers carrying lanterns or those that, like Lily, wanted to admire the moon. Musical notes from the dance clubs and night bars clung to the night breeze and mixed with the soft calls of the frogs, crickets, and night birds. Koh Samui was very much awake even in the dark hours.

Lily was alone here, but she never felt lonely. Each day brought a subtle new discovery or adventure – both in her inner world and her outer world. The hours of meditation had brought an equilibrium to her life, and a pervading calmness. Her panic attacks a thing of the past. She was no longer striving for anything, but things were arriving: a new friend, an exciting conversation. An undiscovered waterfall under a canopy of trees. A revelation.

Despite Alexander Chau SC's attempts to lure her back to work every few weeks with the dangling carrot of a high-profile case, she had no desire to return to Hong Kong. She wondered when he would give up. *Lulama would say that he was a stubborn old goat.* The thought made Lily smile. If there was one person Lily truly missed here, it was Lulama, but since there was no way to contact her, Lily would just carry her memory by reading her latest postcard repeatedly. Once a week, Lily would call Mama on Sundays. The last few times Mama's duty nurse had said that she was too tired to take her call, which left Lily with a niggle in her stomach. *Something's not quite right.*

The simple life that Lily was living felt in tune with the rhythms of the island – stress a thing of the past, and the thing that surprised her most was how little she needed. She was living on investment income and savings, and Luka kept topping up her account. She had written and told him that this was unnecessary, that she was more than comfortable, but Luka had other ideas. He was paying a penance, or at least, that's what it looked like to Lily.

Lily thought about him almost every day since they had met on Lamai beach. He arrived with a shared scent, old song, favourite food, or a memory floating by on a cloud. As though he were by her side, even if he wasn't. She would often talk to him on her late-night walks, tell him about the day, or who she had met, or what she had discovered. This attracted attention from the occasional passers-by, who would give her an odd stare, letting her know, in no uncertain terms, that her behaviour was strange. She wondered when it would stop. After so many years together, the habit of wanting to share a day had resurfaced in her subconscious. They'd had a reset. The anger gone from both. Forgiveness is a miraculous thing.

From time to time. Lily would get on her scooter and risk the windy roads south to reach the Buddhist cave at Kalalaya. She was often on the lookout for Karma Chodron, who was as elusive as a shooting star in the night sky. And like a shooting star, the sight of her brought Lily an absolute, animated joy. She had become a way marker on Lily's path — a sign that all was well. She acknowledged Lily with a nod of the head or a quiet smile, and even when she wasn't present, Lily could somehow feel Karma Chodron sitting beside her in the cave — like an old, old friend who had held her hand for a thousand lifetimes.

On one humid day, as Lily arrived back from a trip to the cave on her new pastel pink scooter, she was greeted by a frenzy of people milling around her bungalow. Along with nosey onlookers, there were four police officers sitting on the deck outside her bungalow with serious expressions. For the first time in months, Lily put on her assertive lawyer voice and marched towards them.

'This is my home. Why are you here?'

'Miss, we come to interview Miss Nova,' the stoical officer replied.

Lily's heart lurched.

'It's okay, Lily.' Nova stepped outside. 'I called them.'

Surprised by the sudden turn of events, Lily grabbed Nova's hand and pulled her aside.

'Nova, are you sure?' she whispered. As much as she wanted this day to happen, she knew the decision would not be without consequence. Fighting for justice is no straightforward thing – especially for victims in cases of rape or sexual assault. In cases without witnesses and DNA evidence, the central issue would be consent – essentially a matter of he says, she says. And the defence strategy for cases like that would often be character assassination. Lily didn't want that for Nova. She had become protective of her – almost motherly.

'Yes, I'm sure.' Nova pressed Lily's hand. 'I'm definitely sure,' she repeated.

'Well, okay then.' Lily hugged her. 'I'm proud of you.'

Unbeknown to Lily, fate had brought Nova an ally. Ubon's uncle was a senior police official from

Bangkok. His distraught niece had visited him, informing him of a serial 'farang' rapist living on Koh Phangan. After some digging, it turned out that there had been several complaints laid by women that the local police on Koh Phangan had dismissed. Yohan had lined the local police's pockets. But now his money wasn't enough to cover his tracks. Yohan's ruse was exposed, along with the corrupt duty officer who had accepted his bribes. His time was up. As buried as truth can be, it often rises to the surface.

Lily was ecstatic that this day had come, and she hadn't done a thing to bring it about, except advise and support Nova. It seemed, at least in this case, that fate was on their side. Yohan's retreat was closed within the week, and Lily slept very well, knowing that justice would likely be served. She wished she could have seen him being led away in handcuffs – the smug assuredness wiped off his face. He had misjudged her, and he had misjudged Nova. And he had misjudged women in general.

When women stand together, mountains move.

Now, there was one fewer sexual predator out in the world – and a generation would be saved from suffering.

twenty-five

BEYOND THE NOISE OF the temple visitors, Lily had found a clearing with a view out over the sea. She was visiting Wat Ratchathammaram, a terracotta-hued Buddhist temple decorated with bas-relief carvings and sculptures depicting sea demons on stormy waves with giant swallowing fish and fierce warriors fighting near the God Hanuman – a smiling Hindu monkey deity depicted dancing on the walls of the Buddhist temple. It made sense, since the qualities that Hanuman represented – perseverance, loyalty, pragmatism, strength, selflessness and above all humour - are the qualities required of an aspiring yogini or Buddhist seeker on the path to nirvana or awakening. Both philosophies are dedicated to attaining freedom from suffering whilst still in human form. And both require its seekers to have formidable determination.

The temple crowds were unsettling, and Lily was relieved to find a quiet spot opposite the main shrine close to the wonderful old tree of spirits that was creaking in the gusty ocean winds. The tree was dressed in a yellow and gold fabric flapping in the breeze, its branches adorned with statuettes and figurines of spirits. Beneath it, in a bad mood, sat a dark faced Buddha his hands in a meditation mudra, gesturing to Lily to follow suit; she sat on the prickly grass beneath the tree, her apple green dress ballooning as she adjusted herself into lotus position.

After some time, the external noises of the crowds and the day faded, and Lily settled into a place she had been accustomed to visiting each morning on her old grass mat. A place of inner quietude undisturbed by the noisy currents and storms of daily life. A place where the heart softens and the barriers between waking life and dreams blur.

The spirits of the temple tree were said to bring back old friends, and today they bestowed their mysterious powers on the human sitting below its shady hand-shaped branches. Lily felt her first and then saw her in a waking dream. When she opened her eyes, she was gone, but when she closed them again, she was there – bright and shining like the sun. She was a laughing meadow, a golden sunflower, a little girl with dark twirls of mahogany hair and dark-rimmed tortoise-shell spectacles. Her laughing eyes making her recognisable as Luka's daughter. She reached her little hand out towards Lily, beckoning her to come closer.

'Mama, is that you,' she called. 'Mama!'

Lily cried, 'Jessie. Jessie.'

And then the dream faded like stars into the morning light – leaving an ethereal residue, a touch of her daughter with her. Lily opened her tear-rimmed eyes; the vision had been unexpected, the shock of it pulsing her heart.

A young girl dressed in jeans and a white T-shirt came barrelling towards her.

'Why you sit here, miss?' she asked, her eyes inquisitive and open like a full moon.

Lily could hardly speak, the child's gaze reaching a place she'd covered.

'I'm meditating, like the Buddha.' Lily pointed at the statue.

Happy with Lily's answer, the little girl skipped away, leaving her to contemplate what she had experienced.

The little girl returned two minutes later carrying a bag of dried red rose petals. She scattered them all over Lily chanting, 'Green Tara, Green Tara, Green Tara Om.'

No, I'm not Green Tara, whoever she is – I'm a mother grieving the loss of a little girl that I don't want to live without.

She smiled at the child and lifted a few fragrant smelling rose petals to her nose. Then she jumped up, gathering a hand full of the petals and began throwing them in the air towards the smiling girl. They both giggled and twirled under the rain of flowers. The child sprang into Lily's arms for a hug. The moment was so touching it brought more tears to Lily's jade pool eyes.

Here under the tree of spirits, she had touched the essence of her lost daughter in a dream, and she had heard her spirit through the laughter of another child.

My life is full of falling roses, all of them, beautiful.

The sky opened, letting down a torrent of water. Lily ran to her parked pink scooter, and the child ran to her mother. Lily knew she would arrive home today soaked and cold and shivering. But most of all, she would arrive knowing that wherever she went, Jessie was always with her.

Monsoon season was coming to the island. The rains began in September and carried on until December. Lily had been on the island for six months and she felt it was time to move on. Nova and Ubon were deep in the rhythms of falling in love. They needed space and their own home to create a nest. Lily suspected that the only reason that Nova hadn't already moved in with Ubon was because she didn't want to abandon her.

Karma Chodron had returned to her nunnery in the Himalayas for monsoon season, and the familiar travelling faces at Lily's favourite lunch eatery had moved on. The winds were whispering – it was time to move on. She didn't know where to go next. She was looking for a sign.

The sign came much sooner than she expected. That very evening. Lily was washing up the dinner dishes when the call came. Lily dropped a plate on the floor – it shattered, making her foot sticky with blood. She cleaned it up with a black striped tea towel. *Mama had a stroke.* She washed the towel under the cold water tap until it no longer turned the water red. She packed the dishes away and plastered up her foot. *Mama had a stroke.* It was time for Lily to fly home to Africa.

Lily saw her. She was sitting on the corner of the bed in the dimly lit hospital room with the African light gently illuminating the walls. *Mama, so frail, all bone. My beautiful, beautiful mama. Where have you gone? Is this really you?*

It had taken her so long to get here, so many airports. Asia to Africa. Dusty roads, several lines through several custom points, bag searches, stifling aeroplanes, dirty smelling public toilets and crowded spaces. Lily was exhausted.

She let her bag fall to the floor, and she walked towards the frail, unrecognisable woman she had once known. It had been three years since Papa passed – time had moved so quickly and time had stolen her mother.

'Mama, it's me!' she called out.

The woman on the bed turned her head into the light and looked up. Lily saw her eyes could no longer open. Those beautiful piercing baby blue eyes. Mama was blind. Lily's heart shattered like the old dish plate she had dropped all over that dusty kitchen floor. Ripping apart into emptiness.

She can't see me. Mama can't see me.

'Mama, it's me!' she called out again.

Mama didn't reply. Instead, she curled up into a ball on the lonely bed with its unkempt sheets. A picture so impressed on Lily's mind; it would never leave her.

She doesn't know who I am. My mother doesn't know me.

Lily broke apart some more. *Was that even possible? When did her heart have time to heal just so that it can break once more?*

Lily covered the old woman with a plaid blanket and sang the songs of childhood. She sang, with her tired, shaky voice – she sang the songs of love that Mama had so tenderly sung to her as a child, the songs of childhood summer sky in the land of burning desert heat and thunderstorms.

Lily couldn't remember when the singing stopped. She found herself in the twilight hours with her arms wrapped around her mother. Mama had become her child, and she never, ever wanted to leave this place again. She had abandoned Mama with her longing for life, and now Mama was abandoning Lily with her longing for death. Lily climbed into the bed, pulled her close, and fell asleep beside her.

She woke up when the African sun warmed her skin through the hospital window. When she looked up, she could see the light caressing them both through the curtain. She knew Mama was looking at her, even though she knew her mother couldn't see her.

And then Mama spoke.

'What are you doing with your life now, my child?' she asked.

Lily whispered, 'Mama, I am still a lawyer, but I've taken a break from work. Luka and I have had some trouble. I have been wandering and feeling lost, not knowing who I am or what I want to do.'

Mama paused, took a deep and measured breath, and then said,

'No, you are not a lawyer, my child. You are a writer. And you haven't lost your way, you're just finding your way back home like me.'

She paused, smiled, and whispered,

'That Luka is a wonderful man.' As though she could see his soul.

Those were the last coherent words Mama ever said to Lily. She knew her child better than her child knew herself.

What a parting gift.

They buried Mama on a warm spring day – brown-veined white butterflies spiralling through the looping hadeda bird calls. Belenois aurota, the African caper white, were migrating from the desert homes in the Karoo and the Kalahari towards the wide oceans of

Namibia and Mozambique. Making many stops on the way to lay their eggs, nobody knows their true destination. Just like nobody knows ours.

They were migrating earlier than usual, perhaps to take Mama's soul wherever it was going.

Lulama's hand reached for Lily's. 'Mama is becoming the sky,' she said.

Dying And Giving Birth Go On

'Dying and giving birth go on inside the one consciousness, but most people misunderstand the pure play of creative energy, how inside that, those are one event.'

Lalleshwari

twenty-six

LULAMA'S HANDS FELT BONY, no longer the meaty cushions that had offered Lily so much comfort during her life. She was fading, like a great old pine that was losing its branches, the skin on her hands becoming fine and translucent.

She sat on her sunken olive sofa, stringing coloured glass beads together for one of her vibrant tapestry creations. She coughed into a hand-embroidered handkerchief. Lily watched as the light ebbed and flowed from the room in waves. The cotton wool clouds covering the Transkei skies were limiting the sunlight in the room. The rondavel had expansive views of the Wild West Coast ocean. High on the hillside, they sat watching the world go by from their crown.

This morning had brought a pod of whales frolicking in vast waves as if they were only ripples. Their sounds and calls were echoing off the cliffs, letting everyone know they had arrived. It was a sight that brought morning emotion. Sometimes beauty does that.

Since Mama had flown with the butterflies, Lily had cried a lot. No longer seeking to be strong, or stay focused, or be the organiser or the resolver of problems, she had let what wanted to arrive – arrive. And she had let her siblings take care of the rest. She cried for Mama, but also for Papa and Jessie.

Lulama said her tears were healing tears that would nourish the earth where they fell. They would grow magnificent flowers. When the tears wouldn't stop, she meditated them away. She was tired of salt; she refused to cry anymore.

She rolled her grass mat on the clean swept concrete floor of the rondavel each morning, afternoon, and evening, sitting cross-legged in a lotus position nearby Lulama's ageing feet. During her meditation, she found the familiar sense of peace, her breath an echo of the rhythmic waves outside. She could access this place of calm, no matter where she was.

Lulama complained she was spending too much time on her mat. She said that Lily would be better off helping Nelson tend the vegetables growing in the garden.

'What use are you to the world, child?' she teased. 'Sitting all day?'

'Why are you searching for yourself when you're here? I can see you.'

Lily giggled. 'You should try meditation, Lula. It brings peace—'

'I have limited time left on this planet; I don't want to waste it half asleep. When I'm dead, I will sleep. Right now, I want to see each day, with all the colour that it brings.' She held up a string of shimmering beads and patted Lily's head. 'Even if it means I must sit here staring at you sitting in that silly position which is cutting the blood flow to your legs. Eish, child, I wish you weren't such a stubborn goat,' she said, with eyes turning up at the corners.

'You love me because I'm a stubborn goat,' said Lily.

'Yes. Yes, that's true.' Lulama stroked her rose oil hair.

'I'm just not used to seeing you like this. So still. We need balance in life. Too much of one thing is bad.'

Despite Lulama's warning, Lily continued to increase the hours of her meditation practice. Sometimes she would sit for three hours in one sitting. She was becoming skilful at separating her thoughts from herself. Skilful at distancing herself from her body, skilful at silence.

Day after day, she would allow herself to fall into a blissful emptiness. The more she meditated, the less inclined she was to live in the 'real' world, but the more connected she felt to it. It was a strange anomaly. To be in the world but not of it.

Lily's memories became distant. Her life was a playbook that she was looking at through a screen. If she maintained this state of being, nothing could touch her, not pleasure or pain. She could just be floating in this space and not care about the future or the past. The outside world had become irrelevant.

She would listen with one ear to Lulama, who would chasten her daily.

'Child, you are too thin. Your flesh has dropped from your bones.'

'Child, your mat is a drug. Stop hiding from the world.'

'Child, your eyes are empty. There is no life left in them.'

'Child, where are you?'

In these moments, Lily longed for the advice of Karma Chodron. It was hard being your own teacher. Lily was ready to join her now. She thought living in solace would be blissful. She didn't need six more months. She was ready. Why had Karma Chodron insisted on a year? She was grateful to have this time with Lulama at her home in this gorgeous African paradise with wild cosmos growing on the hillsides, but she felt an increasing need for solitude. Mama's passing had impressed upon her the sadness of lost moments, and she sensed Lulama wasn't well, so she willed herself to stay until Lulama was better.

Each day, Lulama coughed a little more into her hanky. Occasionally, the intricate embroidered cotton flowers became speckled with pinpricks of blood. If Lily hadn't spent so much time meditating, she might have noticed that.

One Transkei summer day, as Lily was on a rare walk, it turned cold. Dark foreboding clouds turned into the rain, which set off the smell of the African soil. Cooling earth swirling up Lily's nostrils, she headed back to Lulama's rondavel for a warm cup of her favourite rooibos tea. The grass under her feet was brown, mingled with patches of barren red earth, which the rain turned into a malleable clay. Lily scooped some up into a ball. Lulama could work her magic and make it into a cup, or some other interesting object.

The bright red door of the rondavel flapped against the mudbrick of the house, the ominous hollow banging sound an omen for the day to come.

'Lulama,' called Lily, as the earth in her hands turned to clay, 'look what I found.' She was a child again, excited to share her discovery with someone who would acknowledge her joy.

'Lulama,' she called again. There was no reply – all she could hear was the banging of the unsecured door and the gusty winds through the open windows. The curtains were rising and lowering, with waves of air billowing beneath them.

Perhaps she's at Nelson's place next door.

She shut the windows and closed the door. An eery stillness descending inside the round walls of the rondavel. As she did that, she noticed that Lulama's bedroom door was standing ajar. She walked inside and saw the reflection on the wall of a shadow on the ground. She walked to the other side of the bed, and then she saw her, lying on her side on the cold, unwelcoming floor.

'Oh my God, Lulama!' Lily knelt beside her.

There was not even a whisper of a breath escaping from Lulama's lips. Lily grabbed a cushion from the bed and placed it under her head.

Lulama was gone. It couldn't be clearer. There was nothing to be done. She had died with her eyes open, taking in the light. Lily swiped her palms over her Lulama's eyes, closing her eyelids. *There is nothing more to see in the world, Lula.*

She pulled a patchwork quilt off the bed and covered her best friend, her lifelong companion, her mentor, her confidante, her protector. Perhaps keeping her warm would revive her. She walked outside into the rain, finding only a small voice to call to Lulama's son.

'Nelson. Nelso—' Her voice failed her.

Lily started running towards the ocean. She ran kaalvoet down the winding path, small stones digging into the soles of her naked feet. She ran like a goat bouncing down the hillside or a barrelling tumbleweed being blown by the wind.

The giant Wild Coast waves hit the shore with force, white foam spraying spirals metres high into the air. *The rain inside the rain.* Lily felt the sting of the salt water on her face as she stood cold blue feet in the sand, close to the water's edge.

She paused for a moment, breathless, but calm and contemplative. In this world, there are moments that define us – closing moments where we make choices that alter our destiny.

Lula, Jessie. Mama. Papa. I'm coming home.

Lily walked into the wildness of a crazed sea. There were no fisherman here to pull her out. No long boats to rescue a foreigner.

The cold smacked the breath out of her as she dived beneath the waves, letting the weight of her wet garments pull her down. Her body rising and grasping for air, she willed herself to drop below the churning surface. She sank into the echoing silence of stillness.

The last thing she saw was Luka's smiling eyes.

They found her lying like a sleeping baby in a foetal position in an inlet surrounded by black rocks. It seemed the sea had spat her out of its churning waters. While Lily had willed herself to die, the oceans had willed her to live. The first inkling that she was alive came with a seagull picking at her feet and the screams of the woman who was breaking her ribs while performing CPR. Lily vomited sea water, and heartbreak and blood.

They took her to Zithulele Hospital, a small provincial hospital with a tiny staff who knew one another's first names, and secrets. News travelled fast that she was Lulama's 'white' child. The one who had found Lulama's body and had run into the sea.

Nelson's was the first face she saw when she opened her eyes.

'Pikinini, she was our mother.' He closed his fingers around hers. 'And you are my sister, and I need you to stay.' He bent forward and kissed her forehead.

Lily didn't cry, didn't eat, and for a week she didn't speak. They fed her through drip lines and prayed at the end of her bed to a God she didn't believe in. She overheard one nurse tell another that someone had stolen her spirit. *That is more accurate.*

The first time she spoke was to thank a little girl in a white dress wearing jangling bracelets who had brought her a perfect seashell and left it on the austere metal table beside her bed. It was an opalescent shell with perfectly forked grooves and a mother-of-pearl inlay – like the ones she used to hunt for as a child. This one was a real prize. Perhaps a goddess of the sea had returned her spirit to her. A Moana.

After two weeks, they discharged her with taped-up ribs and a prescription for anti-depressants, which she never collected. Instead, she flew back to Hong Kong and checked into a clinic run by her trusted friend, Saima. Luka had heard she was back in town, but she refused his calls. She couldn't face anyone she loved. The thought that she may feel nothing for him was dangerously close to pushing her over a precipice.

She spent her days focusing on lifting the grey cloud that had covered her heart. Lily couldn't feel. There was no laughter, no tears, no pain, nothing but a monotonal all-pervading greyness. Saima had diagnosed her with clinical depression.

'This is just a bump in the road,' she said. 'Lily, you have suffered an enormous loss. It wouldn't be normal if you came out unscathed.'

Saima prescribed anti-depressants and several talk therapies, including Cognitive Behavioural Therapy, which Lily found the most helpful. She was understanding what healthy emotional regulation was, and it was not escapism. This time, she took the prescribed drugs. She trusted Saima. She meditated again – only for short periods. Saima had advised against longer sittings, saying that for now any practices that caused further dissociation could be harmful.

Lulama was so wise; she knew this all along.

After six weeks at the private clinic, Lily smiled when the sun's rays warmed her skin through the old bay windows. The smell of frangipani blossoms in the small courtyard garden drew her outside, and the whiffs of dim sum from the eatery next door stimulated her stomach juices. She was hungry, and she was finding Saima's silly nerdy jokes funny.

'Did you hear about the Italian chef who died? He pasta-way,' or 'I like elephants, everything else is irrelephant.'

Saima's chest would puff up, her dark eyes glinting with mischievousness as she rolled out silly jokes. She was a good friend, as solid and reliable as the ground beneath your feet.

Lily decided she would take Lulama's advice, and instead of spending so much time looking inwards, she would look out at the beauty of the world. Karma Chodron was wise to insist on a year before she would become her teacher – Lily understood why now. She understood, too, that the path to healing was as important as the path to awakening – and you cannot heal by avoiding your pain. The body-mind is a complex eco-system. Suppression is like a pressure cooker that can boil over at any moment. Lily was grateful that the ocean had spat her out, that she'd been rescued from her boiling point. She shuddered when she thought about all those who had not, those who had succumbed to the darkness. As painful as life can be, there is always beauty if you allow yourself to open your eyes and see. Lulama knew that, and now Lily knew that too. She was one of the lucky ones who had been spared by a brief parting of the clouds. And she decided that when it was her time to go, she would go with her eyes open to the world – like her beloved Lula.

Lily spent a week reading travel blogs, looking for the most spectacular places to see. She had no commitments, a steady investment income, and Alexander Chau SC had failed to convince her to return to chambers. Luka lived in their house. Lily wasn't ready to sell. Right now, she needed to come alive, to live and dance and play. What better place to do it than in the cloud forests of Costa Rica? She was desperate to see the magical quetzal bird. According to the blog she was reading, it was the most beautiful bird in the world.

For Ever We Come, For Ever We Go

For ever we come, for ever we go;
For ever, day and night, we are on the move.
Whence we come, thither we go,
For ever in the round of birth and death,
From nothingness to nothingness.
But sure, a mystery here abides,
A Something is there for us to know.
(It cannot all be meaningless)'

Lalleshwari

twenty-seven

IN THE TWELVE CANTON of the Puntarenas Province of Costa Rica lies the Monteverde Cloud Forest. A waking, living dream. The low-hanging clouds hovering in misty swirls around the upper canopy of the dense forest trees condense as they caress the leaves and drip into crystalline streams which keep all the plants on the forest floor well-watered.

This forest is one of the few places on earth where the sky comes down to meet the ground, enabling you to walk through the clouds. Visitors rarely remain untouched when they are surrounded by the beauty of the soft hazy mists, tendrils of trailing foliage, unique plants and epiphytes, and the mysterious calls of strange animals and rare birds. Mother earth, known here as Pachamama, is without a doubt the most talented artist.

Gabriel was looking up, hoping to spot the holy quetzal bird, a mysterious enigma, but one that would bring you light, goodness and maybe even immortality – if you were lucky enough to spot it. The forest guide claimed that the mystical birds were in the canopy.

'They are watching us,' he said.

The group had been walking on the track for an hour, and Gabriel had seen a menagerie of wonderful things: glass see-through tree frogs, glass butterflies that resemble stained glass windows in old churches and frogs wearing distinctive blue jeans with pokey red sunglass eyes.

There were rainbow-coloured humming-birds feeding off wildflower nectar, cawing parrots biting into juicy berries, orange and yellow-billed toucans, reptiles in greens and black camouflage gear, shimmering gold frogs and jewelled butterflies fluttering from one flower to the next. The forest floor was alive under decaying leaves with ants, termites, and a plethora of tiny insects that Gabriel couldn't identify.

If anywhere deserved to be painted on earth, this was it. The bright colours of the forest fauna were a vibrant contrast to the shimmering green of the trees. The earth pulsating with beauty and alive with danger. A turn of each corner on the path bringing the potential to run into jaguars, pumas, tarantulas, green pit vipers, and the deadliest of all – poison arrow frogs that produce a type of batrachotoxin so venomous that only 1/100,000 of an ounce can kill a human.

Gabriel was in awe of the complexity of this unique ecosystem, knowing that he was privileged to witness it as the climate of the Monteverde is changing. The hotter temperatures bringing less precipitation and longer mist-free periods, causing the rapid decline of these unique and distinctive species, which critically depend on the heavy moisture in the air to survive. The cloud forests are dying.

Pachamama is losing her heart.

Gabriel kept his eyes on the canopy – scanning for the mysterious quetzal. A woman at the back of the group let out an involuntary squeal.

'There, look up!'

Gabriel followed her eyeline and was amazed by the sight of an astonishing bird. It sat resplendent on the branch of a wandering ficus, its shimmering emerald wing and crown feathers gleaming in the dappled forest light. Its beak was a golden yellow, and it had a tail of iridescent blue feathers – almost a metre long. Its chest was blood red – in legend the colour deriving from the blood of a brave dying Mayan warrior.

The quetzal stood there, still and observant, his eyes communicating something Gabriel was trying to understand. Gabriel's eyes trailed back down to the woman who had spotted the quetzal – there was something haunting and familiar about her. That desolate look in her eyes. He recognised it. During his years of hollow depression, he had seen it in the mirror.

Gabriel looked back up at the holy bird.

Ah, that's it – it's telling her to hold on. After all, it is the bird of immortality.

As if acknowledging his thought, the quetzal looked across at him and raised his green jewelled wings in a flamboyant display. Gabriel smiled. This creature was a dream come true. He noticed a single golden feather trailing on the back of the bird as it turned around and flew off into the mist. The head rests of Aztec and Maya priests were once adorned with these gold feathers. In these parts, the bird had been sacredly revered for centuries and in Mayan and Aztec times, the penalty for harming one was death.

The quetzal was glorious, and so was the woman who had spotted him – he noticed her damp golden hair falling haphazardly across her face. He loved the wildness of it. Her features were delicate, like a water nymph – her eyes the colour of serpentine. He tried to catch her eye to thank her for spotting the bird, but she kept them looking out into the forest.

She was still searching.

twenty-eight

HER BEDROOM, IN THE Costa Rican bed and breakfast, had walls painted a canary yellow and a duvet cover adorned with waving green palms. It was owned by an American retiree. There was a soft pink dresser beside a bay window, where Lily would sit in the morning and write. Vintage classics filled a matching bookcase. Lily enjoyed waking up to the musty smells of old books mingled with the aroma of croissants and coffee. Her host brought a fresh breakfast tray each morning accompanied by a purple country girl – a delicate indigo orchid.

Each morning she would thumb the pages of an old book and discover new worlds – places she had never inhabited. Here in this new land, Lily found herself free to embark on Virginia Woolf's strangest adventures. The new light had brought a restlessness, an urge to explore. She was still sad, but she was coming to accept that it was okay.

This morning, she signed up for another trek in the forest. She was hoping to spot a quetzal. So far, she had been unsuccessful. Maybe today she would be lucky.

The cloud forest was a magical wonderland of aliveness. Everywhere Lily looked, the colours of the living things around her were glimmering and reflecting in water droplets.

The clouds swirling like coffee cream were close enough to touch. The forest was humming with the most remarkable creatures, her favourite so far a tiny hummingbird the size of her thumb with feathers of shimmering purple and silver. A Tinkerbell bird of the forest sipping honey from benevolent orchids. She resisted pulling her phone out every minute to take pictures. Her line of sight focused on the treetops, scanning for the mystery bird in the verdant canopy.

After an hour of craning her neck, the magnificent quetzal appeared. She spotted him high on a branch of a ficus tree with trailing vines. He wasn't disappointing, his long cobalt-blue tail glinting like the hanging tinsel on a Christmas tree. Lily's eyes became saucers, her heart racing. It was worth being alive just to see this astonishing creature dressed in its emerald gown and red frills. The bird had a powerful presence, making everyone look up. Even the multicoloured tree frogs stopped leaping for a minute. The God of the cloud forest had arrived.

The quetzal was only there for a minute, but everything about him was etched into Lily's brain. Prickly goosebumps covered the skin on her body. *I will never forget this moment.*

It took some time for her feet to feel grounded, but as she walked on the leaf-covered paths, she listened to the guide reiterate that this beautiful cloud forest, home to the God of birds, was disappearing. Lily felt a hollow sadness, tears threatening in the corner of her eyes. She supposed this was a good thing, to feel anything at all.

Buoyed by the sight of quetzal, she spent the rest of the afternoon reading about the fate of the cloud forests in her room. Tears ran down her face as she considered the universal plight of cloud forests and rain forests around the world. It was unimaginable to think that this rare and precious beauty would soon be gone. It was the first time that she had cried since the ocean had thrown her out of its waves. She supposed it was apt crying for the forests of the earth that had saved her. For Pachamama. And after she cried for her, she cried for Lulama. A wail rose from her throat, and her body shook – a volcano of grief. Finally erupting.

She cried until sleep found her and she woke in the morning to find her silver breakfast tray decorated by a single red rose, and a note from her host which read,

'*Wherever there is grief, there is love.*'

It was a sunny morning in Monteverde. Lily went to a local coffee shop with her laptop in hand. She was determined to understand the fate of the forests. Buoyed by caffeine, she joined a local online chat forum set up for raising awareness of the plight of the Monteverde forests. It was full of brainstorming locals and tourists, discussing ways to raise funds for the cause.

A man named Gabriel seemed to have interesting ideas. She messaged him with suggestions. Their conversation flowed effortlessly, and before they knew it, they were on to other topics. Their conversation carried on into the afternoon. He intrigued Lily, and she gave her number to him without hesitation.

Lily kept her phone beside her all day, waiting for the buzz of a new message to drop. That evening, she went out to a local pizzeria for dinner. Her appetite was increasing, and she was happy to have her hips back. Between mouthfuls of soft mozzarella and sticky garlic bread, she typed animatedly on her phone. She had never encountered a human like Gabriel.

He was as enigmatic as the resplendent quetzal. He spoke about things she had never encountered — magical forest plants that could heal souls, shamanic singing rituals in the Amazon, wild indigenous ceremonies where dancers with painted bodies writhed like snakes and whooped like the howler monkeys of the forest. His conversation was dynamic and exciting. It was strange to feel this way about a person you have never seen. By the next day, they were flirting.

And the day after that, Lily agreed to meet and make love to a stranger.

It was the wildest thing she had ever done in her life. So reckless and utterly exhilarating. Lily was losing her fear of the unknown. Perhaps facing death was teaching her to live a fearless life. Saima would call that a problem. But not her sister, Sarah. When Lily messaged her to ask for advice, she said,

'Go for it! He sounds delicious. Your gut will let you know if it's off.'

When Gabriel wrote, she couldn't get enough of his words. His brutal honesty created a whirlpool of wonder in her tepid grey outlook. His words spoke of ideals, ideologies, entheogens. Intimacy. He spoke to her heart, somehow cracking its seal and letting in a sliver of lightness. Gabriel was sunshine.

It seemed they couldn't get enough of each other's words. Why would it be any different in bed? Gabriel's lyric soothed her, and she could feel his infectious energy creeping into her most intimate places. He made her blush. And so, they began their play. Co-writers of each other's story, they made each other feel words in forbidden places. She hadn't felt this type of intimate excitement since Oliver, his memory still haunting, but now, she was stone-cold sober. There was no reality to obscure. This was real, raw, and unfiltered. And totally unexpected.

They agreed to push boundaries. Gabriel made Lily feel bold. They would meet for the first time in person – naked, with no words. They would make love without introduction, there would be no voices. Only the sound of intimacy. Crazy, crazy beautiful. Or simply crazy.

When the agreed day arrived, Lily shook inside. All made up for the first time in months, she hardly recognised the reflection of the woman in the mirror. Her eyelids touched with a delicate blue powder setting of her eyes, her lips with a touch of coral, and her hair dried into soft wavy curls. She climbed into the four-wheel drive she had hired – essential for the potholed mountain roads of Monteverde. The breathtaking landscapes of this new wild country were captivating. The undulating mountain roads, layered in gentle mists with wild raptors circling overhead, made it easy to feel that a benevolent goddess had gifted this day.

Lily arrived at the picturesque cottage down the side of a mountain track. There was a hammock tied to the deck lazily swinging in the afternoon breeze – it had no agenda other than to be there tossed about with the wind. The pace of this place was easy.

Lily was still trembling, unsure but committed as she walked up the gravel drive towards the front door. Someone loved this place. The gardener kept the garden tidy and hung hummingbird feeders in the limbs of a breadfruit tree.

The key was where Gabriel said it would be – underneath a planter beside the door. Lily turned it in the well-oiled lock with quivering hands. The cottage smelt like freshly cut flowers. An arrangement of orchids was used to decorate a small, round wooden table. Lily climbed the creaking wooden stairs to the bedroom, where she laid out a few white candles that she had brought with her. The room was simple and elegant. Dominated by a king-size bed covered in white broderie Anglaise duvet cover with a handwoven throw of rainbow colours over the end, and a window with views out towards the towering cloud topped mountains.

Lily must have gone to the bathroom at least five times to check on her hair and lipstick, before she finally settled down on a brown worn leather sofa in the reception room downstairs. She waited, hands fumbling, heart pounding in her head for Gabriel. She waited as the sun bid farewell to another misty day in Costa Rica.

Gabriel arrived. He burst in with force. His presence was larger than the little cottage could contain.

My Goddess, he is such a beautiful man.

With long hair tied in a bun, striking features, and years of yoga etched on his body, he had freedom written in his serene smile, and wisdom lines around his grey knowing eyes. He was such a contrast to the clean-cut suited men of Lily's past.

Breathe, Lily, breathe.

He looked at her with an uneasy recognition in his eyes, like he was looking at her soul. Lily was all butterflies; her hands and breath couldn't settle. He sat opposite her and gently took her hands in his. Such tenderness. His hands felt a little clammy. He was nervous, too.

And that's when she felt it move through her. The energy that unites lovers. Their hands pushing into each other, dancing into the subtleness that desire can bring. They both wanted to talk, but they had agreed no words. Those were the rules of this game they were playing. Instead, they smiled and laughed and looked at each other and let their hands dance. Until it became too much, and they grabbed their phones and began texting each other.

Gabriel wrote, '*Are we doing this?*'

Lily replied, '*Yes.*'

Gabriel wrote, '*You're beautiful.*'

Lily replied, '*So are you.*'

He led her upstairs to bed, and it was there in the flickering candlelight that they truly spoke for the first time. Without words. Lily felt vulnerable. She knew he could see her. There was no hiding here – no words to cover them. Her naked body leaning into this stranger whom she knew so well. The heat moved between them, rising in urgency, and it was in that urgency that they heard each other's voices for the first time. The sounds of ecstasy vibrating into the walls, through their flesh, and out into the valley beyond. Gabriel's cries were deep and urgent. He made her feel so hungry for him.

She surrendered, not only to Gabriel, but through him, joined to the universe – her cries reaching the mountains. Her body shook with the ecstasy of it. It was a sacred moment. A holy moment. A joyous moment.

When they finally returned to Pachamama after all the lovemaking that night, Gabriel wrapped Lily in his arms from behind and fell asleep that way. Lily lay dead still, listening to him breathe softly into her ear, her body still trembling under the weight of his warm body. Trembling under the weight of what she had just done. This good girl gone bad. Sleeping with strangers. Yet she had never felt so free.

She lay there like that all night, still and feeling. Listening to their heartbeats and moving to the rise and fall of Gabriel's breath. That memory carved into her. Being wrapped up in Gabriel. A feeling so familiar, yet so unknown. The place where their breath met in rhythm. The space that was in between them. It didn't matter to Lily whether this was the beginning or the end of their story.

This *now* was big enough.

When You See Yourself

When you see yourself
and someone else
as one being,

When you know the most joyful day
and the most terrible night
as one moment, then

awareness is alone
with its Lord.'

Lalleshwari

twenty-nine

LILY PUSHED THE TEARS back, but they wouldn't let go, welling in dams behind her eyes. They were ready to flood again. She slipped out from beneath Gabriel's embrace with the call of the first morning bird. Collecting her clothes so as not to disturb him, she sneaked out down the stairs, and out the door to her car. She hoped the ignition noise wouldn't wake him. It wasn't kind to leave this way, but she had no choice. She needed to be alone. Lily couldn't face him. Their intimacy had brought a matrix of confusion. She wasn't ready for a love like this. A closeness like this. She was still healing.

She shut the door of her bed and breakfast room and snuggled into the plush cotton covers of her bed. She lay there, head under the duvet, breathing in lavender fabric softener and contemplating the crazy adventure she had just had. The vulnerability of her coupling with Gabriel had released something, and she was afraid of opening the floodgates. She thought of all she had lost, the laughter and conversations she'd once shared with her loved ones, the warmth of their embrace, the smell of Lulama – now gone forever. She thought of Oliver with his dimpled chin and Luka, his music still haunting. Despite it all, she still loved them. And she wasn't sure that there was capacity in her heart to love anyone more.

Gabriel – she hardly knew him, but he had given her a gift, a pathway back to her heart. In those hours wrapped up in him, she could feel again. And what she had felt was overwhelming. She wanted to stroke his hair, kiss his face, bury herself in his skin – instead she had run away.

It was afternoon when she finally emerged from under the covers. She opened the floral curtains in her room to be greeted by the dance of hummingbirds flitting in the garden. Their jewelled wings shimmering in the afternoon sun as they hovered from one extraordinary flower to the next. Purple Guaria Morada orchids, red ginger flowers, heliconias and anthuriums, and of course Lily's favourite frangipani – but here in Costa Rica they were in colours she had never seen. Watermelon and magenta pinks. New colours for a new day.

Lily picked up the orange bottle of anti-depressants sitting on the dresser, stared at them for a moment, then threw them in the dustbin. Their job was done. It was time for her to get to work. Recalling Saima's advice to come off them gradually, she retrieved the bottle from the tissue-laden dustbin. *Don't be impulsive, Lily.* She would taper off the drugs slowly.

She reached for her phone to see several missed calls and messages. She owed Gabriel a huge apology.

They met for coffee in Santa Elena the next day, sitting opposite each other with eyes like owls. Both taking each other in during the daylight. Gabriel was larger than life, his presence making heads turn wherever he went. His gregarious nature was contagious. He seemed to know everybody, even though he was thousands of miles from his home. A native New Zealander, his accent was both fascinating and hard to follow. Part Māori, he had a distinctive tattoo of spirals and curved shapes in an intricate pattern on his left arm. He had been travelling in the Americas for over a year.

'I'm so glad you've come back. I didn't like it when you ran away.' He took a strand of wayward hair and tucked it behind his ear, his greying dark hair glistening. Lily had a brief recollection of it streaming down his back as they made love. She felt her cheeks warm.

'I'm so sorry, I—'

'You've already explained. No need to apologise for being human. I'm just happy we could meet again.' His smile was gracious. 'I have a confession to make.' Gabriel's eyes twinkled as he poured a thick clump of cream in his coffee.

'Oh, tell.' Lily took a sip of the hot peppermint tea she had ordered, bracing with the touch of the hot liquid. It surprised her he was having cream. She expected him to be a vegan.

'I've seen you before our little silent rendezvous.'

'Really, where?'

'Up in the cloud forest – we were on the same walking tour.'

'We were?' She looked at him quizzically.

'Yes, you spotted the quetzal. I tried to get your attention, but all you could focus on was the forest. I couldn't compete with Papatūānuku.' He smiled.

'Papatūānuku?' she asked.

'Pachamama, Mother Earth. We call her Papatūānuku in New Zealand.'

'Ah.' Lily nodded. 'It was mesmerising in the forest,' she said. 'I didn't want to miss a second. But I can't believe I missed you. You are very noticeable.'

'Am I now?' His playful tone made her heart thump faster.

Much like Lily, Gabriel was an explorer and a seeker. He had crossed a bridge in his life and had taken the road less travelled. His small health food products business ran independently, and he could now explore his unusual hobbies with his newfound wealth and free time. He was obsessed with entheogens, the plants with powerful psychoactive and hallucinogenic properties that have been used by indigenous peoples in spiritual ceremonies since the beginning of time.

He had come to the Americas seeking to learn more from a Shipibo shaman in the Peruvian Upper Amazon. The Shipibo worked with Ayahuasca, a brew made from two distinctive plants, which was said to have potent healing and transformational properties. The shamans were masters of the plant's powers, and they lead their people through rites of passage and healing ceremonies, the bitter brew giving them insights into their life, healing sickness, and connecting them with their ancestors. Gabriel said that if you consumed the mysterious drink, you would be blessed with a meeting with the Goddess. Lily wondered if this was what Luka had been given in Koh Samui. She had never asked, but she knew that whatever it was, it was wholly transformative. And dangerous.

Gabriel connected deeply with the Goddess, his spiritual roots, his power, and his heart. He was the most unique human being whom Lily had ever encountered. After an hour of fascinating conversation and two coffees and two teas, his face took on a serious expression.

'Lily, I hope you don't find this intrusive, but that day in the forest, I saw an emptiness in your eyes. I know it well,' he said. 'I call it the grey ghost. It comes to take your spirit.'

'Yes, my doctor diagnosed me with clinical depression.' Her eyelids lowered, she was looking at Gabriel's bare feet on the floor.

'Don't let that diagnosis define you.'

'I don't. I'm getting better, day by day, moment to moment.' She paused and played with her spoon. 'And after our night together, I'm feeling again. Something has moved. I thought maybe it was you.' She looked away, embarrassed by her own words, but couldn't help saying, 'I ... I thought maybe you were an angel.'

Gabriel laughed and tossed his wild hair to the side. He reached out for her hand. Still chuckling.

'Lily, I'm no angel, rather the opposite, but I can help you. I know a thing or two about the old grey ghost.' His expression was earnest. 'Just let me know when you are ready, and I'll take you where you need to go.'

He swirled the last sip of coffee in his cup and swallowed it down.

Gabriel rose and settled the bill before Lily had a chance to object. A smile on his face, he waited for her at the door. He grabbed her hand. He was taking her somewhere. She didn't ask where, and it didn't matter because she knew she was safe with Gabriel.

After walking through the hilly town, Gabriel led her down a track. It was steep, so she clung onto his shoulders. His steps were steady and confident as he travelled down a path which was familiar to him. They scampered down rocks until they arrived at a crystal-clear rockpool under a small waterfall.

They must've set fairy tales in this whimsical place.

Lily was in awe. Surrounded by towering trees and dragonflies and bright turquoise butterflies twirling overhead – she took time absorbing it all. Gabriel dropped his clothes on a rock and jumped into the blue pool, stark naked, with a giant splash.

'Are you coming in?' he shouted, while doing breaststroke.

Lily, suddenly self-conscious, looked for a tree to hide behind. She slipped off her light summer dress and sandals and edged towards the water, still wearing her underwear.

'Don't get your undies wet,' he teased. 'I'll turn around if you are feeling shy.'

And so, with Gabriel's back towards her, Lily slipped off her underwear and quickly jumped into the mountain pond. Letting out a squeal as she hit the water. It was freezing, her skin covered with goosebumps. Gabriel was behind her in a heartbeat, his breath on her neck. He scooped her up from behind. Lily giggled nervously. She felt like a child, so happy in his arms.

His firmness pressing against her back caused her breath to catch in her throat as the memories of their night together came flooding back. His arm around her waist, he gently propelled them towards the waterfall, with its cascading sound.

They swam under the falls and felt the cool mist on their faces as they arrived at a place behind the wall of water against a rock face. Gabriel turned her around, her breasts above the water facing him. He looked at them shamelessly. He pulled her closer and licked one of her nipples, the blissful sensation shooting through her body. His mouth traced soft lines on her chest before taking in the other nipple, which was firm from the icy water.

He groaned with desire. Lily was on fire despite the coldness of the water.

She reached for him under the water, his hardness in her hand as she brought him closer, slipping him inside of her and lowering herself onto him. She straddled him, rolling her pelvis in waves while his tongue explored her mouth. Their movement was slow and gentle. Every time she tried to speed up, he would slow her down – their passion building in waves.

'There's no rush, Lily. We have all day,' he said, the smile not leaving his face for a moment.

They played like this for what seemed like hours. Sometimes she'd slip away, and he'd chase and catch her. Their laughter lighting up the sky full of hummingbirds and butterflies. They lay on the rocks to warm themselves and then they would slip back into the cool water again for more play.

Until eventually, their crescendo escaped out into the flowing waters. Lily screamed so loud, she thought that someone was bound to come running. Nothing could stop the powerful energy that coursed through her veins like lightning. Gabriel cocked his head back in ecstasy, his low growls like a tiger.

'You sound incredible, Lily,' he whispered.

He kissed her over and over as they lay out in the sun to warm and dry. Lily nearly fell asleep in the summer breeze. She hadn't felt so relaxed in months – as if everything that had been holding her rigid had suddenly coursed away. The water, the rocks, the birds, and the sky were all part of her, drifting through as seamlessly as the clouds above.

thirty

THE DAYS WITH GABRIEL were light, lazy, and beautiful. They'd moved in together into a hilltop tree house in Monteverde that was rented out to tourists — committing to a month's rental. Quite extraordinary for strangers. No expectations, no promises, just presence.

The owners built the tree house of wood, perched it on stilts, and made it float amongst the treetops of the forest. It was a small, round house with a four-poster bed in the centre, a luxurious bathroom with copper taps, and a balcony looking out over the tree canopy. In the dark of night, the howler monkeys would whoop around them, making a tremendous raucous that sounded more like roaring tigers than little monkeys with white faces. The first time it happened, Lily jumped into Gabriel's arms, shaking.

'What the fuck!'

Gabriel laughed and pulled her closer.

'I've got you, sweet woman.' He nuzzled her neck with his nose.

They found a steady rhythm. Morning meditation, and a yoga class at a tiny studio in town, followed by a simple breakfast of rice with beans and fresh fruit. Gabriel spent the early part of the day with a local shaman who ran a centre nearby, helping guests with a plethora of ailments using healing plants.

Lily spent the time reading, researching spiritual traditions, and writing. She had rekindled her love of poetry, and the wild forests of Monteverde were the perfect inspiration. In the late afternoons, they would go exploring. Sometimes forest walks, sometimes a swim in the rock pools, sometimes shopping for fresh produce at a local market. They prepared most meals at home together and evenings were for sunsets, candlelight, and lovemaking. Sometimes Gabriel would pick up a book and read to her as they cuddled in bed, getting ready for sleep. Lily cherished those moments.

She slowly and steadily weaned herself off her anti-depressants. As simple and satisfying as her life with Gabriel was, she still felt a hollow, aching sadness. The place where Jessie once lived was a ghost town. Papa, Mama, and Lulama's eyes haunted even among the heavenly cloud tops. Lily ached with missing. Lily ached for a home that she hadn't found and the quiet pull to disappear still lingered.

Gabriel observed silently when those moments took hold of her, never forcing her – his presence the steady support she required. Until one day, when they were out for a swim, and she stayed underwater for too long, the sorrow in her expression was palpable, the sadness in her eyes shining brighter than the day.

'Lily, it's time to drink the medicine tea. Trust me, it's going to help you.'

She had faith in him but was nervous about consuming anything that might cause her to spiral out of control. Heeding Saima's advice, she felt a reluctance to engage in dissociative practices.

'Gabriel, I'm not sure. I'm trying to do this my own way.'

His frown softened as he traced her cheek with his fingertips.

'And you're doing wonderfully. But you have buried Lily, the grey spirit in your subconscious, not a place you can access easily. The Teacher is gentle with people who hurt. I'll be with you every step of the way. And I'll choose the gentlest medicine. Please trust me.'

'What if it makes me lose it, makes me crazy?' she asked. She'd read enough to know that entheogens were unpredictable. And she'd heard stories of women travelling to these parts seeking salvation through the plants, only to be drugged, robbed, and taken advantage of by men posing as Shamans. She knew that didn't apply to Gabriel, but she was still nervous about an altered state of reality that she would have no control of.

'We're all a little crazy.' Gabriel chuckled. 'I have worked with hundreds of people, and I know who can handle the medicine and who can't. And I promise you, you can handle it.'

He hugged her close, and she heard the steady beat of his heart.

'Lily, you are one of the most capable people I've ever met. But we all need a little hand sometimes, and Papatūānuku, she has everything you need on hand. She's calling you. You wouldn't be here with me if she wasn't.'

'Okay, I'll do it.' She snuggled into his warm embrace.

Relief washed over Gabriel's face.

They chose a quiet Sunday. Lily woke up feeling edgy, like she was walking on a tightrope. She'd been gathering courage for days. It was a glorious day. Cool, bright, a soft breeze blowing in from the open balcony door and the smell of the thick composting vegetation on the forest floor hanging in the air. She walked outside, her eyes drinking in the panoramic views of the canopy.

The cacophony of jungle sounds filled her ears – whooping monkeys, chirping cicadas, buzzing insects, birdcalls, and streams of air whistling through rustling leaves. Memories rushed in, and with them came a whisper of wind, carrying a single leaf that fluttered and settled on the ground near her feet.

While picking it up and twirling it about, she thought about her own journey. Her life in South Africa, London, and Hong Kong. Standing in the remote silence of this place, her previous life seemed so far away. All the boxes she had packed and unpacked. Boxes of dreams, love, and devotion. Dreams of a happy marriage and children were now fading hopes, a decaying leaf on the ground.

She remembered the sound of her heels clicking across the marble floor of the thirty-third floor of the high-rise tower in Hong Kong on the day she packed up her office. What a show it all was. The box files neatly lining her walls containing stories which shaped the lives of so many, now swept up and packed away, and stuck in storage. Her robes, her bands, her precious wig gathering dust. Symbols of achievement now meaningless clutter.

She thought about Jessie. Who would she have been if she had lived? Would she have reached a precipice in her life like Lily had? When the meaningful became meaningless. What would she have said to her daughter on that day?

She heard Gabriel stir, stretching his muscular limbs with a languid yawn.

She stared at him, her eyes lingering on his face. He was gorgeous, with his sleepy eyes and tousled hair.

Yes, I gave it all up. Just to meet you here, so I could do this. I know that now.

She hadn't planned it this way, planned to meet him, planned to be here. It had all happened when Lily stopped resisting her pull towards freedom, towards flow. A flow that moves us all to the places we are meant to be if we listen.

As her thoughts returned to the present moment, she felt her heart quicken – nervous anticipation setting in. She had no more Oud, the soothing oil she had relied upon for so long to settle her nerves. She'd run out months ago on Koh Samui. When she began her meditation practice, she stopped needing it.

She grabbed her pink jute yoga mat, unfurling it across the splintered wooden balcony floor, and wearing nothing but white knickers, she settled into lotus posture. With her eyes closed, she took a slow, deep breath and felt her body relax as she exhaled.

She heard a rustle and peeked through her eyelids to see that Gabriel had laid his very worn yoga mat beside hers. A grey mat that had been his steady companion for fifteen years. Full of holes. He'd kept it; he couldn't let it go. All his hours of yoga had not taught him the very yogic lesson of non-attachment. Lily smiled to herself. He was someone who cherished things.

Sitting cross-legged beside her, his silhouette lit up by the easy morning light, Gabriel was wild and statuesque. His body sculpted by hours of disciplined yoga asana practice, he was physically strong, yet somehow feminine. He was an enigma – not defined by the norms of male or female. A spirit no one could capture. Like the eagles that circled above them in the canopy, he was most magnificent when he was flying free. Definitely an angel, though he denied it.

They had agreed there would be no sexual intimacy today. The first day without it since they met in person. They began their asana practice together, working through a sequential vinyasa – a flow of different yoga postures. Gabriel stopped every five minutes to correct Lily's form, adjusting her arms, or legs, or torso. She recoiled each time he came close. How could she resist him? Today she preferred a little distance. A little indifference. She did not want her desire for him to interfere with the deeper work that was calling them both.

Feeling more relaxed after practice, she had a warm shower and put on her favourite lavender floral dress. A special occasion deserved effort. Gabriel smiled when he saw her emerge from the bathroom.

'You look ready, you smell ready.'

He kissed her on the forehead, inhaling the scent of rose oil.

'I am,' she said with a smile.

Gabriel explained what was going to happen and Lily attempted to remain composed, but she knew Gabriel could detect the fear in her eyes. He was not someone she could hide from.

He took her hand in his and led her to the balcony, where blankets had been laid out and soft pillows surrounded an altar of stacked river pebbles. A heady, sweet smell of watermelon frangipani drifted through the air. He had lit some incense, which was throwing smoke out in a straight line. The morning had become still. Gabriel looked at her with his soul-seeing eyes and Lily knew then, as her stomach flipped, that it was time.

The plant medicine tea that Gabriel had brewed for Lily was sweet. The bitterness of the fungi disguised with honey. She sipped it, the sweet taste of the drink lingering on her tongue. Gabriel had the same, telling her it was important that he matched her dosage. Once they swallowed the brew, there was no turning back.

Nothing could have prepared Lily for the reality of it. Nothing.

She lay herself down on the floor as her internal world dissolved. Gabriel covered her with a blanket as she felt a cold terror creeping in. She was no longer in control of her mind, but there was no turning back now. There was nothing she could do to become sane again. This new reality was on the inside of the inside. A space so foreign, yet familiar. Vast and expansive. Lily didn't know how to navigate it. She had found eternity. This was the great lesson of letting go.

She felt her stomach churning in a knot of nausea as the fear consumed her, her body shaking. She could feel the tension of years of pent-up anxiety.

Making his presence known, Gabriel lay behind her. His arms enclosed her, and the familiar sound of his measured breathing soothed her. Her shaking subsided, and she surrendered to whatever was taking control of her.

As they lay there wrapped up in each other on the ground, Lily watched as her fear moved through her body. She could see it as distinct and separate from her. It had a colour, a texture, a taste, and it moved around her body like a thousand honeybees, a dark mass buzzing and trailing. Lily let the swarm of fear fly, observing it with fascination, until it dissolved into a quiet space beyond her.

If only I could do this in my waking life.

In a single moment. In this mercurial, water-like reality that the plant had created, the dissolving of a lifelong fear was as effortless as blowing out a candle.

A rushing sensation washed over her. A river of calm flowed into a pond of peace, and the gentle ripple of the water was a source of pure contentment. Gabriel was still breathing in a strong steady rhythm behind her, the rise and fall of his chest pressed into her back. Subconsciously her breathing had matched his. Their breath had merged. She recognised this rhythmic dance of Chi, taught by the monks at Kalalaya. It was a yogic pattern of breath designed to shift awareness.

Her literal brain knew that Gabriel was physically there, holding her, breathing. But in the ephemeral reality, neither of them existed. Their bodies had disappeared. They had no edges, no periphery. They were apart in waking reality, yet inextricably joined in this expansive place. Two energies merged as one.

There in breath, there in rhythm, there together. One body of pulsating light. Pure ecstasy.

Lily was home. She had been longing for this place since she was born. The place where she came from and would return to. And she was there with Gabriel.

The extraordinary merging ended as soon as Lily opened her eyes. But began again as soon as she closed them – like the flicking of a switch.

Are we always this close to home?

One breath away, one movement.

When she came back into the room, with eyes fully opening, Gabriel encouraged Lily to get up and walk. He took her outside into the forest, and the first thing she felt was the warmth of the sun on her face as she marvelled at the miraculous plants and the intricate life systems that sustained them. The beings that could fly on currents, the beings that burrowed their way into the chasms of the earth. Microorganisms in the soil hummed with activity, providing sustenance to all other life. The water was like a mirror, reflecting the plants and creatures that lived beneath its surface. The air was filled with the miraculous shapeshifting clouds that wove around the trees, and the mycelia beneath the ground formed a web of energy, allowing the trees to communicate.

She was in awe of the mighty winds, which shaped them all, and the unified, intelligent symbiotic being that every other being on this planet was connected to. She was a child of Pachamama. Papatūānuku. Gaia. Mother Earth. The planet was not just an inanimate object, but a vibrantly alive, intelligent, sentient being. A Great Goddess. Lily felt a wave of awe wash over her as she realised how long she'd gone without knowing this.

They remained outside all day, revelling in the infinite beauty of the forest. As the sun set, painting the sky a warm rose gold, they moved back inside the treehouse, huddling beneath the warm, colourful blankets on the balcony and gazing up at the night sky as the stars, planets and galaxies sparkled above them.

Lily felt the medicine coursing through her veins, and the sudden urge to write came over her. Her tears flowed like a river as the words echoed in her ears. They weren't her words, yet they came from within her. They told her she was breathtaking, but she had never seen her own reflection before this moment, and so she didn't recognise her own beauty. Glass mirrors could never tell her who she was. Only the Goddess could do that. The Goddess who lives in all of us. The Goddess that is us.

How beautiful we are with the scars of lessons learned, the wrinkles of time, the aches of hurt, the shivers of fear, and the emptiness of loss.

We just don't see it. Because we look in the wrong places.

She gazed at the remarkable individual who had shown her the way back to her true self – the person she was before life happened to her. And it filled her with gratitude. He had known all of this all along. This profound and simple truth.

We belong.

Playfully, You Hid from Me

*'Playfully, you hid from me. All day I looked.
Then I discovered I was you,
and the celebration of That began.'*

Lalleshwari

thirty-one

THE ROOF BAR HAD views over the west of the city. Hong Kong's juxtaposition of modern, brutalist and old buildings making a fascinating skyline. The bar patrons, dressed to the nines, mingled – wearing their designer tags. Gorgeous women with gorgeous legs wearing their Louis Vuitton, Manolo Blahnik, Prada, and Jimmy Choos, yet the skyline was the only thing holding Luka's attention.

These places and people once enthralled Luka. Now, it all seemed vacant and uninteresting. He looked out at the harbour, out towards the jungled islands. The wild was calling him. A few months on, and he was still integrating the insights that the plant teacher iboga had given him.

He was here to meet his date, Xiang – the owner of a high-end florist, who radiated joy as she expertly cut and assembled flowers into remarkable works of art. He had walked into her store on an early morning, drawn in by the smells of herbal florals – mint, scented geranium, euphorbia, and eucalyptus in among the sherbet-toned roses, hydrangeas, dahlias and chrysanthemums. Amid the honking horns and exhaust of the city, her shop was a refreshing oasis of beauty and serenity. Not expecting customers at that early hour, she was on the floor surrounded by pruners, floral wire, and flower snips. Covered in pastel petals and loose stems, and flying leaves in her hair, she was irresistible. Xiang was sweet, kind, and funny. Not a pretentious bone in her body. And he adored her.

For months, Luka had been avoiding dating, his heart still hoping that Lily would come back. Hoping that one morning, he would open his eyes to the sight of her silhouette in the doorway of their house. But that day hadn't arrived. He heard the news of Lily's mother Maria's death through a mutual friend, followed shortly by the announcement of Lulama's death. All of his attempts to reach out to her, from calls to texts, emails to letters, were met with silence. On days when longing, aching, and worry consumed him, the thought of her being out there alone and hurting was a physical pain he could not shake. But if he had learned one thing from the plant teacher, it was that you can't control destiny. The more you tried to manipulate outcomes, the less likely they were to arrive. He had to let her go. He had to trust that they were both exactly where they were meant to be. It was a hard lesson.

Luka swirled whisky blocks in a fine crystal glass, the smell of the spirit evoking memories of his wild days. Ever since his life-altering experience with death and iboga, he had steered clear of cocaine, although he would occasionally treat himself to a glass of whisky or merlot. But it was only ever a single glass. He had no desire for intoxication. It was the same with sex. The desire for endless women was gone. There was no more hole to fill and no need to escape – he had faced his pain head on. His music remained, becoming more poignant and filled with a painful longing. The audience was more entranced with him than ever. The cello's notes echoed the feelings in Luka's heart that he couldn't express in words.

As he sat staring above the patrons into the skyline, a man in the bar's corner caught his eye. He was an impressive figure, wearing a sophisticated pinstriped suit and a distinguished expression.

Oh fuck, I know that face. The man that was holding Lily's hand. Oliver. That fucking C— He stopped his thoughts in their tracks. *I know nothing about him, except that he made Lily happy. I should be grateful to him.*

He watched in fascination as Oliver and a woman interacted, their voices blending in a soft hum. She had glossy, dark hair, and her bountiful breasts filled out her shirt.

Ah, he is a tits man, that's why he went for my Lily.

Trying not to let bitterness rise, he looked away into the distance. This emotional equanimity thing took practice. His unhelpful impulses were still there, but at least now he recognised them. Before iboga, he might have taken a swing at him.

Xiang walked in wearing a delicate pink-and-white frangipani in her hair. Luka thought of Lily. *Her favourite tropical flower.* He swallowed his guilt with a sip of woody spirit and a bright, squishy hug for Xiang. Her eyes glinted with a youthful naivete. He needed to tread carefully here. He didn't want to hurt her. She didn't deserve that – she was such a sweet and delicate soul.

'How was your concert?' she asked, as she flashed a bright white smile and leaned in to kiss him on both cheeks.

Luka inhaled the unmistakable scent of Chanel, the perfect accompaniment to her pristine white pant suit and dainty pink pearl earrings. Xiang wore a timeless elegance.

'You were there. Why don't you tell me? How did I do?' he said. His eyes shone with an impish glint.

'You were lovely,' she said. 'You made me cry.'

He pulled her closer and kissed her forehead, taking a glance at Oliver over her shoulder.

'I'm glad I could stir something in you. What would you like to drink?'

'Could I get a gin and tonic with a squeeze of lime, please?'

Luka draped her jacket over the back of the stool before taking a few steps to the bar. Oliver stood up walked towards him. He had noticed him, too.

Shit.

Oliver was direct. 'Look, I know it's uncomfortable to be in the same space, but it was bound to happen. For what it's worth, I'm sorry for the pain I caused you. I can assure you it was unintentional.'

Luka perspired, his white collar choking. This man had gumption. He could see that Lily would respect that. He turned to face him.

'Yes, I suppose it was bound to happen. I accept your apology, but she wasn't yours to experiment with. Married women are off the cards, mate. There is no integrity in that.'

'And there's no integrity in fucking your wife around.' Oliver's eyes were hard.

It felt like a slap in his face, but Luka knew he deserved it.

'Look,' continued Oliver, 'I'm not being sanctimonious. I've made that mistake, too, and it turned my life into a living hell. The thing is, I loved Lily from the day I met her, and I would have been good for her. I sure as hell wouldn't have made the same mistakes with her. But she chose you. She never said it, but I felt it. She was waiting for you to get your shit together.'

Oliver's vulnerability surprised Luka. He was taken off-guard.

'She never chose me,' he replied. 'She chose herself. Lily's wiser and better than both of us. I don't even know where she is, who she's with, what she's doing. You know her mother passed away, and then Lulama.'

Luka felt a lump in his throat. The words just came out. This was the first time he'd spoken to anyone about Lily. How ironic that it was with her former lover.

'Fuck.' Oliver's face dropped. He ran his fingers through his hair. The distress on his face was obvious.

It pained Luka to see it. This man loved his wife.

'Is she okay?' Oliver asked.

'I don't have the faintest idea. I just told you. I don't even know where she is.' He picked up Xiang's gin and tonic from the barman. 'It's killing me. I stuffed up the best thing in my life. And I just … seeing you here, well, let's just say it's not easy,' said Luka.

'It's not easy for me either. You are a reminder of what I lost, too.' Oliver sighed. 'Well, for what it's worth, Luka, I'm glad I ran into you. I wish you well. I see you have a beautiful lady on your arm. Don't fuck it up, eh?'

'As do you.' Luka smiled and looked across at the voluptuous woman sitting at Oliver's table. 'Don't fuck it up, either. And thanks for coming over,' he said, surprised that he meant it.

Oliver nodded.

Luka's head hung low as he trudged away. He was happy to find Xiang talking to a friend.

'Sorry, hon, got distracted.' He apologised and gave her the gin and tonic.

'Is he someone important? It looked serious from here?'

Xiang took a dainty sip of her drink.

'Yes, he is someone important, to someone who was very important to me.'

Xiang smiled, not quite following, but happy that he had returned to her side.

thirty-two

LILY LOOKED OVER AT Gabriel, contentedly sleeping through the loud claps of thunder and despite the violent weather outside, she felt a serene happiness. No matter how biting, and grey a storm could be, it passed.

It had been a week since Lily's plant journey. Dark, oppressive clouds rolled in, and the sky lit up with streaks of lightning and the crackle of electricity. She heard the rustling of leaves above, like the gushing of ocean waves as the water cascaded onto the forest floor.

Gabriel, and his plant medicine, had enabled her to turn her head to the sky, and to see with a clarity that had been so elusive. The sky would always be there, smooth, calm – it was only the weather that changed. Her depression had lifted, and even if it returned, she would have this anchor to get her through whatever she had to face. She felt a sense of peace as she watched the grey clouds gradually become luminous, the tints and shades softly intermingling. A dance of changing colour.

Several days before, she had been filled with pride when Gabriel told her he had been accepted by a highly regarded Shapibo Peruvian shaman to apprentice in the Amazon for two years. He would live in a wooden hut nestled in a rainforest village in Peru, learning the traditional medicine craft of the indigenous peoples. As the rainforests were being destroyed by clear cutting, felling, burning, and being supplanted by plantations and mines, and their remaining parts being lost because of the consequences of climate change, all the healing and remedial magic they contained was also being lost. It was vital that Gabriel gathered as much knowledge as he could as fast as he could. Time was of the essence.

He asked Lily to join him. But that was not her path. As much as she wanted it to be, she just knew it wasn't. And Gabriel knew that, too. He was like the passing clouds, there to teach Lily a lesson, and she always knew their time together would be limited. She was there to love him – she would, no matter where his life took him. He would always exist in her heart alongside the other souls who dwelled there, their brief collision setting off a chain of events that would guide them both to their destinies.

For the first time since she could remember, Lily knew what that destiny might be. She wanted to write, cultivate a tranquil garden, and set up a healing sanctuary. A place of respite for women like her who had experienced the pain of losing a child. She wanted to help them come alive again, to feel joy, to heal. Her days of fighting in courtrooms were over and she was okay with that. She no longer needed to cling to an identity that didn't align with her heart.

Their departing was bittersweet and came sooner than she had expected. When the great shaman called, you answered. She watched Gabriel pack his sparse belongings, everything into one well-worn navy backpack. His holey grey yoga mat rolled and tied to the bottom. She breathed in his smell, which was so distinctive. A heady mixture of plants and soil and clean sweat. Gabriel was deeply rooted in the earth, his feet firmly planted, confidently knowing which way to go.

In that moment, they clung to each other, their tears dampening each other's cheeks in a way that opened up to each other without words. They both felt the gritty texture of salt on their tongues as they kissed for the last time. What they felt for each other was something indescribable. Gabriel's impact was so immense that Lily felt like her heart had expanded and she was reborn. And Lily had given Gabriel certainty. If he could help her, he could help anyone. She was a testament to the effectiveness of the medicine. She was the seed of his well spring and he loved her. Lily was the spark that said he could.

'I'll see you when I see you,' he said.

'See you then,' she replied, knowing that he was only ever one movement, one heartbeat, one breath away.

As she took in the magnificent views of Monteverde on her last day, she knew it couldn't have been more perfect. The sun was beaming, casting its light on the wildlife that flourished in this extraordinary environment. The iridescent shimmers of the birds and butterflies twinkled in the air, the multi-coloured tree-hopping frogs plopped into the rain puddles, and the fruity herbaceous smells of the forest lingered in the air.

Lily was folding her clothes and placing them in her bag, which was laid out on the bed. The only material things she had left of Gabriel were a bright red vest with his earthy smell, and the mala made of beads that he wore wrapped around his wrist. He had placed them on her bedside table. The dark beads were made from the seeds of the ultramarine blue rudraksha fruit. There were one hundred and eight of them strung together on a red thread, each with its own unique markings – traditionally used in Shaivism, in a mantra practice honouring Lord Shiva, the God who represents the awareness in which all things arise or the ever-present primordial silence.

He left me the sky without the clouds.

Lily smiled and strung them over her neck. They would be a reminder of how to find home if ever she got lost again.

Before she left, she knew she had to write one last message – though it had been lingering in the back of her mind for some time, she couldn't put it off any longer. She pulled out her phone and typed an email. She told Luka of her plans to set up a retreat, and asked him to sell the house as agreed. She needed the proceeds to make her dreams happen.

Announcements echoed through the airport as she made her way to the next destination. The cold grey metal seat in the departure lounge was abrasive against her skin, the chill digging into her legs. Lily was checking her emails. She was waiting for Luka's reply. The shrill ping of her phone made her body tense.

Oliver.

She had not heard from him since the day he'd walked away, leaving his folded napkin on the restaurant table. The memory was so powerful, it had been sealed in her mind with glue. With trembling hands, she read the words on the screen.

His message was gentle and thoughtful, expressing his heartfelt concern and care. Oliver was worried for her, his stomach in knots from the news of Mama and Lulama's passing. He hadn't taken a sip of alcohol in months, and he had a partner who was committed to helping him stay sober. He was reconnecting with the man he had been before the tragedy of losing Sadie and their unborn child. His last lines read:

Lily, please don't run like I did. Please don't waste years of your precious life. Find a home, a place to face the sorrow. A place where grief and hope exist together. A place where I can visit you one day, and we can sit and look at the stars together and say we did it. All the hard things. And we got to the other side. In the present I love you with a love that goes deeper than any words. We will never lose each other. It's not our choice either way, to either hold on clutching on for dear life missing each other, or our choice to say goodbye. It simply isn't. The love that flows between you and me doesn't care about those things. It just exists.

Yours always,

Oliver

She felt the cold of the chair on her back, and the warmth of her heart – a welcome sensation as relief flooded and tears streamed down her face. She cried a lot lately. The thought of this remarkable man courageously facing the tough challenges life throws at us left her overwhelmed with emotion. There he was, healing and happy. She would keep him tucked in a pocket of her heart, a reminder of the way he had made her feel loved and seen. A reminder of the eternal nature of a love that flows between soul mates.

She heard her flight number announced over the intercom before seeing it come up on the board. The time had come to bid farewell to the verdant cloud forests. They had given her so much. Lily had one more travel adventure ahead before she chose the place that she could call home.

Patience To Endure Lightning and Thunder

'Patience to endure lightning and thunder, Patience to face darkness at noon, Patience to go through a grinding-mill. Be patient whatever befalls, doubting not that He will surely come to you.'

Lalleshwari

thirty-three

THE KASHMIR VALLEY IS fragrant with the sweet scent of its many flowers. Shrouded in mystery, the wild beauty of the Vale of Kashmir is only rivalled by its soul. The snow-capped Himalayas are a majestic backdrop for its beating heart, which is said to be filled with a powerful Shakti – the creative energy of the universe. Lily was awestruck by the towering mountains that surrounded her as she sat on the steps of one of many colourful houseboats beside Dal Lake, her hands in the water creating a ripple effect that spread out across its seemingly endless deep blue expanse.

The lake was milling with Shikaras – wooden boats with canopies designed to transport passengers. Lily, like many tourists, waited patiently for a ride – an hour-long float on the still waters reflecting the remarkable white peaks that shimmered above them.

When her boat arrived, she was fortunate to find that the only other passenger onboard was a weathered old woman with sun-darkened skin, her face lined with the stories of her years. She grinned at Lily, a gap in her teeth evident, and her eyes darted away to the horizon. She wanted to be silent, and so did Lily.

Covered with a cashmere shawl she had just bought from a market, Lily made herself comfortable as she gazed out towards the sky. While in Costa Rica, she had read so much about this holy place, and was full of gratitude, just to be here floating on its waters.

The beauty was undeniable, yet this land was permeated by the lingering effects of religious wars and power conflicts. Everyone desires the land of milk and honey. This fertile valley was no stranger to the decomposing bones and flesh of the murdered, tortured, and oppressed. Earlier in the day, Lily had walked past a funeral pyre, the sound of lamentation and grief filling the air, the smell of acrid flesh rising in her nostrils. In this place, death was not hidden but could be felt mixed in with the laughter of children, the milling of domestic animals, and the falling of rain. Death was palpable in the heart of the living, competing with the sounds of vendors hawking their goods, flowers being sold, and wedding celebrations. Here, bodies were caressed with ghee, honey, milk, and yoghurt. Essential oils were dripped on the faces of corpses and their palms were placed in a prayer position, big toes tied together. Here, dying was holy and a poignant reminder of the fragility and sanctity of life. Death was revered but was as normal as living.

And that is one of the reasons Lily was here.

In this place, grief was as welcome as joy. There are few places in the world like that.

Lily's boat swayed on the water, its gentle motion almost lulling her to sleep. She had also come here to pay homage to the Goddess who had blessed her with the powerful energy she had felt in the stifling building in Hong Kong, the tranquil and expansive wave that had embraced her in the cave in Koh Samui, and the healing peace she had found in the plant teachers of the cloud forests of Monteverde. She was here to give thanks to the Goddess who was full of mystery and creativity, yet resided in the mundane of everyday life. The Goddess who walks among the painters and poets, her radiant presence filling them with creativity and inspiration, and her comforting touch bringing solace to the woman cradling her dying child. The Goddess who celebrates life in all its beauty and all its pain, and all its grief.

The Goddess who asks nothing of us, other than to be alive.

In this Kashmir valley, from the seventh to ninth century, a group of outrageous (for their times) Goddess-revering men and women documented the potency and practices of Goddess Shakti in sacred and secret texts. Prior to that, generations of mystics and seers kept the spiralis magic alive, their teachings passed down from the siddhas and yoginis – one to the next, in an oral tradition that spanned centuries. An inexplicable intuition stirred those beings to etch their sacred rituals into paper, so they wouldn't be forgotten. And it was indeed a fortuitous decision to do so, as the religious wars that were to come in the following centuries wiped out many of the Goddess mystery schools and practices in the region. Today, some of these sacred texts still remain, held by and interpreted by Sanskrit scholar practitioners in the philosophical tradition of Non-dual Tantric Kashmir Shaivism, Sufism, and Tibetan Tantric Buddhism.

Lily wanted to take in the same landscape that had so powerfully touched the hearts of the Goddess's people long before patriarchal religions had come to be, and to experience the same sky and mountains and water that had stirred the Goddess to unleash her potent Shakti.

As Lily gazed upon the mountains, she had no doubt that the ethereal women who had taught the transformative practice in Hong Kong were bearers of the divine wisdom that originated from this very place. She was aware of the Goddess in the subtle susurration of the wind, the splendour of the sky, and the grandiosity of the trees – her plants, the carriers of an ancient wisdom, a message handed down by indigenous shamans for generations across the earth.

A message that echoes through the air, an unyielding presence that can never be silenced. It is the giver of life and the hand of death. The ancient power of creation and destruction, expansion and retraction, light and shadow. And underpinning it all is the very essence of existence – love.

As Lily floated along in the Shikara, she felt that love. It was all pervading. It had come to her through the living and through the dead, through silence and through pain and chaos, and she would carry it with her until her body was burnt on a pyre, and then it would alchemise into a miraculous stardust which would light up the sky for the next generation.

The boat steadily glided towards the shore, nearing the end of its ride. As they drew close to the jetty, Lily noticed the old woman sleeping, the movement of her chest rising and falling beneath her blanket. A sense of tranquillity surrounded her, the air around her still and silent. Lily's hand brushed her shoulder as she reached over to tap her.

'Madam, it's time to wake up. We have to alight.'

The women slowly opened her eyes, her lips curling into a warm smile.

She politely inclined her head in acknowledgement and thanks. The woman stood up as they drew into the jetty, her regal stance belying her years. She stepped off the boat and onto land with a steady gait. The wood creaking beneath her feet, she spun around and extended her arm to help Lily out of the gently rocking boat. Her hand felt rough and calloused, perhaps from years of hard work. Labour had taken its toll on her nails, which were now scuffed around the edges. Like the lines on her face, her hands bore the markings of a full life. Lily was grateful for her help.

As she stepped onto the jetty, Lily caught a whiff of her perfume. She detected a delicate yet intoxicating aroma of sweet notes and the faintest hint of her favourite scent – roses.

'Your perfume is wonderful. Do you mind telling me what it is?' she asked.

The woman stared at her quizzically, her eyes wide with confusion. She didn't understand English.

Lily tried to communicate her message as best as she could with hand gestures and facial expressions. With a sigh of relief, the woman felt around in her handbag and pulled out a plain bottle and a card with a carefully printed address. She gave the card to Lily. The business card featured a delicate rose embossed with the name The Rose Oil of Srinagar. Lily expressed her gratitude with a nod and handed the card to the nearest taxi driver. She was off on another adventure.

The shop was in the old city of Srinagar. It was next to a food market dotted with umbrellas of every colour, and food carts piled high with fresh produce. Opposite stood a grand white domed shrine – Khanqah-e-Maula. Lily peered through the window, her fingertips grazing the cold glass as she marvelled at what she saw. The shop was a cacophony of smells, with a rainbow of glass bottles of all sizes. The bottles in the store were arranged in even rows, the glint of their labels visible along the walls. This was an old shop with an old story. The shelves were coated in a thick layer of dust, and the small curtains that hung over some of the top windows were tattered with holes. As she looked around, she noticed some of the glass bottles had gone opaque with time, and there were cobwebs drifting between the wooden floorboards. A greying man sat near a table wearing a loose-fitting long-sleeved tunic in white, his head adorned with a skullcap.

'Good afternoon, miss, can I help you?' he said as he spotted Lily peeking through the window.

'Yes. I'm after some of your rose perfume. I noticed it on a woman today. It's wonderful. She gave me your card.'

'We don't sell perfume. Only oils, waters, and healing syrups. You must have smelt an oil. Come inside and you can try a few,' he said, as he walked towards her, his manner very direct. He retrieved several bottles from a drawer in his desk and positioned them on a worn table near the window.

Lily removed the corks from each and breathed in their aroma, one after another. The smells were ambrosial. After fifteen minutes of contemplation, she opted for the one that was most akin to the aroma of the woman.

The shop owner smiled, his fingernails gently brushing against his thick, bushy beard. 'You have a good nose,' he said.

'We distil this oil from our finest Kashmir rose.' He was pleased. 'You know, nothing matches our roses. Their colour is more beautiful and their fragrance is much more pleasant than the roses produced anywhere else in the entire world.'

Lily smiled. She knew a thing or two about Kashmir roses.

'Ah, this oil is gorgeous,' she said, savouring its delicate fragrance.

His eyes sparkled with pride.

'We've been manually distilling these oils in the same way for centuries. My ancestors came here from Turkey, over four hundred years ago. You will never find another oil like this.'

Lily believed him.

'How many bottles of this oil do you have for sale?' she asked.

'Twelve,' he said.

'I will take them all,' she said, and eagerly reached for her wallet, not even enquiring about the cost. She knew she had stumbled on something priceless and unique. As she counted out rupees, she heard the tinkle of the shop door. New customers had arrived. She looked up to see a swathe of turmeric robes. Monks, and among them, wearing her recognisable smile of serenity, stood Karma Chodron.

Three Times I Have Seen the Lake

*'Three times I have seen the lake
of the universe overflowing.*

*Once, I remember seeing
the only existent place
as a whirling without form,*

*And once, as a bridge over this
that is now Kashmir.
and seven times, I saw the whole
as emptiness.'*

Lalleshwari

thirty-four

THE CORNERS OF KARMA Chodron's mouth twitched upwards in a surprised smile. Her eyes lit up as she opened her arms to embrace Lily.

'Well, this is unexpected!'

'I can't believe it,' said Lily. 'I thought about getting on a train and travelling for sixteen hours just to see you in Himachal Pradesh. The alternative was an expensive seven-hour taxi ride through the winding mountain roads, and I wasn't thrilled about that. After studying your monastery's visiting hours, I realised it was a lost cause.'

Karma Chodron's embrace was like a hug from the sun. Lily was ecstatic.

'I'm only here for five days, so this is miraculous!' said Lily.

'It certainly is synchronous,' said Karma.

'What are you doing in Kashmir?' asked Lily.

'We were invited to a celebration this evening at the Ishwar ashram. We will be returning to the monastery tomorrow. And what about you? What are you doing here?'

'A personal pilgrimage, I came to give thanks to the Goddess.'

'That's certainly a good reason to be here.' Karma Chodron was pleased.

The store owner's eyebrows furrowed in confusion. It wasn't often that his store was the location of such a joyous reunion.

'I also came to pick up some rose oil,' said Karma. 'This is one of the region's finest makers. You must have caught wind of it. You always smell of rose oil.' She glanced at Lily for confirmation.

'No, I didn't know about it at all until I ran into a woman this morning out on Dal Lake. She smelt incredible. I asked her what she was wearing, and that's why I'm here.'

'The Goddess works in mysterious ways,' said Karma as she ran her finger down a dusty carafe leaving the clear line of her finger on the glass.

'She sure does,' said Lily. 'She sent you to me!'

Karma chortled. 'Or the other way round.'

'Are you free until this evening? Can we go for a walk?' asked Lily.

Karma conferred with a monk beside her. 'Yes, let's do that. Meet me in the Chashma Shahi Garden in an hour.'

The garden was set in the foothills of forested mountains, the sun filtering through the trees and casting dappled shadows. Constructed around a holy spring in 1632AD, the garden was the vision of a governor of the Mughal Emperor Shah Jahan. Now termed 'Chashma Shahi' meaning 'Royal Spring', the spring was initially named 'Chashme Sahibi' in recognition of the family lineage of a venerated female saint of Kashmir, Rupa Bhawani, who discovered its magical waters. Rupa was a Kashmiri poet, yogini, and a saint. Lily only knew about her because she had done some research before coming here. It was apparent that this garden was not exempt from the obliteration of Her Story.

Since arriving in Kashmir, Lily had also learnt about a great mystic of Kashmir Shaivism who was also a Sufi saint – her mystical teachings and mystical poetry known as Vakhs (speech) were an inspiration to the mystics of many philosophical schools and religions, though she was beyond all of that. She had little words for scriptures – words about the way were not the way. Her name was Lalleshwari, or Lalla, or Lal Ded, and she'd wandered naked in forests, dancing and singing in ecstatic bliss, the stars her lights, the earth her blanket, the forest her food.

Born in Pandrethan (ancient Puranadhisthana), four and a half miles to the southeast of Srinagar in the 1300s, she was married off at twelve and escaped her unhappy marriage in her mid-twenties to run wild and devote herself to the eternal mysteries. In legends, she

317

appeared across the ages to spiritual seekers in the forests wearing a gown of transparent, glowing green and gold – to guide them on their path to awakening.

Each morning since Lily had learnt about her, she had lit a candle and thought about her, and about all women who had to escape the societal norms of the world to discover who they were, and who they always had been. And she bowed her head, and for the first time since Lulama had passed, she prayed. She prayed to the Goddess; she prayed for their freedom; she prayed that all women would become rivers running to the sea; she prayed that they would run free.

The sound of the freshwater spring filled the garden, and Lily observed it as it ran through terraces in the centre. This holy bubbling water, amid the fragrant flowers, created a peaceful ambiance. Lily sat on a bench, taking in the sight of the colourful array of roses planted nearby. Leaning over to smell one, she noticed a peculiar thing. Kashmir roses are devoid of thorns.

'Beautiful. Aren't they?' Lily looked up to see Karma Chodron smiling.

'Stunning and look. They don't have any thorns.'

'Beauty without suffering,' Karma said, 'or beauty without protection?'

Lily thought for a moment.

'It's a matter of perception, I suppose,' she said. 'How you feel in the moment.'

'Indeed, it is that. There is the truth, and then there is our perception of it.'

Karma sat down beside her. Her presence had a way of making everything feel right in the world. She was one of those people who you could be silent with. Lily noticed her gardener's hands and wondered just how many flowers she had brought to life. She was thumbing mala beads she had pulled from her robe pocket. Flicking them as she looked up into the mountains. The cooling air swirled above them, the condensing liquid creating a mist that prevented Lily from seeing the peaks.

As if reading her mind. Karma said, 'Life requires faith. And hope, and an inordinate amount of patience if we want to see that mountain top.'

Lily nodded and said, 'And a whole lot of love.'

Karma smiled, her gentle eyes radiating approval and warmth. 'Tell me,' she said, 'Do you still want to join me at the monastery, to be a nun? I think you would make a rather good one.'

Lily studied her, her gaze holding a thoughtful expression. 'No, I don't think I do.'

'And why is that?' asked Karma.

'Because I want to fully inhabit the world. I don't want to escape it. I want to dance and paint and write and make love. And I want to grow a garden. Like you.'

Lily waved a buzzing bee away from her face. 'I don't feel a need to escape my suffering. I'm okay with it now. I think it makes life more beautiful.'

Karma placed a loving hand over Lily's. Her hand felt like home, like the place she had visited with Gabriel when their souls had danced in eternity.

'You have come a long way, Lily. You're living proof that we don't need a monastery to awaken.'

'Oh, I'm not enlightened, far from it.' Lily's curls bounced as she shook her head. 'I'm not like Tenzin Palmo, Lalleshwari, or the saint Rupa that discovered this spring. Or you. I've just experienced a few extraordinary things that have helped me navigate this very difficult human journey.'

Karma released a thoughtful sigh.

'Lily, enlightenment is a Western construct. There is no super-wisdom or permanent higher state of consciousness that elevates one above humanity. There is simply bodha. Realising who you are and who you always have been, and abiding in that knowledge. And my dear…' she paused and squeezed Lily's hand, 'just by looking at you I can see you know who you are.'

'Yes, yes, I suppose I do.'

Both women were smiling and content. They sat surrounded by Kashmir roses, drinking the beauty in with their eyes. Karma's fingers curled into a mudra as she meditated with her eyes wide open, drinking the glorious day.

In all her searching, Lily found that for women, their spiritual lineage had been all but eradicated by patriarchal, monotheistic religions, their history told through lenses that weren't their own, and their stories stolen and manipulated. Patriarchs stripped matriarchs of their power, both literally and metaphorically, on stakes of fire. So then, to find out who we are as women, we have to embark on a voyage of self-discovery, and maybe that is the blessing, because on that journey we realise that it's the human experience – the small, steady strides we make with our feet firmly rooted in the ground, the gifts of sorrow, and affliction and liberation that take us home to ourselves, and to the sacred knowledge and cosmologies that were present long before the feminine was demeaned, and overpowered by religious structures trying to dominate, control and rule. These cosmologies can be found in every corner of the world – woven into the land, the sea, the sky, the flora, and the very air we breathe. Our hearts know the truth, the earth knows the truth, and it echoes in our souls. Here in Kashmir, amid the world's highest peaks, the people once knew that. Lalleshwari knew that. Awakening is possible through our cells, and our tissues and our bones. We can dance ourselves awake. We can sing ourselves awake. We can grieve ourselves awake. It's not only when we transcend the body that we discover God. God lives in us.

She is ever present and only a heartbeat away.

Karma Chodron stirred from her meditation. The mists parted, revealing a majestic snow-capped peak, illuminated by the last rays of sunlight. With ease, she leaned over the side of the bench and pulled a brilliantly coloured rose from its bush. It was a kaleidoscope – touched with pinks, oranges, and a delicate shade of indigo. The colour of dawn.

With a gentle gesture, and a wink, she handed it to Lily and said, 'Here, another rose for your collection.'

Dance, Lalla, With Nothing On

Dance, Lalla, with nothing on but air:
Sing, Lalla,
wearing the sky.
Look at this glowing day!
What clothes could be so beautiful, or
more sacred?'

Lalleshwari

thirty-five

IT TAKES DETERMINATION AND focus to make dreams a reality, and eventually the hard work pays off. After two years of painstaking planning, complicated consents, hiring builders, managing the build and finally hiring help, Lily stood admiring the light spilling through the open, textured wooden front door of her retreat.

She stood gazing through to the courtyard, taking in the beauty of the large pond full of koi, the sparkling rock fountain, and the pastel-coloured lotus lilies floating on the pond. She had noticed several days ago the first arrival of two bright green frogs, one lazing in the sun on a lily leaf, and the other tucked away in the velvet pink of a flower, its curious eyes peeking out from above the petals. Lily beamed, her heart bright with happiness as she surveyed the perfect scene. She breathed in the feeling of stillness, and knew she had created a place that was all she ever dreamed it would be.

After weeks of her hands in the dirt, the garden was finally beginning to show signs of life, with the buzzing of insects, whispers of butterfly wings and singing vibrant colours. The anthuriums, yellow hibiscus, and spider lilies were nestled amid bamboo grasses, orchids dangled from the tree branches, and potted roses and bougainvillea lined the deck overlooking the tranquil lily pond. There was a separate area at the back with a fragrant, circular herb garden. The bright, wild colours and herbaceous smells of the garden made guest's faces light up with smiles.

The retreat had four en suite rooms for guests, all with a picturesque view of the central pond, a fully equipped communal kitchen, dining and lounging area, and a calming meditation and therapy room. The décor was a mix of modern and traditional Balinese styles, with rattan furniture, bamboo accents, and soft white fabrics. It was a modest design, but its beauty was undeniable, and Lily couldn't help but love it.

With the aid of a psychologist, and a somatic, trauma-informed yoga therapist, Lily ran a meditation programme and arranged weekly retreats for a small group of women who had lost their children.

To Lily's delight, Nova and her partner Ubon had joined her in Bali. Nova had found a job teaching English at a local school, while Ubon was in charge of the retreat's administration, filling the dining room with the smell of her aromatic cooking, and helping wherever needed. This evening, as the sun set, they were having a gentle and solemn remembrance ceremony for the guest's lost little ones – a tradition they kept at the end of each retreat. Ubon was sitting in the courtyard meticulously folding origami rice paper into boats which they would release on ocean waves as the Balinese sun brushed its unique gold across the evening sky.

Saying goodbye was difficult; Lily had gone through the motions of saying farewell many times in the past years, but life still had beauty and purpose and joy to be found. And the essence of all those she loved remained with her. Every morning, as the sun climbed higher in the sky, she thought of them, the scent of incense drifting through the air as she lit the little altars that decorated the retreat.

Gabriel called often, filling her in on all the crazy details of his daring adventures. He was a dancing sky spirit, radiating light and joy as he moved around the world with an infectious exuberance. He was Lily's dependable confidant. Their lives did not fit together, but their souls continued to dance. If she was having a hard day, Gabriel seemed to sense it, and a message of love and support would arrive through the mysterious ethers of the universe. Or on Instagram.

Oliver had remarried. His relationship with his daughter had been restored and strengthened and his new wife had given birth to a vibrant baby girl, whom they named Sky. Lily met them when they came to visit, and one evening, as they looked up at the Milky Way, Oliver and Lily had the closure they had both been seeking.

'We did it, Lily, we stopped running,' said Oliver.

'We did. We stopped running and healed the hard things,' replied Lily.

Embracing from side to side, they clinked their cups of steaming herbal tea.

Oliver's family was beautiful, and Lily was confident that no matter what life threw at them, they would remain strong and face it all together.

Things had been different with Luka. Communication between them was sparse. After the length of their relationship, Lily assumed it would take more time to heal. Settling the property had gone off without a hitch and Luka had been true to his word by honouring all of his financial commitments. When Saima had told her he was seeing someone else, she'd felt a pang of sadness, but she was simultaneously really happy for him, and that is how she knew that she really loved him. Sorrow and joy sometimes live side by side.

Every time she enquired about the progress of their divorce, he avoided giving her a definitive answer. She sighed as she thought of the paperwork that he'd no doubt discarded – he was always consumed with his job and his cello. She hadn't pushed the issue either. Things would happen in their own time.

For the last two years, she had been devoted to constructing the retreat, her ambition leaving her feeling fulfilled. The sound of daily laughter and the feeling of support she received from the small community she had created and the women she served filled her up. Some evenings as the crickets chirped, she would lie in bed, in that stillness between wakefulness and sleep, and her thoughts would drift to Luka, wondering what he was doing. Sometimes she wondered how things would have been if they hadn't lost Jessie. But they had, and that was something they had both come to accept. They had become feral in their grief, wild and disoriented and lost, yet it had also connected them to a deeper part of themselves. They both knew who they were now. And they were both happy.

Lily loved her life on the island. It was simple and purposeful. She wouldn't have it any other way. There was a silent contentment that sustained her each day.

A serenity that originated from her heart and reached out to others – and, of course, into her books. Now an aspiring novelist and poet, Lily was content as she learned a new craft, making each day even more fulfilling. She was in love with the beauty of life, the rhythm of words, the tranquillity of gardening, the purposeful work she was doing, and the warmth of her friends and family who visited frequently.

Alexander Chau SC and his entourage would arrive for a weekend escape, regaling her with his thrilling tales of legal drama, trying to entice her back to the law. Until, one day, he looked up out over the Balinese waves, with a margarita in hand and said,

'I may not be happy about it, but I can't deny that you did the right thing. There's a light in your eyes I've never seen before.'

'Yes,' Lily replied. 'It's the same light that shines in your eyes on your way to a raucous trial, especially when you get to argue with a judge – then you're literally on fire.'

They both gave a joyous chuckle.

Your Way of Knowing Is a Private Herb Garden

'Your way of knowing is a private herb garden. Enclose it with
a hedge of meditation,
and self-discipline, and helpfulness to others.
Then everything you've done before will be brought as a sacrifice
to the mother goddess.
And each day, as you eat the herbs,
your garden grows more bare and empty.'

Lalleshwari

thirty-six

LUKA CLASPED XIANG'S DAINTY hand in his. His words felt like lead in his mouth, and he knew they wouldn't be easy to say. He loved her. In a world full of cynicism, her gentle and child-like nature glistened like a rare gem. Xiang was the moon peeking through the clouds, and she had been a wonderful companion for the last two years. But when she'd announced her desire to conceive a child yesterday, Luka knew deep down that he didn't share the same dream. The realisation hit him like a gust of icy wind, cold and stinging. He didn't want to cause any pain to this delicate and kind woman.

He already had a family. The sound of Lily's laughter was home. He was aware she didn't want him anymore, but he had to make a last effort. He couldn't stand the thought of not trying. Luka felt empty in her absence. The idea of creating a human life with someone else made his heart hurt.

Xiang deserved more than he could give her. He was certain that she would find what she desired. Every man she encountered was completely enamoured with her.

'I'm so sorry,' he said. With tears in his eyes, he swallowed the lump in his throat.

'Luka, it's all right,' she said. 'I've known this for a long time. I verbalised the thought of having a child yesterday to solidify it in my mind.' She reached up and carefully brushed a strand of Luka's hair away from his eyes. 'I'm not ready to become a parent right now, but I wanted to know that I'm with the right person when I'm ready in the future.'

'Oh, you surprise me,' he said.

Luka looked at her with admiration in his eyes.

'I've never been as naïve as you think, and Luka, there is something else.' She stared at him with an unwavering gaze.

'Something else?' He felt his stomach drop.

'I've met someone. He has been coming to the shop, especially at lunchtime, bringing me food. He's a chef from the restaurant upstairs. Nothing has happened yet, but I have developed feelings for him and I … I've been so confused. I am the one who should be sorry.'

Xiang's shoulders were slumped in despair.

Luka tenderly pulled her close, planting a gentle kiss on her forehead.

'I am happy for you. All I want, all I've ever wanted, was for all of us to be happy. You deserve the best, and I owe you the world for putting up with my dreary soul for the last two years.'

'Luka, I wouldn't change a thing. We have helped each other grow.'

'Yes, we have.'

He pulled her even closer, his face nuzzling against her neck. He couldn't deny the sting of her having moved on before he understood he didn't want to stay – but he knew it was the right thing for her, that some benevolent force was looking after her vibrant and gorgeous soul. That night he cried unashamedly, big tears that rolled off his cheeks like boulders. Even if they weren't meant to be together, saying goodbye fucking hurt. And iboga had taught him that hurting was okay. Picking up his cello, he filled the room with the sound of an old familiar song.

Over the years, Luka had heard of Bali referred to by many terms – the Island of the Gods, The Last Paradise, the Land of a Thousand Temples and The Morning of the World – which encapsulate the beauty, magic, and awakening that can be found on its mysterious shores. But, to him, it was simply Lily's Island. The abode of his love.

The landscape is a mosaic of coconut trees lazily swaying in the wind, dormant volcanoes, verdant rice terraces, and rolling mountains that smell of earth and grass and flowers. The beaches are abundant, mostly white, set against the backdrop of wild waterfalls, connected by rivers that run like a tapestry of veins through the land and crystalline lakes that glimmer in the plentiful sunshine.

But the true beauty of the paradise lies in its spiritual heart – on a quiet day you can hear the thump of its beat beneath your feet. You can see it in the eyes of its inhabitants, the wild menagerie of long-tailed macaques, dragon lizards, blue-striped snakes and calling birds, and its unique and beautiful people.

Everywhere you look on the island, there are deities, standing as a testament to the long and rich history of Balinese Hinduism. Spirituality is intrinsic, a way of life in Bali where the people, gods and goddesses live in balance and harmony with nature. It is a sacred relationship that is honoured every day. On the vibrant, Balinese streets, offerings of colourful flowers, fragrant incense, and freshly cooked rice and fruit are made to the deities multiple times a day, making even the pavements holy.

Luka peered out of the window of his hotel car, watching as his driver skilfully manoeuvred around a family on a scooter, the mother, father and child, along with their daily shopping all precariously balanced on two wheels. The scooters were like darts, crisscrossing and weaving in and out of the hot and dusty traffic. This was a place where chaos and calm coexist.

Luka's eyes were drawn to a beautiful goddess statue, draped in a shimmering saree, her gold jewellery and pearls glinting in the light. She sat atop a lotus, flanked by two proud white elephants – the driver informed him she was Lakshmi. Wealth, luxury, beauty, fertility, and auspiciousness were all personified in this goddess and honoured by her many devotees.

As they drove through the maze of roads, he noticed a new goddess on every corner. Luka's eyes creased in the corners, turning up into a soft smile.

I know why she chose this island as home.

The car pulled up to the resort town of Canggu, and the bright pinks and purples of newly planted bougainvillea cascading up the freshly painted white wall of the building were the first thing he noticed. The tall black gate was adorned with a wooden sign, the white calligraphy adding a delicate touch. It read: 'Lily's Pad'. Luka gave the buzzer a single, sharp ring. As he waited, he noticed frangipani trees lined the entire street, their blooms drifting on the currents of the warm breeze, leaving a spectacular carpet of flowers on the ground.

A woman with an English accent answered. 'Hello,' she said.

'Hi, is Lily home? I'm an old friend coming to surprise her,' he said.

Luka's palms were slick with sweat, and his stomach was tied in knots.

'Just a minute,' she called.

He heard a buzzer click, and the gate opened. A dark-haired woman with a wild mane of curls appeared, her presence as light as the flying frangipani. She thrust her hand out joyfully, her face beaming.

'Hi, I'm Nova, and you must be Luka.' She wore a triumphant smile, her lips curving with satisfaction as she gave him a vigorous handshake.

'How do you know?' He gave an amused laugh.

'Let's just say you've been described a thousand times.' Nova winked with a mischievous twinkle in her eye. She ushered him through the gate into a courtyard, filled with a dazzling array of flowers, and the sound of trickling fountains and a lily pond gleaming a brilliant turquoise. He heard frogs croaking and splashing in the water. An oasis of aliveness.

'Wow, it's gorgeous,' he exclaimed, his eyes captivated by the intricate details of the space. Each corner presenting something delightful.

'She's done an amazing job,' said Luka.

'Yes, she has. We are very proud of our healing space.' Nova had eyes that showed kindness.

'Is she here?' Luka asked.

'I'm afraid Lily's out. She is with our guests. They are having a remembrance ceremony down on the beach.'

'Remembrance?' Luka narrowed his gaze.

'For the children they've lost. We hold one at the end of each retreat – it helps our guests find closure,' she replied.

'Ah, of course.'

'Why don't you join them?' she asked.

'I'm not sure that would be the right thing to do.' Luka absentmindedly ran his hands through his soft, wavy hair.

'Of course it is. You've lost a little one too.'

Luka was startled by how much she knew about him, and it made him uneasy. She was direct and to the point.

Nova squinted her eyes, scanning the area for something.

'We are all out of rice paper origami boats. Lily must have taken the whole basket. You need an offering for the ceremony.'

She pressed her pointer finger to her lips, deep in thought.

'There's a florist on the corner. Buy some flowers, and send them out to sea with the tide. Tonight's the night. It only comes around once a month with the full moon.'

Luka sensed he had no choice. Nova was adamant.

'Leave your things here. It's a ten minute walk to the beach,' she said as she walked over to the hotel car and grabbed his bags from the trunk before he could protest. The women were assertive around here. Luka smiled. This was definitely Lily's pad.

thirty-seven

FOUR WOMEN STOOD ON the white sand, the sound of the waves lapping the shore in the background as they held handfuls of sweet dried petals and held one another.

The full, pink moon illuminated the sky with its light as it rose in the west, highlighting flecks of gold and umber. These women had taken this journey of remembering together. Remembering who they were before their loss defined them.

Each woman carefully plucked a rice paper origami sailboat out of the tightly woven palm basket. Sinking calf deep into the shallow lagoon, the salty smell of the sea filling the air, they carefully placed their paper sailboats on the small rippling waves and scattered rose petals into the sea. Every sailboat, a personification of a soul, floated peacefully out into the deep ocean beyond, dissolving into the great expanse of serenity as the silvery moon bade them farewell.

Lily watched from afar, with salty tears staining her cheeks. This ceremony moved her deeply each time she attended it. The ritual of letting go, letting be, and creating just a sliver of space for the new to arrive. The crack of heartbreak gently opening to the light. This was a special type of grace.

She smiled as the women playfully threw petals over each other as they returned from the water, the sweet scent of flowers and deliverance filling the air as they gathered in a huddle on the beach. They lit candles – big ones and small ones – and sat in a circle, each taking turns to read a letter they had written to the babies they had lost. Some wrote poems, some wrote stories, some wrote letters, and some offered only a single word. The standalone was usually, *Thank you. Thank you for visiting me for a brief moment in time, so our souls could connect for an eternity. Thank you for teaching me how to love. Thank you for showing me how much love I am capable of.*

Lily's intention behind these gatherings was to offer these women an avenue to tap into the sacredness of grief, helping them grasp its significance in preparing them for life's encounters with death and loss. It is in these darkest hours that sorrow's touch fractures us, revealing hidden depths within our souls. The wild nature of grief alchemises anguish into a space of potential. Sorrow brings us an understanding of our own existence and our mortality, making every moment we have here more sacred. In moments of grief, our true human nature is laid bare, exposing our vulnerability. Grief is the heavy burden that compels us to confront the depths of our soul with unwavering honesty. It transforms us from the inside out. Some of us survive the transition and some of us don't.

Here on this holy night, these women had gathered to befriend their grief so that they may survive it, and this brave journey brought new friends, their loss the thread of connection that would make them old friends. The bonds forged in the fires of sacred grief, creating a lifetime of support.

Lily felt a wave of joy wash over her as she watched the touching scene before her.

Tonight, her work was done.

Gathering up the empty basket, Lily made her way to the pathway that led home, with the sound of distant waves echoing behind her. She was proud of these women, whose resilience was clear in their bravery and in their words. It takes a certain type of courage to face a grief that big. A courage that had taken her years to find.

thirty-eight

IN THE DISTANCE, LILY observed the silhouette of a man clutching a flower as he walked. He took long strides out to the lagoon and gently set the item in the water, keeping his eyes fixed on it as it floated out with the tide. A single flower, a meaningful yet simple display of love and emotion. She wondered who he had lost.

As he turned around and looked towards her, the woven basket she had been carrying fell from Lily's hands, leaving an intricate weave pattern in the brilliant white sand.

His face was touched with age; he had never been more beautiful.

Beyond the horizon, she could see the white sails of distant ships, slowly growing brighter as night fell. Lily squinted against the last rays of light as the figure she knew so well drew nearer. His smile was unmistakable, with laughter lines crinkling the corners of his eyes. Luka, never an angel, walked barefoot on the beach sand towards her, his jeans rolled up and his waving arms framed by the setting sun.

'Lily, Lily,' she heard him call.

Two and a half years can add lines to a face, but it can't erase a love. Lily's chest was tight with anticipation as she blinked rapidly, trying to confirm that what she was seeing wasn't a dream. She carefully smoothed out the wrinkles in her white cotton dress, running her trembling hands through her greying hair to steady her breath.

'I found you,' he said in a voice choked with laughter and tears.

'You did.' She smiled, her hands still shaking.

He reached his arms out with a hopeful smile, asking, 'Do I get a hug?'

'Of course you do,' said Lily.

Luka swept her up in his arms and spun her around in a dizzying circle. She felt a flood of nostalgia and joy as she melted into his arms. He smelled of freshly sanded wood and citrus – a smell she didn't recognise.

'Let me look at you,' he said, as they came to a stop, the warmth of his breath still touching her neck. His eyes swept over her, admiration and recognition in his gaze, and he said, 'Beautiful as ever.' He caressed the slivers of moonlight in her hair, the delight in his eyes unmistakable.

The air was heavy with emotion as they returned to an intimacy that had been broken for so long. Bystanders watching would never know just how long and hard the years between them had been.

'What brings you to Bali?' Lily barely choked out her question.

'I came to see you,' he said.

'You came all this way to see me? You could have just called. Is everything okay?' She was suddenly concerned. 'If this is about finalising our divorce, I would have preferred to do it through our lawyers. It keeps things clean.'

'Lily, it's not about that, and I'm fine. I just wanted to see you.'

His statement brought a comfort that she didn't expect. It was only now that she realised the truth – she didn't want to sign anything that would make the ending of their relationship official. A deep, instinctive part of her had refused to let go, and that's why she hadn't insisted on him signing.

'Why now, after all this time?' she asked.

'Because it's the right time. Shall we take a walk together?' His voice was soft and inviting as he extended his hand out to her. She let him take her hand, the texture of his warm, cello-calloused hands so familiar, even after all this time apart.

The sound of the waves gently crashing against the shoreline filled their ears as they walked towards the water's edge, the cool water lapping at their feet. The rhythmic motion of the waves bringing a sense of serenity to both of them.

'Are you going to tell me what this is about?' she asked, her curiosity bubbling as the water lapped at their toes.

Luka slowly turned to meet her gaze, his obsidian copper-flecked eyes catching the moonlight. He paused and whispered, 'Missed you,' his voice quivering. He tenderly brushed his fingertips along her cheek, pushing a curl out of her face. 'Wow, Lily, it's so good to see you.' His eyes teared over. 'It's been so long. How did we let all this time pass?'

'I missed you too.' She swallowed hard. 'I don't think we had a choice. Destiny is a peculiar thing.'

He nodded.

'You missed me!' he said.

'Of course I did. We had a lifetime together. Those memories don't disappear. They live with you.'

He ran his fingers agitatedly through his tousled hair, his face darkening.

'Lily, are you with someone?'

'No.' She shook her head. She felt the soothing sensation of the incoming tide washing over her calves. 'And you, are you with someone?' she asked.

'Not anymore. I was in a relationship for almost two years, but that's over now.'

She felt a sudden wave of sadness. 'Sorry to hear that, Luka.'

'Don't be sorry, Lily, it wasn't meant to be. We wanted different things … And you? Why aren't you with someone?' he asked, as his eyes searched hers.

'You are so full of questions, Luka,' she teased.

'Lily, I need to know.'

'Why?'

'Lily, please just tell me.'

She let out a sigh of resignation and tugged on his hand. The tide was coming in. The beach was about to disappear, so they had to get going.

'Luka, it's high tide, let's go to my place. We can have this conversation over dinner. Ubon has left some food in the fridge. Unless you are in a hurry?'

'Sure.' He smiled. 'I'm definitely not in a hurry.' He was content to go anywhere with her.

As they strolled for ten minutes, Lily pointed out all the trees and flowers of the neighbourhood, their feet crunching on the sand of the beach side roads. She was so happy to show Luka the sights of the place that she loved. They chatted away, their voices merging in the same comfortable harmony they had shared since they were students.

As they arrived at her gate, Ubon and Nova welcomed them with a cheerful hug. They both looked dazzling, dressed to the nines in their party clothes. Lily assumed they were going somewhere special.

'We're going dancing. Dinner's on the kitchen island,' Nova said, 'it's warm and there's enough for two.'

'Thank you,' said Lily, catching the mischievous glint in her eye. 'Have fun, dance up a storm.'

Ubon gave Lily a knowing smile as she said, 'You have fun, too.'

They settled in Lily's private lounge room. Lily lit candles and incense on a shrine beneath the goddess statue of Saraswati in the corner, filling the room with a sweet, musky aroma. She carried the warm, fragrant dishes out from the kitchen and placed them on the coffee table. They sank into plush Balinese silk cushions on the floor as they devoured the sticky mango salad and pad Thai Ubon had left them. Both of them were ravenous, eating without talking. Lily carefully poured two glasses of a crisp white wine. She seldom touched alcohol these days, but tonight she needed something to still the trembling in her hands.

Luka broke the silence.

'That meal was incredible. This whole place is incredible,' he said, scanning his eyes around the room.

'Thank you. Ubon is an amazing chef, and I am an amazing interior designer.'

'You're pretty good at a lot of things, Lily.' Luka laughed at her bragging.

'I am.' Lily's eyes were playfully twinkling.

'So, are you going to tell me? Why is a talented and beautiful woman like you single?' His eyes searched hers, as if he were trying to read her thoughts.

'There's been a love in my life, Luka.' She felt the tension radiating from him as he absorbed what she was saying. 'Someone who helped me heal and who

I'm very grateful for. We were on different journeys. Different paths. And after him, I haven't had space for anyone. My life has been so full, and I've loved every minute of the last two years. I'm happy.' She paused, the subtle sound of her glass clinking as she took a sip of her wine.

'I guess I needed to be there for myself. I needed to find a reason to live after everyone left. And after a lot of soul searching, I found that reason,' she said.

'I never left.' Luka was overcome with emotion as he watched the soft, flickering candlelight in the corner of the room.

'You kind of did. You became someone else, someone I didn't know.' She felt a lump rise in her throat, and she forced it back down. The truth hurt, but it mattered.

'Oh fuck, Lily I'm so sorry, you lost so much, and instead of being your rock, I became the thing that pulled you under.' A single tear slipped down his cheek.

'I hurt you. I was insane. I was an addict.' He stared, glassy-eyed and overwhelmed, his expression one of devastation. Lily reached for his hand.

'People go insane with grief. Humans fail, Luka. All the time. You lost so much, too. Losing a child is devastating. Nobody teaches us how to navigate that kind of grief. We are left in a solitary wilderness trying to find our way out, and some of us survive and others don't.' She lifted his hand to her lips and kissed his fingers tenderly. The pent-up tears falling from her eyes.

'We made it, Luka. I'm so happy we did, because there was a time when I didn't want to make it. I really wanted to leave this world. I found it unbearable.'

'You wanted to leave?' Luka shook his head, the soft sound of a whimper escaping from his throat. 'Oh my god, Lily, no. You wanted to leave?'

'I came a hair's breadth away from leaving, Luka. I spent months recovering.'

His face was contorted in shock, his mouth hanging open in disbelief. 'What did you do, Lily?'

'I walked into the sea.'

Luka's chest heaved as he tried to control his emotions. He pulled Lily into his arms, and they both cried really hard tears. The sound of their pain carried into the air, out beyond the doors of the retreat and into the night sky. A pain that big has a long way to travel. They cried until the serenade of the crickets and the frogs and the nightbirds stilled them.

'God, Lily, I love you,' he whispered. 'You can't ever do that again, do you hear me?'

'I won't. Luka, I won't.' It was a relief for her to know that she really meant it, and it was also a relief to know that Luka knew now. 'And I love you too, Mr Perez,' she said.

Luka stroked her cheek with his finger. They both gazed at the dancing candlelight.

'I don't want to be a flicker in your life, Lily. Do you think we can try again?' he asked.

'I'm happy here Luka, I'm not going back to Hong Kong.'

'I'm not asking you to. I'm just asking if you have space for me in your life. We'll figure out the rest.'

Lily looked at the shadows cast on her wall by the dancing flame. She didn't want her light to come from anyplace other than inside of her. But she had space for love, and she couldn't imagine loving anyone else as much as she loved this man, with all his flaws and all his beauty. They had the type of love that endured fires. There was only one thing that might make their love impossible.

'Luka, I can't conceive. I've been to a dozen specialists. That part of me is broken.' She felt the tears rising again.

'I don't need you to conceive. I left Xiang when she told me she wanted children because I realised you are my family. You are everything I will ever need. It's always been you, Lily. Always.'

He pulled her closer, and she snuggled into his familiar embrace, wanting to breathe every part of him in.

'It's us, Lily, and our lost angel. She's still with us. She is us. I gave her a rose tonight. I sent it out into the sea. I know she appreciated it, and I know Jessie is right here with us tonight and she's happy. She's happy we're here together because that is where we are meant to be.'

The rose he'd bought from the florist was miles out now. Part of the great wide ocean, where it would float until it decomposed and then it would feed a new cycle of life.

'Well then, yes, Luka.' Her eyes were brimming with happy tears now. 'Yes, I have space now.'

Lily felt the joy burst from her chest, like a dove, freed from a cage.

Their lives had come full circle, and they'd been given another chance. No one knew how their story would end, but Lily was certain that it would begin again.

Sorrow and guilt and pain had left indelible marks on their faces, but with forgiveness and time they found that the love they always had for each other remained unchanged.

And they were both kinder, wiser, and better people now.

thirty-nine

ON THE BEACH, THE sun shone brightly around Luka and Lily as they stood facing each other with their hands clasped and their feet slowly sinking into the soft sand.

Alexander Chau SC stood in front of them, his voice booming through the air with his usual eloquence. He had become a part-time celebrant. He said that it was the perfect way to find equilibrium in his life. Spending so much time with the underbelly of society, he needed a counterbalance and what more uplifting thing to do than join people in love. This afternoon, he had the honour of officiating a renewal of wedding vows.

The sound of laughter filled the air as their loved ones gathered near for a simple, heartfelt ceremony. Lily looked out at the many faces that had brought her so much warmth and kindness. Her heart was filled with a profound sense of gratitude. The Goddess had blessed her with an abundance of love. The day was filled with a beauty that stayed with her long after, making it one of the most memorable days of her life. It was a day that made all the hardships of the past seem worthwhile.

With each passing week, Luka and Lily felt the harmony of their lives coming full circle, finding peace in the rhythm of their new life together. Luka had an apartment in Hong Kong which he would stay in while he worked, although he had reduced the amount of hours he was working – now his role was more of an advisory position. Despite his part-time commitments to the Hong Kong orchestra, he had also begun a quartet in Bali. His music had become sweeter. No longer heavy with melancholy, it was touched with a magic that uplifted the hearts of those who heard it.

When Lily's pad was empty of retreat guests, it was full of musicians, poets, yoginis, and artists. The colours of their new life together were like a rainbow, vibrant and harmonious.

Until one afternoon, when an oppressive heat was pierced with the sound of Luka's past coming back to haunt them. A moment in time that had the potential to unravel the fabric of their new life.

Through extensive investigation, the New York Child Protection Service was able to locate Luka. His tumultuous romance with Imani had resulted in more than just heartache. There was a child, a daughter.

Tragically, Imani had succumbed to her drug addiction and had left behind a toddler with no living family members apart from Luka. The agency had investigated and discovered that his name was listed on the girl's birth certificate as her father. She was now three years of age.

Luka's face was ashen as he entered Lily's room to tell her the news. The ghost of his past left an eerie silence on Lily's face. The carefully crafted reality they had created was about to be broken apart. Acknowledging that she would remain childless was something that had taken years for Lily to come to terms with. She had eventually made her peace with it. Now liberated and feeling a newfound sense of purpose, she happily embraced her life just as it is. She was unsure if she could bring herself to love a child who would be a lasting reminder of Luka's past, a child who belonged to another woman. She had a choice to make. A choice that had the potential to break Luka and her apart, no matter what the conclusion.

Luka was resolute in his decision. His commitment to the child was unshakeable. He would never turn his back on his own flesh and blood. And Lily loved him for it, even if she didn't know if she could survive it.

As the sky darkened that evening, she lit incense in reverence of the Goddess Kali, who is known as the destroyer of worlds, the bringer of death, yet also the ultimate source of liberation. After spending several hours deliberating and reflecting, she concluded if love had been the driving force behind her getting this far, then she would have to trust that love would guide her home.

In a tender embrace, Luka and Lily cried together once again. Whatever this new journey would bring, they would face it together.

If Lily was worried that the child would serve as a reminder of Luka's dark night of the soul, her fears were unfounded. She could not have been more off the mark.

The moment her eyes connected with Serenity's, she felt a warmth that filled her with a love unlike anything she had ever experienced before. The sound of Serenity's voice followed Lily everywhere, the pitter patter of her feet and her childlike laughter ringing out: Lalla, Lalla. Hearing Serenity's mispronunciation, Lily remembered the name she used to call Lulama – Lula. The miraculous strands of life were weaving back together.

Initially, Serenity was a very timid child, but with the patience, love, and care of those around her, she soon gained the confidence to blossom. She was an adventurous and talented soul, blessed with both her mother's and father's natural gift of music. Serenity was the cherished centre of Luka's and Lily's lives. She was not only beloved by her parents, but the entire Canggu community was enamoured with her.

Everywhere she went, the people she encountered, from the florist to the greengrocer to the man selling sweet pancakes at his market stall, all had a great fondness for her. People couldn't help but smile when she arrived. She was a sliver of sunshine.

Serenity was raised among the tranquillity of the temple halls, the rolling waves of the ocean, and the fragrant beauty of the Balinese gardens. Each morning, Lily and she lit incense together and laid out offerings of sweet-smelling flowers, plump fruit, and hot rice at the Goddess shrines dotted around the retreat.

As a young girl, she was deeply aware of the elements of the earth: fire, air, metal, earth, and wind, feeling most alive when surrounded by the natural world.

Serenity knew each goddess by name. She spoke with them as she would with Lily, and with the feathered, winged and honey-making animals. She admired the flowers and fish, and whispered secrets to the trees. She sang with her one unique and hauntingly beautiful voice in the wind.

Far from being a harbinger of pain, she was the greatest blessing and the most cherished love of Lily's life. Fate had brought them together and blessed them all.

forty

LUKA AND LILY WATCHED in wonder as Serenity's confident little legs carried her forwards into the aquamarine water, her dark skin glimmering in the late afternoon sun, her raven-black loops and curls fluttering in the breeze coming off the sea. An African goddess with skin like velvet, her beauty startling and undeniable.

There goes my moon child, dancing in the water. Lily's eyes were soft and full of pride, overflowing with a mother's love.

Serenity's swimming stroke was powerful, way beyond that of a nine-year-old. She could outswim both of her parents. She cut through the waves, her body gliding effortlessly as she sent sprays of saltwater into the air, like a graceful dolphin delighting in its play.

She frolicked in the water for hours. When it was time, when the water receded back to the horizon, on the twilight shore, she emerged with a reckless purpose, with a wild abandonment that stopped for a moment the heartbeat of a little bird. Because there is nothing more beautiful than a soul knowing exactly who she is.

The End and the Beginning

The Soul, Like the Moon

'The soul, like the moon,
is now, and always new again.
And I have seen the ocean continuously creating.
Since I scoured my mind and my body, I too, Lalla, am new,
each moment new.
My teacher told me one thing, live in the soul.
When that was so,
I began to go naked, and dance.'

Lalleshwari

Acknowledgements

I WANT TO THANK everyone who has supported me on my writing journey. My family, friends, and all those who offered kind words of encouragement have played a significant role in this story. I am especially grateful to my partner, who patiently listens to hours of my writer's ramblings. Special thanks to Alex Smith, an incredible writing coach who taught me the importance of perseverance and to my beta readers for dedicating their time to helping me and providing valuable feedback.

Thank you to Claire Strombeck – a book is nothing without an editor. And to Katherine Stephen for her sharp, eagle eyes.

We all have stories; I am so grateful to have found the voice, the words, and the support to share mine.

About the Author

GWEN IS A FORMER lawyer, who lived in London and Hong Kong before moving to Aotearoa, New Zealand, to establish a wellness retreat. While in Hong Kong, she encountered many stories, and now, she's channelling those experiences into her writing.

Born in South Africa, she moved to London at twenty-one and juggled raising two toddlers with her legal studies and career. As well as being the mother of two dearly loved sons, she mothers one bearded collie named Huxley and several goofy ducks who roam her and her partner's little sanctuary in the rolling hills near Hobbiton, where they grow strange and wonderful things.

To connect with Gwen and keep up to date with her books and offerings, go to www.gwenb.com.

To receive the free bonus prequel of Falling Kashmir Roses, which tells the story of Lily and Luka's serendipitous meeting, sign up for Gwen's newsletter here – www.gwenb.com/newsletter-signup

If you have enjoyed the book, please consider leaving a review. This is very helpful to independent authors. It puts food on the table and helps us to focus on the things that we love to do best – write stories for you!